FOLLOW THE SHARKS

Twelve years ago Eddie Donagan was the fastest-rising pitcher the Boston Red Sox ranks had ever seen. Now he is a lonely divorcé selling running shoes at the Burlington Mall. Then his ten-year-old son E.J. is kidnapped and the family turns for help to Eddie's former agent, Boston lawyer Brady Coyne. It seems the kidnappers are out for more than money—revenge. But why? The FBI is determined to do the investigation by the book; Brady decides to take the matter into his own hands before the trail grows cold. Then a critical mistake compounds the kidnapping with a shocking murder, and Brady realizes it's easy to drown when you're following the sharks.

FOLLOW
THE SHARKS

William G. Tapply

ATLANTIC LARGE PRINT
Chivers Press, Bath, England.
John Curley & Associates Inc.,
South Yarmouth, Mass., USA.

Library of Congress Cataloging in Publication Data

Tappley, William G.
   Follow the sharks/William G. Tappley.—[Large print ed.]
      p.   cm.—(Atlantic large print)
   ISBN 1–55504–346–1 (soft: lg. print)
   1. Large type books.   I. Title.
   [PS3570.A568F6 1988]
   813′.54—dc19   87–20159
                        CIP

British Library Cataloguing in Publication Data

Tapply, William G.
   Follow the sharks.—(Atlantic large
   print books).
   I. Title
   813′.54[F]   PS3570.A568

   ISBN 0–7451–9306–4

This Large Print edition is published by Chivers Press, England, and
John Curley & Associates, Inc, U.S.A. 1988

Published in the British Commonwealth by arrangement with
William Collins Sons & Co Ltd and in the U.S.A. and Canada with
Charles Scribner's Sons

U.K. Hardback ISBN 0 7451 9306 4
U.S.A. Softback ISBN 1 55504 346 1

© 1985 William G. Tapply

To Michael, Melissa, and Sarah

PART ONE

EDDIE

CHAPTER ONE

Sylvie Szabo normally speaks with the careful diction and precise grammar of one whose English is a second language, but when she's a little sleepy or drunk or wants to tease, her speech tends to betray her Slavic origins.

So when the phone rang that Saturday morning, she grunted, sighed, disentangled her leg from mine, picked it up and said, 'Allo?'

She listened for a moment, frowned, jabbed me with her elbow, and said, 'Bradee, are you awake?'

'Is that your idea of foreplay?' I replied, yawning.

She smirked and handed me the telephone. I put my hand over the receiver. 'We have a rule, Sylvie. When we're at my house, I answer the phone. At your house, you answer. Remember?'

She cradled my face in both of her hands and bent so close that the tips of our noses

1

touched. Her green eyes peered solemnly into mine. 'Sylvie's sorry,' she said. She kissed me hard on the mouth, then rolled away and stood up beside the bed. 'Sylvie will make coffee.'

'Stop talking that way,' I hissed to her, mindful that someone was waiting to speak to me on the telephone. 'And put on some clothes,' I added.

She winked at me and minced out of the bedroom. I marvelled at how little her body had changed in the thirty years I had known her. She turned heads when she was fourteen. She still did.

I put the phone to my ear. 'This is Brady Coyne,' I said.

'It's Jan. Sorry if I interrupted something.'

'Aw, Jan...'

'Never mind. It doesn't matter.' There was a catch in her voice, as if something were lodged in her throat.

'What is it, Jan? What's wrong?'

'It's E.J. He's not back from his paper route. I'm worried sick.'

'What time does he usually get home?'

'On Saturdays, seven-thirty at the latest.'

I glanced at my wristwatch. 'Jeez, it's not even nine-thirty now. He probably stopped at a friend's house or something.'

'That's what I thought at first. But I called

everyone I could think of. And he did deliver all his papers. I checked that, too. I drove all over the neighbourhood. He always comes right home. He's only ten years old. I know. You think this sounds paranoid. But I'm telling you, something's happened to him.'

'What—?'

'I don't want to say,' she said quickly. 'I don't even want to think about it.' Her voice caught again. 'But—but I *am* thinking about it. Brady, damn it, if something has happened to E.J. . . .' There was an urgency to her tone that hovered near hysteria. I had known Jan for a long time. She wasn't an hysteric.

'You're jumping to conclusions,' I said. 'Look. It's a beautiful summer day. E.J. probably went to the playground to play ball or something. He's getting to be a big kid. Feeling his independence. A little heedless, like kids will be. Believe me, I know. I don't think you should worry about him.'

I heard her sigh. 'That's what my father said.'

'If you're worried, call the police. They'll keep an eye out for him.'

'Yeah. Yeah, I guess I could do that. That would be something.' Abruptly she sobbed. 'Brady, I am a wreck. I really am. Do you—will you come over?'

'Call the police, Jan. There's nothing I

can do.'

'You *could* hold my hand.' She tried to laugh, but it broke into a sob. 'You think I'm being silly. But E.J.'s my little boy.'

'I didn't say you were silly. I understand how you feel. But you don't need an attorney.'

She was silent for a moment. Then she said, 'Right. Sure. Sorry to bother you.'

'Jan, wait. Is Sam there? Let me talk to him.'

'Sure. Hang on.' Anger seemed to have replaced the anxiety in her voice.

A moment later I heard Sam Farina's rich tenor. 'Brady, that you?'

'Yes. What's going on?'

'Janet is absolutely beside herself. She seems to think you can make things all better.'

'You couldn't calm her down?'

'I told her not to call you. Hey, she's my little girl. What can I say? Her husband already ran out on her. She dotes on that boy, you know that. Anyway, I gotta tell you, I'm a little worried myself. I can't console her.'

'I can, huh?'

'You can. You know you can.'

'Sam, what the hell can a lawyer—?'

'Screw the lawyer, Coyne. You're her friend.'

'I see.' I groped on the bedside table for a pack of Winstons, shook one loose, and

4

plucked it from the pack with my mouth. Then I lit a match one-handed, a trick I learned in college. 'Okay,' I said. 'I'll be there in an hour or so.'

'Appreciate it, friend.'

'By the time I get there E.J.'ll be back.'

'I'm not so sure, Brady. Jan's right. This isn't like the boy. Not at all like him.'

I sighed. 'Call the police. I'll be there in an hour.'

Sylvie was sitting on one of the aluminium patio chairs on my balcony when I wandered out of my bedroom. I stood in the kitchen to look at her. She had slipped her arms through the sleeves of one of my dress shirts. She wore nothing else. She had her feet up on the railing and was scanning the Boston harbour, which lay spread out beneath us from my sixth-floor oceanfront apartment. She trained my binoculars on the horizon, where a big LNG tanker was inching its way to port. Beneath us dozens of tiny sailboats skittered across the water like white bugs. The summer breeze that riffled the surface of the Atlantic had brushed my shirt off Sylvie's body, baring her breasts and all the golden rest of her.

I checked the coffee pot. Sylvie had already loaded it and plugged it in. It was chugging and belching on the counter. I went back into my bedroom, pulled on a pair of Levis and a

5

white polo shirt, and then shuffled into the bathroom to run the electric razor over my face. When I went back into the kitchen the coffee pot had fallen silent. I poured two mugs full and took them out on to the balcony.

'Your coffee, Madame,' I said, setting her mug on the table beside her. I remained standing, leaning back against the sliding glass doors.

'Zank you,' said Sylvie, still peering through the glasses.

'Sylvie, will you please for Christ's sake stop talking like a Hungarian refugee.'

'But, Bradee, Sylvie *is* a Hungarian refugee.'

'Can you see the people on the boats clearly with those glasses?'

'Oh, yes. I can see their faces. Very good glasses, these.'

'Did it occur to you that the people on the boats may have binoculars, too, Sylvie, and they might like to look at the people on the balconies?'

She giggled. 'Zay might like to look at Sylvie, no?'

'They might like to look at Sylvie, yes. Why don't you at least button the shirt, if that's all you're going to wear?'

Sylvie took the glasses from her eyes and pouted at me. 'Bradee is an old poop,' she

6

said. She tied the tails of my shirt together
across her flat stomach, which did little to
cover her up.

'Sylvie, you're an exhibitionist.'

'Zis is not foreplay, Sylvie knows that.'

'Sylvie is right.'

'The lady on the phone, she seemed
distraught.'

'Yes. She is distraught.'

'She is angry because Sylvie answered your
telephone?'

'No. That's not it.'

'Brady is angry, though.'

'No, I'm not angry.'

'Because Sylvie wouldn't want to spoil
Brady's love life.'

I bent to kiss her forehead. 'Sylvie *is*
Brady's love life,' I said.

'Bool-sheet,' said Sylvie, her green eyes
smiling.

'We're going to have to cancel our picnic,' I
told her.

'Brady got a better offer, eh?'

'No. The lady was a client. She has a
problem.'

Sylvie must have read something in the tone
of my voice, because she frowned, held my
hand against her bare breast, and said, 'Is it
something serious?'

All traces of her accent had disappeared.

'I don't know. It sounds like it. Eddie Donagan's little boy didn't get back from his paper route when he usually does.'

'The parents must be very worried.'

'The mother is. The father doesn't live with them.'

Sylvie still held my hand, absentmindedly massaging herself with it. 'So you must go to the mother, then?'

'Yes. Jesus, Sylvie, don't do that.'

She grinned up at me, then lifted my hand to her mouth and kissed my palm. She used her tongue and her teeth. It made me shiver. I repossessed my hand. It took enormous strength of character. My hand seemed to have acquired a will of its own.

'Who is this Eddie Donkey, anyway? Has Sylvie heard of him?' Her accent was beginning to creep back.

'It's Donagan. Eddie Donagan. You would have heard of him if you had been following the Red Sox back twelve years ago or so instead of wasting your time on those boys in tights and codpieces. Eddie Donagan, for a couple of years, was the best right-handed pitcher I ever saw. He was as stylish as Marichal, he was as mean as Drysdale, he had more stuff than Bob Gibson, and he was more colourful than Dizzy Dean.'

'Sylvie doesn't know those men.'

'No, I suppose Sylvie doesn't. That's her loss.'

CHAPTER TWO

I met Eddie Donagan for the first time one soft May afternoon on a baseball diamond at Fitchburg State College. The year was 1970.

It began with a phone call to my office from Sam Farina.

'What's up, Sam?' I said.

'Little business trip. I want to take you to a ball game.'

'Business, huh?'

'Trust me, Brady.'

I laughed. 'No one trusts you, Sam.'

'Aw, come on. Have I ever lied to you?'

'Not so far as I know.'

'Okay, then. I'm taking you to a ball game, and it's business. You're my attorney, right? I pay you a ridiculous retainer, right? Our definition of business is when I say it's business, right?'

'Right, right, and, yeah, I guess so.'

'Pick me up in an hour.'

'Is this an offer I can't refuse, Big Sam?'

'That Godfather shit ain't funny, Coyne.'

'I'll be right over.'

9

Sam Farina lived in a twelve-room showplace in Winchester, near the Lexington line, with his wife, Josie, and his daughter, Jan, who was then finishing up her junior year at Mount Holyoke College. Sam owned a chain of liquor stores and four racehorses and a half-interest in a casino in St Maarten. He kept several law firms busy defining the cutting edge of legality for him in his businesses, while I handled his personal affairs. Mostly I gave him advice and directed him to specialists when he needed real legal expertise. He enjoyed my company and trusted my discretion, and if he sometimes treated me as if he owned me, I didn't mind. I liked him, and he never asked me to do anything that violated my conception of the spirit of the law.

I drive a BMW now, but back in May of 1970 it was a Chevy wagon, as befitted a young attorney with a young family. Sam was swinging a five-iron on his front lawn when I pulled into the circular drive. His thick forearms were sticking out of a short sleeved white shirt and a cigar stuck out of his mouth. Sam was built like a refrigerator, and somehow managed to look more like a well-conditioned offensive tackle than a pasta-fed businessman.

He climbed into the front seat beside me

with the five-iron propped between his legs.

'I thought the Sox were in Detroit,' I said to him.

'They are. They're facing Denny McLain tonight and Mickey Lolich tomorrow.'

'Then where are we going?'

'Get on to Route 2 west.'

About an hour later we took the Fitchburg exit and Sam directed me to a ball field. I parked the wagon behind some bleachers and looked at Sam. 'Now are you going to tell me what this is all about?'

Sam hooded his eyes and turned his face away from me so that he could stare down at me along the lumpy slope of his big nose. He'd done that to me before when I asked him questions about some income he wanted to invest, or a line on a tax form, or the losses he was declaring on his horses. It was Sam's way of saying, 'Just don't ask, and then I won't have to tell you.'

We climbed up into the bleachers. The game had already started, and the stands were sparsely populated with college age kids smoking marijuana and wearing shoulder-length hair and tee-shirts and blue jeans cut off high on the thigh. Both the boys and the girls. You could tell the boys because they wore their hair a little longer.

It was a big game. Fitchburg State against

11

North Adams State. I suppose it was a great rivalry. 'What the hell, Sam?' I complained.

'Watch the game. Shut up. Trust me,' said Sam.

Sam slouched back into the bleachers and propped his elbows up on the bench behind him. He rolled his dead cigar butt around in his mouth and gazed placidly out on to the field. I clearly had no choice but to follow his example.

The May sunshine warmed my face, and the perfect geometry of the game commanded my attention. I knew none of the players. I had no interest in learning whether North Adams or Fitchburg might win. Sometimes baseball is a better game that way. Once in a while I'll pull over beside the road to watch a bunch of Little Leaguers or a men's softball game, always amazed at the symmetry of it, no matter how well or poorly it's being played.

Baseball is a game of absolutely flat planes, perfect right angles, precise distances, measured velocities, and beautiful parabolas. Euclid would have loved baseball. The field is a grid laid out in white lines against emerald green. It contains dozens of little contests of inches and feet-per-second, all so equalized that a millimetre's alteration would destroy the entire balance of the game. Baseball demonstrates repeatedly all the physical laws of motion. It could have served as Newton's laboratory. The fact that it's played by flawed and unpredictable human beings creates a classically dramatic tension between the physical and the emotional, the fixed and the random. A single game of baseball is a whole repertoire of one-act morality plays. The good guys win about half the time, which seems to me to reflect the ways of the world.

For several innings I allowed my mind to ponder the abstractions of the game. But after the players had taken a few turns in the field, I began to pay closer attention to the pitcher for the Fitchburg team. He habitually hunched his shoulders and compressed his neck into them as he received the sign from the catcher, much like a turtle beginning to retreat into his shell. Then he'd bend, dangling his arms for a moment before bringing them over his head to initiate his windup. He kicked high, his right arm reaching behind him nearly to the ground, before arching his body like a bow and zinging the ball quick as a dart towards the plate. The North Adams kids, I realized, were completely overmatched. One of them dumped a blooper in back of first base trying to hold back his swing. An innings later another beat out a topped roller down the third-base line. And that was it.

Not only did he get batters out with

13

effortless grace, but the Fitchburg pitcher had what actors call 'presence', and what, in a politician, would be termed 'charisma'. He was always in motion. He sprinted to the mound to begin each innings. He got down on his knees to pat and pack the dirt around the rubber. He yelled and gestured to his fielders. When he struck out a batter he thrust his right fist into the air and yelled, 'Yeah!' loud enough for me to hear from the stands. Once the first baseman scooped up a low throw from the shortstop, and the pitcher ran over to him and patted him on the ass. Between pitches he sometimes turned his back on the batter and held the baseball up in front of his face. It looked as if he were talking to it.

I reached over and poked Sam on the arm. 'That kid out there—that pitcher. He's good. You notice him?'

'Shut up. Enjoy the game,' he growled.

In the middle of the eighth innings a stocky, deeply suntanned guy wearing a blue knit shirt and a Red Sox baseball cap climbed up into the bleachers and settled beside Sam, imitating his slouch. Neither of them spoke until the innings ended. Then Sam said to him, 'He's doin' okay, huh?'

'Sixteen K's, one innings still to go. Two goddam bleeders. No walks. Okay, I guess,' said the man. He appeared to be in his late forties. His face was crosshatched with deep creases that could have been smile lines or old knife wounds. His hands were square and powerful. His teeth were astonishingly white and he showed them often.

'This is Brady Coyne,' said Sam, jerking his head in my direction. 'Brady, meet Stump Kelly.'

I reached across Sam to take Kelly's hand. He squeezed hard and showed me his teeth.

'My friend Stump here is a scout for the Red Sox,' continued Sam.

'You're interested in that pitcher, I'll bet,' I said.

'Betcher ass,' said Kelly. 'Thanks to Big Sam.'

I frowned my confusion.

'Sam put me on to the Donagan kid,' explained Kelly. 'I been birddoggin' him all spring. The kid's got it, no question.'

'He's in the wrong league, I'd say.'

'Betcher ass,' said Stump Kelly. 'Good head, great arm. Throws BBs. For strikes. Got a curve'd put a stripper to shame. He could be in Triple A right now, still mow 'em down.'

In the top of the ninth the Donagan boy, rolling his shoulders, wheeling his arms, lecturing the baseball, and grooming the pitcher's mound, struck out the three batters

15

who faced him. He made the game look unfair.

After he had swatted palms with his teammates and absorbed their slaps to his backside, Donagan took off his cap and wiped his face with his forearm. He looked around momentarily, saw us in the bleachers and trotted in our direction.

He wore his reddish hair fashionably long, over his ears and collar. His nose was short and sunburned. His grin was broad and ingenuous.

Sam waved at him, and he climbed up into the bleachers. 'Hey, Mr Farina,' he said.

'Nice game, Eddie,' said Sam. 'You know Stump Kelly.'

'Sure,' nodded the boy. 'Hiya, Mr Kelly.'

'And this is Mr Coyne, who I was telling you about.'

Eddie Donagan reached over and engulfed my hand in his big mit. 'Thanks for coming, man.'

I frowned, but just nodded. 'My pleasure. You pitched very well.'

'Yeah, I had the good gas today, man. And, let's face it, North Adams ain't exactly the Red Sox. A salad team.' He glanced at Sam and Stump Kelly and grinned. 'A little cheese for the kitchen, a yakker for the kudo, and it's sayonara North Adams. Know what I mean?'

16

I smiled at him. 'I'm not sure.'

'Kid's gonna make a million bucks some day, right Stump?' said Sam.

'Yup. Million bucks. Betcher ass.'

Sam turned to me. 'The boy needs some counsel, Brady. Already things are complicated.'

'You mean an agent?'

'That's it. Whaddya say?'

'Me?'

'I'm giving you first refusal, being as you're my lawyer and I trust you and you can use the dough.'

I shook my head. 'You should've mentioned this to me on the phone and saved us both the trip, Sam. I don't know anything about being an agent.'

'Of course you do. You know contracts, you know how to protect somebody's rights, and you don't try to screw people. You'd make a helluva agent. Tell him, Stump.'

Kelly took his Red Sox cap off and rubbed his head, which turned out to be as shiny and hairless as a light bulb. 'Sox'll draft Eddie in June. Probably wait 'til the third round, not because he ain't a first-rounder but because he's only a junior and nobody else's heard of him yet. Eddie wants the Sox. Right, Eddie?'

Donagan grinned and nodded.

'Betcher ass,' said Kelly. 'Okay. So we draft

17

Eddie. Now, Big Sam here's wondering about the rest of his education. I'm tellin' him he can get all that stuff into a contract—deferred payments, big signing bonus, loans, tax shelters, tuition payments, long-term guarantees if Eddie hurts himself—God forbid. I mean, the contract is standard, and the Red Sox are fair. But Sam's right. Business is business, and they'll take him as cheap as they can get him. Betcher ass. Bein' as Sam and me go way back, and it was Sam put me on to Eddie in the first place, I let Sam know how it was. Eddie oughta have an agent.'

I shrugged. 'Makes sense. I don't see why I couldn't do that.' I looked at Sam. 'Though I'm not sure Eddie shouldn't finish up his education first.'

'Tell ya what,' said Kelly eagerly. 'Eddie waits a year, say. Everyone's heard of him. TV, *Sports Illustrated* fachrissake. Bound to happen. Right? Okay. We draft him this June and he don't sign, all the others start comin' around to see what we were so interested in. Get it? Then it's the damn Mets or the Twins or somebody picks him first. End of Red Sox career. Anyhow, s'pose Eddie slips on the mound at Bentley College or Salem State, hurts his arm or whacks out his knee. Hell, million things could happen. No career, no

18

dough. We pay him, we take good care of him. He's an investment. He gets good coaching, weight training, proper diet. If Eddie don't hurt himself, he'll be up with the big club two, three years at the most. Betcher ass.'

'What about it, Eddie?' I said.

He grinned. 'All I wanna do is play ball,' he said. 'Get me some of that iron, get out of these crusty threads.'

'Well, I'll be your agent, if you want me.'

'Mr Farina said you would. He said you wouldn't chill me. So thanks, man.'

Eddie's hand devoured mine again, I shook with Kelly, who mumbled something that sounded like, 'Betcher ass,' and Sam and I climbed into my Chevy wagon.

When we had turned back on to Route 2 heading to Sam's place in Winchester, I said to him, 'So what's your interest in Eddie Donagan, anyway?'

'The kid's good, isn't he?'

'Betcher ass,' I said.

Sam grinned. 'Stump Kelly's an old friend. We were in Korea together. Stump was a POW for three years. Cost him a career in the big leagues. So the Sox made him their chief scout for the region. He's supposed to be pretty good at it. They put a lot of stock in what Stump Kelly says. He recommends a

19

kid, they'll generally try to draft him. He's also a kind of trouble-shooter for them. Works with some of the minor leaguers. Special cases, you know? I put him on to Eddie. Favour to a friend, you might say.'

'That explains Kelly, all right. But it doesn't explain Donagan.'

'Eddie? Didn't I tell you? My little girl's gonna marry him.'

CHAPTER THREE

Eddie Donagan signed with the Red Sox in June of 1970, a comprehensive contract, with a nice balance of incentives, guarantees, and options, up front and deferred. I was proud of that contract. We held a little ceremony in Sam's living-room. Stump Kelly was there, and Sam and Josie, his wife, Jan and Eddie, Farley Vaughn from the Red Sox, with whom I had negotiated Eddie's contract, a photographer from the *Globe*, and, at Eddie's insistence, Mr and Mrs Jacob Grabowski from Lanesborough, Massachusetts.

The Grabowskis grew corn and raised cattle on their hilly little spread out in the Berkshires. They scraped and sweated enough money out of that rocky, unyielding earth to send their only son to college. Johnny Grabowski enrolled at Fitchburg State College. He wanted to become a teacher. The college assigned him a red-headed baseball player named Eddie Donagan as a roommate. Donagan had no parents and Johnny Grabowski had no friends, so they struck the obvious bargain. Eddie spent his vacations with the Grabowskis, and Johnny followed Eddie around to parties.

When Johnny Grabowski was drafted, Eddie wanted to sign up to go to Vietnam with his friend. Johnny wouldn't let him. 'You stay home and take care of Ma and Pa,' he told Eddie. 'And keep that arm in shape. I want to see you in a Sox uniform when I get back.'

Eddie kept his part of the deal. But Johnny didn't keep his. The helicopter he was riding in was blown out of the sky. He had been in Vietnam for nine days when it happened.

So when Eddie signed his contract he insisted that Jake and Mary Grabowski be present, and after all the signatures had been inscribed and witnessed, Eddie glanced at me, and I said, 'Eddie has a little announcement he'd like to make.'

Eddie went over and stood between Jake and Mary Grabowski. He draped his arms around their shoulders and said, 'Jake and Mary have been like parents to me. And

21

Johnny was my brother. I love them. I can never repay them for everything. But I wanted to do something. Here's what I'm trying to say. Me and Mr Coyne worked out this thing. It's a scholarship to Fitchburg State in Johnny's name. It's for a needy boy who wants to be a teacher. The Johnny Grabowski Scholarship. Mr Coyne fixed it up with the school, and everything's all set.'

Mary Grabowski's thin body shook as she cried softly, and Jake pumped Eddie's hand.

'You should all know,' I added, 'that the money for the scholarship comes out of Eddie's bonus. It's enough to cover room and board and tuition for four years.'

That's how Eddie Donagan was back then. Generous, warm, simple. He loved baseball, Jan, and Jake and Mary Grabowski. He'd never had any money, so giving a lot of it away didn't strike him as a big deal.

Eddie played for the Red Sox farm club in Jamestown, New York, that summer of 1970, and in September he and Janet Farina were married at St Eulalia's in Winchester. Jake Grabowski was his best man, and I was an usher. Sam held the reception under a big tent on his side lawn. Most of the guests were his business associates. It looked like the opening scene from *The Godfather*.

That winter Eddie took a couple of courses

22

at Boston State, but he didn't finish them. He worked part-time in one of Sam's liquor stores. He and Jan lived at Sam's house in Winchester.

One Saturday night that winter Gloria, to whom I was still married then, and I took Eddie and Jan to a concert at Memorial Hall in Cambridge. The Harvard and Radcliffe orchestra and chorus were performing Beethoven's Ninth Symphony. It was Gloria's idea to invite Eddie and Jan—she had a kind of missionary zeal about bringing culture to the unwashed masses, into which category she automatically lumped all professional athletes like Eddie and weekend golfers like me. Jan, with the benefit of her Mount Holyoke education, seemed thrilled at the prospect, and Eddie went along good-naturedly. His idea of classical music was something melodious by Simon and Garfunkel, and when the musicians filed into the hall, the men in their black tuxedoes and the women in frilled white blouses, he leaned across Gloria and whispered to me, 'It only takes four Beatles to do a tune. Look at all those musicmasters up there! Man, this song must be something!'

Gloria patted his arm. 'It is,' she said. 'It's a great song.'

Jan looked embarrassed. 'Eddie, shh!' she said to him.

23

When the orchestra began to play, Eddie leaned forward. I could see his eyes studying the moves of the conductor. His head bobbed to the rhythms of the music. At the beginning of the second movement, he leaned towards me, his hand carelessly balanced on Gloria's knee and his eyes bright with recognition, and whispered, 'That's Huntley-Brinkley music, man!'

A little later, when the chorus was singing 'The Ode to Joy', I glanced at Eddie. He was leaning back in his seat and his eyes were closed. Tears glistened on his cheeks.

After the performance the four of us paused on the steps outside the hall to turn up our collars and huddle into our heavy coats against the winter air. Eddie had one arm around Jan's shoulders. He grabbed my hand and pumped it. 'Man, that was beautiful. A great show!' He looked down at Jan. 'We gotta get that record,' he said to her.

Stump Kelly had been right about Eddie Donagan's talent. He played Double A Ball for Pawtucket the following spring, and in August he was called up to the Triple A club in Louisville. His combined record with the two minor league teams in 1971 was fourteen and three. The papers began to hail him as a cinch to make the Red Sox in 1972. He was added to the forty-man roster in the winter and went to spring training with the Boston team.

He called me collect one afternoon that March. I was in my office staring out at the grey city that was suffocating under layers of clouds, fog, and slush. Eddie was in Winter Haven, Florida.

'They're sending me back to Pawtucket,' he said. 'What a bummer.'

'They can do that, Eddie. You'll be back.'

'How the hell can they do that to me? Nobody's hit me all spring. I shut out the Tigers for three innings day before yesterday.'

'That's the business you're in. Stick to pitching. Do your stuff. You'll make it.'

'I'm gettin' chilled, man. It's bogus. A real turnoff.'

'I can't help you. Keep your mouth shut and throw the hell out of the ball.'

'Yeah,' he grumbled.

'How's Jan?'

'Oh, she's okay, I guess. She doesn't like living in a motel. The other wives chill her. I guess if I'm headed back to Pawtucket she'll be home in a week or so.'

'Give her my love. And Eddie?'

'Yeah?'

'Do your job. Pitch, don't bitch. Okay?'

'Sure. Ten-four.'

'So how's the weather down there?'

25

'The weather? Oh, you know. Florida.'

'By the way, Eddie. Spalding wants to sign you up.'

'Yeah? Is that good?'

'I don't think so. They figure you're going to make it. They try to sign minor leaguers up cheap, lock them in, so that when they do make it, it won't cost them a bundle. I suggest you wait. There's Wilson, Rawlings, all the rest. We can do better when you're a big league pitcher.'

'I don't know, Brady. I could use some of that iron.'

'You don't need money now. It's up to you. I say you should wait.'

I heard him sigh. 'Sure. You're the lawmaster. I'll wait.'

'Smart decision.'

He laughed. 'See you later, Counsellor.'

The Red Sox were in the thick of a pennant race when they called Eddie Donagan up in July. Fenway Park was sold out the night he started his first game. For Eddie it was what he called a 'Bogart'—a big game. 'My first debut,' he said. Sam and Josie and Jan and I sat in seats Eddie got for us behind the Red Sox dugout. And Eddie pitched the same way he had that first time I watched him at Fitchburg State College, hunching his shoulders, bending like a bow, and zipping

26

the ball with the speed and accuracy of an arrow. The fans loved him, a gangly local kid, big-shouldered and open-faced and red-headed. He pawed and scraped at the mound, cheered his fielders, chatted with the baseball, and bounded on and off the field like a boy on his way home from school for summer vacation.

The White Sox hitters looked about as skilled as those college kids from North Adams State had looked that first time I'd seen Eddie pitch. They waved at his 'yakker', swung late at his 'cheese', and after eight innings he had a one-to-nothing lead. He had given up four singles, one walk, and, by Sam's count, had struck out six.

When Eddie sprinted to the mound to begin the ninth innings, the people in Fenway Park all stood and began to applaud. The sound of thirty-five thousand pairs of hands clapping for Eddie Donagan made me shiver. I glanced at Sam and saw that his eyes were shining. Eddie stood awkwardly, flipping the ball back and forth from his hand to his glove while Carlton Fisk, the catcher, pretended to adjust his shin guards. I could see Fisk grinning at Eddie's discomfort.

When the first Chicago batter stepped into the box the fans continued to stand and applaud. When he hit Eddie's second pitch

27

hard on the ground into centre field, the applause shifted into a chant, 'Ed-die, Ed-die,' and grew in volume when Eddie Kasko, the Red Sox manager, hopped out of the dugout and jogged to the mound. Fisk walked out, his mask tucked under his arm, and the three of them talked for a moment. From where I sat I could see them smiling. Eddie nodded his head vigorously, and then Kasko slapped him on his ass and walked back into the dug-out.

When the next Chicago batter came to the plate, the noise in the park suddenly stopped. It was Dick Allen, a fearsome slugger in those days, and destined to be the American League's Most Valuable player that year. One by one the fans sat down to watch the confrontation.

But there was no drama. Allen hit Eddie's first pitch high into the misty Boston night, over the left field wall, over the screen atop the wall, and the ball was still rising on the ascending arc of its big parabola when I last saw it. I turned to look at Eddie. His body was still facing the plate, his legs planted in his follow-through, but his head had swivelled around to follow the flight of the ball, and his finger was the barrel of a gun pointed at his temple.

The silence in the ballpark was as awesome,

28

in its way, as the applause of a few minutes earlier had been. Then a guy sitting somewhere behind me yelled, 'At's okay, Eddie-boy. At's okay.' And the chant built again, 'Ed-die, Ed-die,' as Kasko climbed out of the dugout and moved slowly towards the mound. Eddie started to walk towards him, and they met by the third-base line. I could see the back of Kasko's neck redden as he thrust his jaw at Eddie. I couldn't tell what the manager said to him, but Eddie's chin sagged on to his chest, and he trudged slowly into the dugout and out of sight without looking up or acknowledging the cheers.

Later that evening we all met at Sam's house. Sam kept pounding Eddie on the back telling him what a great game he pitched, and Eddie grinned shyly and didn't say much of anything, and Jan hugged his arm. Josie kept running in and out of the kitchen where she had a vat of pasta bubbling.

'Tough one to lose,' I said to Eddie, when I found myself momentarily alone with him.

'Man, I was stylin', when all of a sudden that Allen went ding-dong. Took me to the bridge.' Eddie took a big gulp from his Budweiser.

I smiled. 'What did Kasko say when he came to take you out? He didn't look too happy.'

'He said, "When I come out to get you, you wait for me. You wait right there on the mound 'til I get there. Don't you ever make me look bad again."'

'What'd you say?'

Eddie flashed his Huck Finn grin. 'I told him not to sweat it, he wouldn't have to get me any more.'

'And what'd he say to that?'

'He said if I was in Pawtucket it wouldn't be a problem.'

Eddie didn't go back to Pawtucket. He took his spot in the Red Sox pitching rotation, and when the season ended he had won six games, lost only that first one, and the Red Sox lost the pennant to Detroit by a single game. Even though he had played only half the season, Eddie got several votes for Rookie of the Year, which his teammate Fisk won. He had the city of Boston, as Sam liked to say, 'by the short hairs'. Everywhere he went he was recognized, welcomed, loved. The Red Sox sent him to visit sick kids at Children's Hospital. He did publicity for the Jimmy Fund. He spoke at Little League banquets and Rotary Club meetings in places like Andover and Bridgewater. I got him some easy endorsement money from a Somerville Pontiac dealer, and we signed a five-year exclusive contract with Rawlings, who wanted

30

to manufacture a full line of Eddie Donagan sporting equipment.

Eddie started off the 1973 season about where he had left off—and it wasn't until sometime in June when I first became aware of the change. It didn't even seem important, because Eddie was still winning, and the sportswriters loved his ingenuous antics and inventive language. But he was starting to give up runs. The Sox had plenty of hitters, and they lived with the tradition of outslugging their opponents. In comfortable little Fenway Park, the Red Sox expected their pitchers to give up runs, so at first they didn't seem to care that Eddie's five-to-nothing games had become five-to-three or four. Kasko was making trips to the mound to bail Eddie out of ninth-innings trouble quite regularly, and a few times the relief pitchers failed and the runners Eddie had left on the bases scored, and then he was a loser.

I was with Eddie one night after he had blown a three-run lead in the eighth innings and was lifted from a game that the Sox eventually lost in the eleventh. Jan had gone to bed, and Sam and Josie were away, so it was just Eddie and I at the kitchen table sipping beer.

'You got a sore arm or something?' I asked him.

'Hey, you ever lose a court case?'

'Sure. Somebody's got to lose. Sometimes I don't have a case that can be won.'

'In baseball somebody's got to lose, too.'

'Don't give me that crap. Baseball's different from the law. You're not pitching the way you can.'

'This ain't an easy game, lawmaster. Everybody gets beat sometimes. It ain't like Fitchburg. No salad teams. These guys are all major leaguers. There's no margin for error.'

I sipped my beer and said softly, 'You seem to be erring a lot lately.'

'Christ, man, I ain't a machine. So I'm making a few bad pitches. I'm still a winner.'

'You don't look like a winner out there.'

He slammed his beer can on to the table. 'Okay, man. Get off a my back, will you? You're my lawyer, not my fuckin' manager. You just take care of my iron and leave the baseball to us ballplayers. Okay?'

I shrugged. 'Okay, Eddie.'

He cocked his head at me, his eyes blazing. I smiled and gave him the finger. Then he grinned. 'Up yours, too,' he said. 'Ah shit. I'm sorry, man. I'm taking all kinds of horseshit these days, and it just don't seem fair, know what I mean? What's the matter with Eddie Donagan? I hear it everywhere. I see kids on the street, they yell, "Hey, Eddie,

32

what the fuck's the matter with ya?" The papers they're sayin', "What happened to Donagan? How come he's givin' up runs and hits and even losin' a game now and then?" Now the coaches are startin' to screw around with me, like I was some kind of little machine. They say, "Here, shorten your stride, you're overstriding, Eddie." So I shorten my stride and it feels fucked up, and I tell them, and they say, "Look, kid, we're big coaches, we've been around for a long time, and you're just a young wise-ass, so you just do what we tell ya to do and we'll make a pitcher out of you. Yessiree." Shit. I was a pitcher without them. They tryin' to tell me I'm too—you know, eccentric. They tell me I gotta stop talkin' to the players and fixin' up the pitcher's mound. They want me to try the, whatchacallit, you know, Bob Turley, the . . . ah, shit . . .'

'The no-windup delivery? They want you to do that?'

'Yeah, that's it. Hey, that ain't Eddie Donagan. One of 'em's even sayin' I oughta get another pitch. Wants to teach me the fuckin' forkball. Hey, I don't need no forkball, or a knuckleball or a palm ball or a goddam spitter. I just wish to hell they'd leave me alone, is what I wish.'

I lit a cigarette. 'I'm sorry I mentioned it.

You're doing fine. Pitch a shutout for us sometime, though, will you?'

'Man, I feel one comin' on,' he said. 'Watch out, you Indians.'

But he didn't pitch a shutout against Cleveland. He walked two batters leading off the seventh innings and Kasko yanked him. Eddie threw his glove into the dugout as he walked away from his manager. Later, Kasko told a reporter he was thinking of taking Eddie out of the starting rotation and putting him in the bullpen so he could, as he put it, 'work out his problems'.

I was watching on television the night in Detroit that it all blew up in Eddie Donagan's face. In the first innings he walked the leadoff batter on four pitches. The fourth actually went behind the batter, who glared at Eddie as he jogged to first. Eddie hit the next batter on the foot with his first pitch. His next pitch bounced in front of the plate and caromed past the catcher. The runners moved to second and third. That's when Kasko came slowly out of the dugout. The television camera zoomed in on Eddie as he stood on the mound to wait for the manager to come take the ball from him. Eddie's forefinger was pointed at his temple.

He called me collect later that night. 'I'm all fucked up, man. I don't know where the fuck it's going. Oh, man, am I fucked up.'

'You been drinking, Eddie?'

'Damn straight I've been drinking, man. Oh, shit, I can't do nothin' any more.'

'It was just one of those things. You'll be fine. Forget it.'

'Just one of those things,' he sang. 'Yeah. Ha, ha. Forget it, he says. Listen, lawmaster, you ever try to talk and nothing but gobbledygook come out of your mouth? Huh? That ever happen to you, you gonna talk to the jury, be all eloquent and do your lawyer thing, and nothing but noises come out? You ever talk to a judge and hear yourself barkin' like a dog? Huh?'

'Jesus, Eddie. It must be frustrating.'

'Frustrating! Ha! Know what they call it? Oh, big joke. It used to be a big joke. Something that happened to other guys. The Steve Blass disease. Remember Steve Blass? It means you're a big league pitcher who wakes up one day and finds out that he doesn't know where the fuck the ball is going to go when he lets go of it. Well, man, I got it. I got it bad. A bad case of Steve Blass. Terminal case. Eddie Donagan's sick, and all the guys, they stay away from me now. They think it's contagious. Don't go near Eddie Donagan. He's got the Big C. Cancer of the head. Even the coaches, they don't look at me when they see me. All of a sudden they don't wanna

35

come near me. They think if they try to help me somebody'll blame them for what happened. Ah, shit, man, am I ever fucked up.'

'How's the arm? Is your arm okay?'

'Oh, man, the arm is beautiful. Still got the gas. I can throw the ball nine hundred miles an hour. I can still bend off a yakker that'll come right back to me. Shit, after I came out of the game I snuck out to the bullpen. Know what? They could've propped the glove up on a stick and I would've hit the pocket every time. Shit. Perfect. I was fuckin' perfect.'

'Well, then, it sounds like you're fine. You'll get over it. Just one of those things.'

'Naw. I was doin' that before the game, too. Warming up I was great. Perfect. My head is messed up. Soon as the game starts I'm thinkin' about my stride, and bending my back, and the hips and the shoulders and cocking the elbow and man it won't go where I'm aimin' it at all. I got bit by the Steve Blass bug and there ain't no cure.'

His next start Eddie threw the first pitch over the middle of the plate, then nine consecutive balls not even close, and Kasko took him out. He didn't pitch for eleven days. He worked out every day with the bullpen catcher. He threw the ball perfectly. When he next pitched he came into the sixth innings of a game the Red Sox were losing by five runs. He walked a batter and threw the next pitch shoulder high and out over the plate. It disappeared over the centre field fence. For a major league pitcher, I knew, that home run pitch was just as wild as any of those that hadn't been strikes.

Eddie spent the rest of the season back in Pawtucket. The Sox sent Stump Kelly down to work with him. They were even talking about trying a hypnotist. I talked to Eddie on the phone now and then. He said he was throwing the ball as well as ever—except in games. In games he had no control.

While Eddie was in Pawtucket Jan remained in Winchester with Sam and Josie. It was only an hour and a half drive from Pawtucket, but Eddie never made it. Jan said she understood. Eddie needed to work things out. Baseball was his profession. Right now, baseball came first. Eddie didn't call her, either. Once in a while she phoned him. She told me Eddie was distant and even surly with her.

'He's drinking a lot, I think,' she confided to me one day. 'I think he's got a real problem, Brady. He doesn't want to see me. They won't let him pitch. He just gets dressed every day and throws on the sidelines and takes a shower and goes to that room he's living in and drinks. Will he get better, do you think?'

'I don't honestly know. He's got lots of people rooting for him. He's young. His arm is still good.'

'But that's not what I mean,' said Jan, snapping her head to toss her hair away from her face. 'I mean, if he can't pitch any more will he get better?'

I touched her hand. 'I don't know.'

CHAPTER FOUR

The Red Sox advised Eddie to take the winter off, stay completely away from baseball. That seemed to suit him fine. He hung around the house, made a few appearances, and after Christmas he and Jan went to Bermuda for two weeks.

'I've got this thing licked,' he told me the February morning he left for spring training. I was there to see him off. He had a new station wagon loaded with duffel bags and suitcases. He and Jan had decided that she'd fly down to join him after a few weeks so that Eddie could concentrate on baseball. He was scheduled to begin working out with the minor leaguers, but he professed not to mind. He stood there in Sam's driveway, one arm thrown carelessly around Jan's shoulders, grinning that big hillbilly grin of his, and said, 'I can feel it, man. The old feeling, it's there. You'll see. All of them, sayin' Eddie Donagan's washed up. Just wait.'

Jan looked up at him, and I read more fear than love in the smile she offered him. He squeezed her shoulder, kissed the top of her head, then thrust his hand at me. 'See ya, old buddy. You get a bunch of them contracts ready. People gonna be wantin' Eddie Donagan's John Hancock.'

We shook hands. 'You just work on your pitching. I'll take care of business.'

'And take care of my little girl, here, too,' he said, giving Jan another squeeze. He raised his hand in a kind of salute. 'Well, people, I'm gone.'

He climbed into his car. Jan and I stood in the driveway and watched him back out and pull away. She found my hand with hers and gripped it hard. 'I think he's going to do it this time,' she said. 'He's so confident. I think he's going to be okay.'

I nodded. 'I think so, too,' I said, with more conviction than I felt.

The pitchers and catchers were expected to arrive in Winter Haven on Saturday. The following Monday morning I received a phone call in my office from Farley Vaughn.

'Where's Donagan?' he said.

'And a cheery good morning to you, too,' I said. Vaughn was the guy with whom I had negotiated Eddie's Red Sox contract. In the couple of years since Eddie had signed with the Sox I had consumed at least a gallon of Jack Daniels with Vaughn, and he twice that amount of various fruit and vegetable juices, while we debated semicolons and subordinate clauses. He was a straight shooter, an old-fashioned baseball man who had once been a class D in-fielder who couldn't hit the curve and had sense enough to get himself an MBA from the Tuck School at Dartmouth. Farley Vaughn was smart and tough and fair, and I liked doing business with him.

'Your boy's late, Coyne. He's accumulating a pretty good-sized fine. It's all there in his contract.'

'I'm familiar with the contract,' I said. 'He didn't show up? That's funny. He left a week ago. Hm. He probably got thrown into the can for speeding in Virginia. They do that down there. Didn't he call you?'

'No one's heard word one.'

'Me neither. Let me call Jan. I'll get back to you.'

All I accomplished in calling Jan was upsetting her. She had heard nothing from

40

Eddie. I called Vaughn back and told him.

'Five hundred bucks a day it's costing him. Figure he's shacked up with some tootsie in South Carolina? Gonna be a pretty damn expensive toss in the hay.'

'I don't know. He was rarin' to go when he left here. Maybe he had an accident. There has to be an explanation. I'm sure he'll turn up.'

'He can't afford this. Professionally, I mean.'

'I know, Farley,' I said. 'He knows it, too.'

The Red Sox contacted the State Police all along Eddie's probable route from Winchester to Florida. He hadn't been arrested, or injured in an accident, or admitted to a hospital. He hadn't even gotten a speeding ticket. His absence from training camp was, they concluded, voluntary.

Three weeks passed with no word from Eddie, at the end of which Vaughn informed me he was invoking Section IX, paragraph C of Eddie's contract which, in effect, voided the agreement and put Eddie into the category of suspended without pay.

'You know damn well there are extenuating circumstances,' I told him. 'We'll have to litigate this when Eddie comes back.'

'And you know that if Eddie comes back we'll work something out. We want him to pitch for the Red Sox. Right now, though, we've got no choice. You know, we've got a couple of Latin American players who have trouble every year with their visas. And there's always somebody whose wife's about to have a baby. We're not unreasonable. But we've got to draw the line. Look. Get Eddie down to Winter Haven. We'll work it out.'

Eddie called me at my office— collect—two days later. After I told the operator I'd accept the charges, I said, 'Eddie, where the hell are you?'

'I'm okay, old lawmaster. Tell Jan I'm okay. That's the message.'

'I talked to Farley Vaughn. He says—'

'Don't hassle me, man.' And he hung up.

I became adept at saying 'no comment' to the inquiries of the Boston sportswriters. Jan stopped taking phone calls. Even so, the papers ran speculative stories about the mysterious disappearance of Eddie Donagan, which they spiced with indiscreet quotes from Eddie's teammates and coaches.

The snow melted, March became April, and the baseball season arrived. The Red Sox flew to the West Coast to open with the Angels. The minor leaguers dispersed to Pawtucket and Bristol and Winston-Salem and Elmira. Eddie Donagan accompanied none of them.

On the morning after Patriot's Day I was sitting at my desk cradling a mug of coffee and wishing I was fishing when the phone rang. It was Eddie.

'I'm back,' he said.

'Where's "back"?'

'Here. Home. Jan said I should call you.'

'Are you all right?'

'Sure. Of course.'

'Oh. We were kinda wondering.'

'I'm fine.'

'Well, I hope you won't think I'm getting too personal if I ask you where the hell you've been for the past couple of months. You know, several people were mildly curious. Like your family. And your employer. Not to mention your attorney.'

'I've been around. Thinking.'

'Oh, good.'

'Yes. I decided to quit.'

'I think you've already been fired.' I paused to light a cigarette and recover my composure. 'Look. Why don't you meet me at my office tomorrow. I'm pretty sure we can work something out with the team.'

'You weren't listenin' to me, lawmaster. I quit. I'm done with baseball. There's nothing to work out with the team. I got no uniform to turn in or anything.'

'Eddie, what the hell . . . ?'

43

'The Steve Blass disease, man. It got me. I just ran out of control. Used it all up. Like a car out of gas. I'm out of control. None left. That's all.'

'You're out of control, all right. That why you had to disappear for two months?'

'Don't crowd me, man. I'm back, Okay?'

'How do you know you can't pitch if you never went to spring training?'

'I know.'

I sighed. 'Sure. Meet me tomorrow, anyway. We've got some things to do.'

'Okay,' he said cheerfully. 'I'll be there.'

Eddie was immovable in his decision. We met with Farley Vaughn and arranged for a press conference.

The three television stations who attended had cameras in the Red Sox conference room. About a dozen reporters were there, armed with pencils and notebooks and tape recorders. Eddie wore blue jeans and a plaid shirt and scuffed cowboy boots. He sat between Vaughn and me at the table, his arm hooked casually around the back of his chair. He smiled and nodded at the sportswriters. A cluster of microphones crouched on the table in front of him.

Vaughn stood up and said to the reporters, 'You boys all set?'

Murmurs of assent came from the double

row of reporters sitting in the folding chairs.

'Okay. Eddie has a statement for you.'

Eddie leaned forward on to his forearms to get his mouth close to the microphones. He read from the paper we had prepared for him.

'This morning I informed the Boston Red Sox Baseball Club that I have voluntarily retired from professional baseball. I have done this for personal reasons. I have always been treated well by the Red Sox, and I regret any inconvenience I may have caused them.' Eddie looked up from the paper. 'That's it, guys. No questions.'

Eddie and I left Farley Vaughn in the room to deal with the chaos of questions from the reporters. When the door shut behind us I said to Eddie, 'I still think you owed it to those guys to stay and face them. You should have answered their questions.'

'Ah, the hell with them. Goddam vultures. Love you when you're going good. But they like it better when you're down. Screw 'em.'

For a couple of months Eddie Donagan was a big story in Boston. One of the local talk shows invited a panel of psychiatrists to speculate on the psychopathology of the Steve Blass disease, Eddie Donagan, of course, being Exhibit A. They invited Eddie to participate. He refused. A book publisher approached me with a contract worth twenty-five grand for a ghost writer to put together a quickie paperback about Eddie. They thought they'd call it *The Eddie Donagan Story: A Tragedy in One Act*. They were 'ninety per cent certain' they'd be able to sell the rights for a made-for television movie. I advised Eddie to turn it down.

The *Globe* did run a three-part story a couple of weeks after Eddie quit. It was written by one of the staff sportswriters, who based the piece mainly on interviews with baseball people. All of them had a story to tell about a kid they'd once known—the shortstop who mysteriously began to imitate a croquet wicket when a ground ball came his way, the third baseman who compulsively heaved baseballs into the stands in back of first, the catcher who refused to give the sign for the curveball, the outfielder who could not persuade his body to slide into a base, and many, many pitchers who, like Eddie, 'ran out of control'. All gifted athletes whose careers collapsed into neurosis. Eddie laughed when he read the article.

'They think I'm upset about this,' he said. 'Shit. I'm the happiest guy in the world. I know that I'm gonna wake up tomorrow morning and I won't hafta throw a baseball. I can play golf, and if I start hooking no one's gonna start asking, "What's the matter with

Eddie Donagan?" And when I go fishin' and don't catch nothin', nobody's gonna say, "Oh, oh. Looks like Donagan's lost it again." I can do anything, and nobody expects nothin', and I don't hafta play baseball. What more could a guy want?'

And outwardly, at least, Eddie really did seem at peace with himself. He stopped drinking. He began to travel with Sam, 'learning the business', as Sam liked to say, although I believe that Sam just enjoyed Eddie's company. Sam called him his 'administrative assistant', paid him a good salary, gave him a car.

I suggested to Eddie that I might be able to win him some money by claiming a work-related disability. As I tried to explain it to him, his problem seemed to me legally identical to a torn rotator cuff or broken leg. If he'd been forced out of baseball because of a physical injury, I could have invoked a clause in his contract which would have required the organization to pay him what would have amounted to a comfortable annuity.

Eddie flatly refused to let me try it. 'I just can't do it any more, that's all,' he said. 'They pay me to get batters out. I can't get batters but. That ain't their fault.'

'I'm sure I can make a case,' I said.

'I don't want you to make any case. I want

you to forget the whole thing. I don't want anybody pokin' into my head, talking to people about me, analysing my problems. I can't do the job. So I quit. That's fair. That's the way it should be. That's the way I want it.'

'The only difference,' I argued, 'would be that you'd have some guaranteed income. Better to have it than not to have it.'

'Why don't they give it to me then?'

'Because we have to go to court to make the case, first.'

'That means there'd be testimony, right? Guys who knew me, coaches. You'd bring your witnesses, and they'd bring theirs, and you lawmasters would examine them and cross-examine them and make them say things they didn't mean. And their witnesses would say bad things about me, and yours would say good stuff. Right?'

'More or less. And we could have doctors, who could testify as to the nature of your problem.'

'And they'd have their doctors, too.'

'Yes.'

'No fuckin' way. I want none of that. I don't care about the money. I just want to forget the whole thing.'

'Okay. We'll forget it.'

And with that, my professional relationship with Eddie Donagan ended. He no longer needed an agent. He had no need for an attorney. We remained friends. I took him fishing with me a few times, and occasionally he and Sam played golf against my friend Charlie McDevitt and me for beers. I continued under retainer for Sam.

A year or so after Eddie quit baseball, he and Jan had a baby. They named him Edward Joseph, after Eddie. They called him 'E.J.'. Shortly after that they moved out of Sam's place in Winchester into a little hip-roofed colonial in Bedford. Eddie worked full-time for Sam Farina, while Jan stayed home to raise their son. Sam started mumbling about retiring, now that he had someone he could trust to take over the business. And before long Eddie Donagan had become the answer to a trivia question.

★   ★   ★

And that's how things remained until one winter afternoon a little more than three years ago, when Sam Farina called me.

'That son of a bitch has walked out on her,' was how he put it.

'Which son of a bitch has walked out on whom?'

'Him. Donagan. Who else?' Sam sounded as if he were hyperventilating.

'If you don't calm down I'm going to hang up.'

'Calm down, he says. My only daughter is here in my house bawling her eyes out, and my only grandson is here wondering what in the hell is going on and where his goddam daddy went to, and you want me to calm down. Let me tell you something. I want that bastard picked clean. Understand? When we get done with him I want him jay naked.'

'Sam, will you for Christ's sake tell me what's going on?'

I heard him take a deep breath. 'I don't *know* what's going on. Jan doesn't know what's going on. All I know is he didn't show up for a couple of days at work, but I, you know, didn't think too much about it. The hell, we got a loose arrangement. I leave the kids alone. Eddie has his work to do, he generally does it. Then this morning my Jan calls me, says her Eddie's gone. Packed a bag and walked out. He was away from the house a couple of days and nights, but she wasn't worried because he told her he was gonna be out of town. Okay. Then he shows up, packs, says he's leaving and not to say anything or ask any questions, just that he's leaving her and she should get a divorce and give the kid his love.'

'Was he drinking?'

'She says no. She says he was perfectly sober, rational, calm. The bastard hugged her and kissed her and said not to worry it was nothing she did, nothing to do with her. He's gone.'

'And—?'

'And I want you to pick his bones, Counsellor.'

'No.'

'What do you mean, no?'

'I mean, I'm not going to represent Jan in any divorce proceeding. I'll be happy to recommend a good attorney for her. I'll do the same for Eddie, if he asks.'

'Wait just a goddam minute,' said Sam, his voice a growl. 'You're my attorney.'

'Don't even think about threatening me, Sam. I'm Eddie's attorney, too, in case you've forgotten. I make it a policy not to take sides in domestic disputes when I have a personal relationship, or a professional commitment, with both parties. Anyhow, you should be thinking in terms of reconciliation, not divorce. Every marriage has its ups and downs.'

'This kid is a bona fide wacko, Brady. When he was playing ball it was kinda colourful. But he's supposed to be a grown-up, now, with responsibilities. I'm in favour of a divorce.'

'It's not your life, Sam.'

'Like hell it ain't. Jan's happiness is my happiness.'

'Then let them work it out. He'll be back. I'd put money on it.'

*   *   *

I would have lost my money. Eddie and Jan Donagan didn't work it out. Eddie disappeared for several months, just as he had when he quit baseball. And, like the previous time, he called me collect to assure us all that he was all right. When I mentioned reconciliation, he hung up on me. They were divorced a year later. Sam got Jan an attorney of his own choosing, and they did pick Eddie clean. Jan got the house, custody of E.J., and about everything else that wasn't actually attached to Eddie's body, though I think Sam had designs on certain functional portions of his anatomy, too. Eddie refused to contest it. Jan, for her part, decided not to demand child support or alimony, reasoning, logically, that Sam would take care of her and her son and that Eddie didn't have much of anything left to share, anyway. Besides, she still loved him. Her reaction to the entire process was one more of bewilderment than of anger or even sadness.

Once the divorce was finalized, Sam helped Jan to sell the house in Bedford and set up a suite for herself and E.J. in his Winchester home. Meanwhile, Eddie turned up living in an apartment in Medford and working in a sporting goods store in Burlington. Eddie Donagan, who once had looked to me like the reincarnation of Bob Feller, was a sneaker salesman.

And he and I lost touch with each other. He had no business with me. Sneaker salesmen hardly ever need agents. Still, we had been friends. I called him a few times, suggesting we get together. He had excuses. I suppose he was embarrassed at the changes that had befallen him. Sam told me that Eddie mailed a couple of Christmas presents to E.J. the first year after the divorce. But he forgot his son's birthday. Every few months, according to Sam, Eddie apparently had a bout with his conscience and called Jan and E.J. on the phone. He made vague promises to visit, to take E.J. to a ball game or fishing. E.J. would lie awake nights waiting for Eddie to appear. But he rarely did.

A few months before Jan called me to tell me E.J. was late from his paper route, I had called Eddie and he agreed to meet me for lunch. I hadn't seen him since before his divorce. He was waiting near Faneuil Hall at the kiosk where they sell discount theatre tickets. He was wearing blue jeans and a denim jacket over a faded flannel shirt. He had grown an ill-kempt beard. Lines had been carved into his forehead and at the corners of his eyes that I hadn't noticed before, and it startled me until I realized that Eddie Donagan was thirty-four or thirty-five years old.

Shaking hands with him still reminded me of sticking my mitt between the rollers of an old-fashioned washing machine, and Eddie's Huck Finn grin was broad and welcoming.

We walked inside the crowded market to Regina's booth and I bought us big slabs of pizza. Peppers and mushrooms and extra cheese for me. It was late March and dense little mounds of grey snow huddled against the shady sides of the buildings. Eddie and I wandered around the brick-paved mall area. We appraised the ladies, peered into windows, and munched on our pizzas. We didn't talk until we finished eating. Then we sat on a concrete bench in the sun. I tapped a cigarette out of my pack and offered one to Eddie. He shook his head.

'Naw, man,' he said. 'One thing I still don't do is smoke.'

'All the other sins, huh?'

'Most of 'em.'

'So how's the job?'

'Oh, man, you can't imagine. Bending over people's feet all day. They come in, these fat, wheezy old beefs, they want to spend sixty or seventy bucks on a pair of sneakers, for God's sake. Excuse me. Running shoes. We gotta call them running shoes. Not sneakers. And they want to be fitted just so, as if they were actually gonna run somewhere. Hell, they'd fall down dead if they ran six steps, most of 'em. No question. And the kids. Look around the playgrounds sometime. What do you see? Nikes. Pumas. New Balance. You think these kids shelled out fifty, sixty bucks for leather Nikes? You gotta watch 'em all the time.'

'Sounds like you love your work.'

Eddie's laugh was dry and mirthless. 'Quite a comedown, huh? Don't know what the hell I expected. Shit. Guess I'm lucky to have a job.'

'They're not lining up for your autograph, I guess.'

'Nope. They're not. That's a fact.'

'So what're you going to do, Eddie?'

'Do?' He grinned. 'Hell, lawmaster, I don't think about what I do. I get up, I go to work, I come home, pound a coupla Buds, maybe get lucky with a broad, more likely I don't, go to bed, get up again. Like that.'

I stamped out my cigarette. 'Sounds like quite a career.'

55

His elaborate shrug was meant to convey indifference. It didn't fool me. 'I guess I already had my career,' he said. 'I read somewhere everybody's got their fifteen minutes of fame. I already had mine, that's all.'

'Ever think about finishing school?'

'What I mainly think about, you want to know the truth, is going to Alaska. Build me a cabin way the hell up on one of them big rivers, shoot bears and caribou and catch salmon, chop wood all day.' He cocked his head at me and chuckled. 'Get me a squaw. One of them Eskimos that chew blubber all day and can't talk back because they don't know English. Live offa walrus meat and seal oil. Rub bear grease in our hair. Build an igloo in the winter. Wear animal skins. Sleep with the dogs. Walk around on snowshoes, ride sleds. Maybe even pan for gold.'

'Sounds perfectly idyllic,' I said.

'Hey, I'm half serious. A man can start all over in Alaska. Beats the hell out of Medford, I can tell you that. Some day I'm just gonna do it. I'll just be gone. Ta-ta.'

'What about the family?'

'Family? You mean E.J. Look. I've been a shitty father. I know that. Done the kid more harm than good. I don't see him much, I guess you probably know that. It's not easy, going

56

there. Sam won't even be there when I go, and all Jan does is glare at me out of the corner of her eyes like she's gonna start crying. And being with E.J., that's real weird. He's always kinda crouching, all tense, like he's ready to run away from me. It's almost as if he thinks I'm gonna hit him or something. So, I admit, it takes more guts than I usually got to go see him. I keep meaning to. I think about it a lot. And I call him and tell him I'm gonna take him somewhere or come out and visit. But then—hell, I just chicken out. It's like I was butting in. He seems like he's putting up with me because somebody told him he had to, and I keep thinking he's relieved when I don't go.'

'I know,' I said. 'I went through it myself with my two boys. I remember the feeling. But I don't think that's the way E.J. feels. It's not the way I hear it.'

Eddie flapped his hands. 'Yeah, I know. That's Jan. Maybe she thinks I should see him more. Maybe she's just makin' the point that I'm a bad guy.'

'Are you really prepared to give him up?'

'Looks like I already have. Can't very well take him to Alaska can I?'

'Not very well.'

Eddie thrust out his arm and glanced at his wristwatch. Then he stood up. The old grin was back. 'I gotta get to the shop,' he said.

'Lots of sneakers to sell. Good to see you again, man. Thanks for the pizza.'

'I hear they have great pizza in Alaska,' I said.

He squinted at me for a moment, then shrugged. 'I'm half serious,' he said.

PART TWO

JAN

CHAPTER FIVE

I promised Sylvie I wouldn't be gone long and left her sitting on the balcony outside my apartment. She continued to study the maritime traffic through my binoculars, still clad only in my shirt. I extracted from her a promise not to try to tidy up the place while I was gone. I had everything just the way I wanted it—in complete and comfortable disarray.

In addition to Sam Farina's Lincoln and Josie's Porsche, a nondescript blue Ford sedan sat in the driveway when I got to Winchester. I parked behind it and went to the door.

Sam had built his house on five acres of prime land on a hilltop near the Lexington line back in the Fifties. It was constructed of glass and vertical cedar sheathing and surrounded by flowering fruit trees and bark mulch paths which wound among formal rose gardens and goldfish ponds and fountains.

There was a kidney-shaped pool out back and a putting green on the side lawn. Sam built his place right after Jan was born, in anticipation of the big family he and Josie hoped to raise. It had seven bedrooms, each with its own bathroom. But Josie miscarried a couple of times and they never had any more kids after Jan.

Josie opened the door just as I was ringing the bell. She must have seen me drive up. Sam's wife was a slim, stately woman who looked ten years younger than her age of close to sixty. Her silver-and-black hair was pulled back loosely in a ponytail, accentuating her high cheekbones and good jawline. She wore tailored white slacks and a pale blue sleeveless blouse that did full justice to her trim tennis figure.

I kissed her on the cheek. 'Hi, gorgeous,' I said.

She made a quick attempt at a smile, then gave it up. 'Inspector Basile just got here,' she said. 'Come on in.'

I followed her into the big glass-walled living-room where Sam and Jan were sitting side by side on the sofa talking to a man I had never seen before. He wore rimless glasses, a shaggy blow-dried head of red hair, a bushy moustache, and a cheap summer-weight suit.

Jan stood up and came to me. Her smile was

60

unconvincing. She put both arms around my bicep and reached up to kiss my cheek. 'Thanks,' she whispered.

I disengaged my arm so I could put it around her shoulders as I walked towards the sofa with her. I said, 'He's still . . . ?'

'We don't know where he is,' she said. She gestured towards the red-headed guy. 'This is Inspector Basile. He's from the police.'

I nodded to him and said hello to Sam.

Jan and I sat on the sofa beside Sam. Basile hitched his chair closer to us, while Josie took another chair beside him. The policeman cleared his throat and produced a notebook and ball-point pen from a pocket inside his jacket. He opened the notebook on to his knee and peered up at Jan over the tops of his glasses.

'Okay. Let's get started,' he said. 'First off, I want you to understand that, from the police point of view, this sort of thing happens all the time. It's almost always just a misunderstanding. Kids wander off. They lose track of the time. They go exploring in the woods or downtown or something. I want you to try not to worry.'

Jan was staring at him, shaking her head. 'E.J. wouldn't do that.'

'Well, there's always a first time,' said Basile gently. 'Okay. Let me get some

61

information, anyway, and we can start looking for him.' He peered into his notebook for a moment. 'When did you last see him?'

Jan smiled quickly. 'Last night, actually. See, he has a paper route, and he always gets up early to do it. The truck leaves the papers at the end of the driveway. On Saturday he goes out about six-thirty. It takes him about an hour. He's usually back by seven-thirty. Quarter of eight at the latest. He's very responsible. Gets himself up in the morning.'

'Do you know if he left late today?'

'I was up,' said Sam. 'He left at the usual time.'

Basile made a notation in his notebook. 'Which was . . . ?'

'Six-thirty, like she said.'

'Okay. And you said that you checked and he finished his route, right?'

'Yes,' said Jan. 'He starts right next door, at the Bradleys' house, and goes all the way down the end of the street, then up Oakmont to Royal Ave. He ends up with two houses down on Maple Street.' Jan smiled at Basile. 'See, when E.J.'s sick I do it for him. Anyway, I called all his customers. They all got their papers.'

'Maple Street's a main road,' said Basile, talking, it seemed to himself. 'Okay. So then what? He walks home, right?'

'Yes,' said Jan. 'He comes straight home. He always does. The whole thing takes him less than an hour. He's only got nineteen papers. Seventeen on Saturday, actually, because two of his customers get the *Wall Street Journal*. They don't print a paper on Saturday.'

'Yes,' said Basile, smiling perfunctorily. 'How does he usually come home?'

'He just turns around and comes back the way he went.'

'Is there a shortcut he takes?'

Jan hesitated. 'He can cut through backyards and end up on Royal Ave. But he's not supposed to. I told him I want him on the sidewalks, not in people's yards.'

'But he might have taken a shortcut today?'

'I told him not to.' She frowned at Basile. 'Yes, okay, I guess he could have. But I don't see . . .'

Basile shrugged, scratching into his notebook. 'Okay,' he said without looking up. 'Describe your son for me.'

Jan sighed. 'He's about four-feet ten, eighty pounds. Red hair, like his father. Something like yours, actually,' she said to Basile. 'Not carroty red, but sort of brownish.' She put her hand on my knee and squeezed it. I covered it with my own. 'He's got greenish eyes. Impish. He smiles a lot. He's a happy child, he really is. He's very cute. He looks just like Eddie. A little turned-up nose . . . Oh, God!'

Jan put her face against my shoulder. I could feel her body shake.

'Take your time,' said Basile.

Jan sniffed and looked at him. 'I'm sorry.'

'Can you tell me what he was wearing today?'

'I can,' said Sam. 'He had on a yellow tee-shirt. It says Brother's Pizza across the back, and it's got a picture of a slice of pizza on the front of it. And jeans, I think. And sneakers.'

'Blue jeans?'

Sam nodded. 'I think so.'

'What kind of sneakers?'

'Nikes,' said Jan. 'Leather Nikes. He wears them everywhere. Eddie gave them to him. They've got this red stripe on the side.'

'He's how old?'

'Ten. Ten and a half, almost. He'll be eleven in February.'

Basile was writing into his notebook. 'I'll want a photo. I assume you can get me a photo.'

Jan smiled. 'I've got a million photos of my boy. He's very photogenic.'

Basile returned her smile. 'Yes. Now, what about his friends? Can you tell me who his friends are?'

Jan reeled off ten or a dozen names.

64

'These are neighbourhood kids?' said Basile, scribbling into his notebook.

'No, not all of them. Some are from school. The district is pretty big. I can get you all the addresses. But I've already called their homes. All those boys were home, and E.J. wasn't with them.'

'Sure,' said Basile. 'But we might want to talk with them. Maybe some of them have an idea where he might have gone.'

'I'm telling you, he didn't *go* anywhere. He wouldn't without asking me.'

'There's always a first time,' Basile repeated automatically. He riffled through a few pages of his notebook. 'Okay, now I have to ask you some more difficult questions. I don't want you to get upset. Okay?'

Jan stared at him. 'I'll try.' Her hand tightened again on my leg.

'Has E.J. been upset recently about anything? Did you have an argument, or did you punish him? Anything that might have made him angry?'

Jan looked from Sam to Josie. 'I don't think—'

'Eddie,' said Josie. 'Eddie was supposed to come over last week. He called and said he couldn't make it. It was Thursday. His day off. E.J. was upset about that, remember?'

Jan nodded. 'Yes, but that's happened

65

before.'

'What were they going to do?' asked Basile.

Jan shrugged. 'I don't think there was a plan. Eddie can only take E.J. away on weekends. He's only come to see him a few times in the past couple of years. This was nothing new.'

'But he *was* upset,' said Josie.

Jan nodded. 'He's always upset when that happens.'

'That was Thursday?' said Basile.

'Yes. Thursday.'

'And where does Eddie live?'

'Medford. Do you want the address?'

'Yes.'

Jan told him, and he wrote it down. 'Anything else?'

Again Jan appealed to Sam and Josie. They both shook their heads. 'No,' she said. 'I haven't punished him or anything. He was fine last night. We watched TV together. He was fine.'

Basile nodded, then peered at Sam. 'Difficult question for you, but I've got to ask it.' He paused, and Sam nodded. 'A wealthy man like yourself is bound to make an enemy or two along the way. Can you think of anyone—?'

'Who'd kidnap my grandchild?' Sam frowned. 'What a question,' he muttered.

'No. No, I can't think of a soul that evil. Nobody I know.'

'Well, if the FBI gets involved, they'll want to talk to you about that, so think about it.'

I felt Jan sag against me. 'The FBI? Oh, Jesus!'

Basile regarded her benignly. 'We have a lot of resources.'

'But that means . . .'

'One step at a time. Ninety-nine per cent of the time the kids show up. Look. Just last week I went through exactly this same thing. Boy was missing. Friday afternoon. Know what happened?'

'No,' Jan whispered.

'He spent the weekend in New Hampshire. Swimming, water skiing, having a grand old time. He was with friends of the family. Didn't get home until Sunday afternoon. The mother was absolutely frantic. We were about ready to call the FBI. Turns out the kid had talked to her about it and she said it was okay and then forgot about it. So when he kissed her goodbye she just thought he was going out to play. It just slipped her mind. It can happen.'

'I wouldn't forget,' said Jan.

'I'm not saying that. Just that boys, especially, seem to be missing and there are almost always logical explanations. If he's

67

missing for twenty-four hours we can call the FBI. Depending on the circumstances, they might get involved right away or not. And we have the State Police to help, too. I just want to have as much information as possible, so that if we do have to involve these others, we'll be able to give them what there is and save you the trouble of going through this all over again.'

'I can't think of enemies,' said Sam. 'I really can't.'

'What about the father?'

'Eddie?' Jan snorted. 'The problem with Eddie is that he doesn't care about his son.' She hesitated. 'Is that what you're thinking? That Eddie . . . ?'

'It happens,' said Basile. 'The non-custodial parent takes the child. Yes.'

Sam was shaking his head. 'That's not Eddie. He did a lousy thing, running off. But he wouldn't do something like this. Not Eddie.'

Basile cleared his throat. 'Has anybody spoken to Eddie today?'

Jan shook her head.

'I'll call him,' I said quickly.

Basile closed his notebook. 'Do that, will you?'

I went out into the kitchen, found Eddie Donagan's phone number in the little book I

68

carry in my hip pocket, dialled it, and let it ring a dozen times before I slapped the side of my head. Eddie worked on Saturdays. I found a phone book on a shelf beside the phone and looked up the number for the Herman's store at the Burlington Mall. The girl who answered was reluctant to get Eddie for me until I told her that it was police business. Several minutes passed before I heard Eddie's voice say, 'Yeah?'

'It's me,' I told him.

'The lawmaster himself. How're you doin', man?'

'Okay. Just wondering if you've talked to E.J. today?'

'No. 'Course not.' He paused. 'Why? Wait a minute. What the hell's going on?'

I decided not to beat around the bush. 'I'm at Sam's. E.J. didn't come back from his paper route yet. Nobody knows where he is.'

'What the Christ do you mean, nobody knows where he is? What happened?'

'We don't know. I hoped you might.'

'Well I don't. Jesus, Brady. I don't understand.'

'I'm just telling you what I know. The police are here now. I guess they'll look for him. Listen, if you talk to him or anything make sure you let us know, will you?'

'Of course I will. God! He's missing?'

'Right now he's missing. That doesn't necessarily mean . . .'

'He's been kidnapped or something, hasn't he? That's it, isn't it?'

'I don't know, Eddie. The police don't seem too concerned. They seem to think he'll turn up. He might've just gone somewhere to play and didn't tell Jan. Or maybe he decided to run away.'

'Run away?' I heard him take a deep breath. 'God damn it, Brady. What's the matter with them, anyway?'

'What's the matter with who? Whom?'

'Jan. Sam and Josie. Can't they keep track of a ten-year-old kid?'

'I really don't think it's useful for you all to start blaming each other.'

'They're blaming me, right?'

'No, not really.'

'Yeah. Right. I understand.' He sighed. 'I can't get off. I gotta be here 'til six.'

'That's okay. There's nothing you can do. I just wanted to make sure you didn't have him with you. And I wanted you to know what was going on.'

'Yeah. Thanks, man. Look, let me know, okay? No one else will. So keep me posted. If—when they find him, call me. Okay?'

I assured him that I would, and went back into the living-room to report my conversation. Basile suggested that no one use the telephone, and nobody seemed inclined to ask why. He went out to his car, saying he'd be back in a minute or two. Josie wandered into the kitchen to make sandwiches, a knee-jerk reaction for her. Sam and Jan and I remained sitting. We didn't have much to say. It reminded me of a hospital waiting-room. There we sat, the three of us together on the sofa, dreading the moment when the surgeon would come out, his mask lowered from his mouth, tugging at his rubber gloves and avoiding the eyes of the next of kin.

After a few moments I excused myself to go outside for a cigarette. Josie had cleared all the ashtrays out of her house a few years earlier, having issued an edict to Sam and his cigars, and I wasn't about to challenge her.

Basile met me on the porch.

'I'm just going in to say goodbye,' he said. 'I've called the station, and they're getting the boy's description around. They'll let the Medford and Woburn and Lexington and Arlington police know, too.'

'What about the State Police?'

'No sense in telling them anything now. If he doesn't turn up by tomorrow . . .'

I nodded and shook a Winston from my pack. I offered one to Basile. He hesitated, then took one with a sheepish grin.

71

'I quit five weeks ago, damn you. Still can't turn 'em down.'

'Sorry.'

'Don't be. After a session like this I need one.'

I held my lighter for him while he lit up. He dragged deeply and exhaled with a loud, contented sigh. 'Oh, man, is that good.'

We sat on the porch steps. 'What do you think?' I said. He grinned. 'You mean, what do I *really* think?'

'Yes.'

'I really think what I said in there. We have this kind of thing all the time. Kids will be kids, as the man said. This boy's probably playing ball somewhere in town. We'll find him.'

'But that really isn't like E.J., you know.'

Basile squinted at me through the smoke of his cigarette. 'It never is. Look. You know kids. I mean, at some point they start doing things they didn't use to do. They get more independent. Or just more irresponsible. It's all part of growing up.'

I nodded. I had helped to raise two boys of my own. Like Eddie, I had to do a big part of it as an absentee parent. I had experienced the agony of seeing them grow up and grow away from their parents. What parent hadn't gone through some version of what Jan was experiencing?

'But there are other possibilities,' I said.

'Sure. Sure there are.'

'You think he might've run away?'

Basile shrugged. 'It's common. It wouldn't surprise me if a cruiser picked him up as he was trudging towards Medford to visit his daddy. Or found him in a bus station or trying to hitch a ride on Route 3A.'

I nodded. 'I guess that would make sense.'

'Does he know where his father works?'

'Sure. At least, I assume he does.'

'So he's headed for the mall. Or maybe he's already there, wandering around looking for his old man's store. I've already had the Burlington police alerted. Those guys'll keep an eye out. Hey, there are close to two million kids reported missing in this country every year. The statistics say that between ninety and ninety-five per cent of them are runaways. Okay?'

'How many of them are found?'

Basile took a long last drag on his cigarette and snapped it towards a clump of bushes. 'Most of 'em. Especially the young ones, like E.J. When they're fourteen or fifteen they sometimes have the savvy—and the real desire—to get away. The little ones, they tend to chicken out. Or else they just go to a friend or a relative.'

73

I flipped my butt in the same direction Basile had. 'What are the other possibilities?'

'Well, of course, there are sickies out there. We like to think we know who they are, but ...' He shrugged. 'There are the ones, the women, who just wanted to have a kid. You know, they go around with a pillow tied on to their belly pretending they're pregnant. The ones who dress their poodle up in diapers and feed it through a bottle. Sometimes they'll snatch a child.'

'A ten-year-old?'

'No. Usually a lot younger. Then you have the bastards who do it for profit. The guys who make porno movies. And the baby sellers. Very lucrative black market for babies. Not ten-year-olds, though. The porno moguls, they like ten-year-olds, though. Kiddie porn. Ever see kiddie porn?'

'No,' I said.

'You're lucky,' he said. 'And then we've got the old-fashioned ransom kidnappers. Since the FBI got itself involved, there's not so much of that any more. But it happens. Or kids are held hostage. That's usually a political thing.'

'God,' I muttered.

'Then, of course, we have the pedophiles,' he continued. 'Sex nuts. They're the worst of all. They usually murder the kids. Like the

74

one in Florida a few years ago. Maybe you read about it. Six-year-old boy. Disappeared in a Sears store. They found his head in a canal two weeks later.'

'I can see why you didn't go into all this inside,' I said, gesturing back towards the house.

'There's more,' Basile said softly. 'Let me have another cigarette, will you?'

We both lit up again. 'The Atlanta case awhile back,' he said. 'Twenty-nine black kids disappeared. All murdered. They convicted a guy on two of them.'

I shivered. 'So it could be anything, couldn't it?'

He nodded. 'It could be, sure. But, understand, I still think it's going to work out. It usually does.'

We finished our cigarettes in silence, then went back into the house. Basile told Jan he had to get back to the station and that he'd keep in touch with them, and then he left. I watched him go, wishing I could go with him. I wanted to get back home before Sylvie left. And I guess I'm flawed as an attorney, because I'm just not that good with other people's tragedies. I hoped this wasn't going to be a tragedy, but it didn't feel good to me.

So I stayed for the afternoon, sipping the beer that Josie brought out and ignoring the platter of sandwiches she had made. Nobody seemed to have any interest in food. My own stomach felt as if it had been whacked with a Louisville Slugger. The beer helped a little.

We waited for the telephone to ring. It did, a few times. Business for Sam, which he dispensed with quickly. Jan stared out the window while I held her hand. Josie kept moving. Sam sat on the sofa with his head thrown back against the cushion, his eyes closed. He looked like he might be sleeping, but I knew he wasn't.

It took me all afternoon to summon up the courage to leave. I didn't get back to my apartment until nearly seven. Sylvie was gone. As I had requested, she hadn't cleaned up at all. The coffee pot was still plugged in. It smelled like burning rubber.

I poured myself half a tumbler of Jack Daniels, dropped in some ice cubes, and found the Chicago Symphony playing Beethoven's Sixth on WCRB–FM. Somehow the music failed to conjure up pastoral images of sheep grazing on verdant pastures. I kept seeing Jan Donagan's haunted eyes accusing me, it seemed, of all the evil in the world.

The booze settled in my stomach like a handful of buck shot. I realized that I hadn't eaten all day. I found a glob of hamburger in my refrigerator, which I beat into a couple of patties and fried. They tasted like Brillo pads—not that bad, with lots of catsup.

I was fiddling with the dial on my television, looking for an old Charlie Chan movie to get me through another Saturday night, when Eddie Donagan called me.

'You drunk?' I said.

'Not yet, old lawmaster. The night is young. You gonna tell me what's goin' on? I called Jan. All I got out of her is E.J.'s still gone and it's gotta be my fault.'

'You didn't see him today, then?'

'No.'

'That's all we know, Eddie. I'm sorry.'

'Oh, man . . .'

'The police are confident they'll find him, or he'll turn up. Try not to worry.'

'Yeah. Right.'

'There's nothing you can do.'

'I feel as useless as tits on a rooster, know that? I can't stand sitting around waiting for something to happen. Not my style.'

'Are you home?'

'Such as it is.'

'Stay there. Maybe E.J.'ll call you. At least, if anybody hears anything they'll know where to reach you.'

'Make sure I know, will you?'

'I will.'

'You're the only one who will.'

But I didn't hear anything, not that night and not all day Sunday. I talked to Sam a couple of times, pretending not to get his hints that Jan would like me to be there to hold her hand. He told me that Inspector Basile had contacted the State Police and the FBI. He didn't know what, if anything, they would do. Feeling the need for a little hand-holding myself, I tried Sylvie's number, but she either wasn't home or wasn't answering. So I went to bed. The next day was Monday, and then, at least, I could go to my office and feel useful.

I wondered who was going to do E.J. Donagan's paper route in the morning.

CHAPTER SIX

I was on my first cup of coffee and staring at the accumulation of weekend mail on my desk when Julie, my secretary, buzzed me.

'It's a woman. Claims it's urgent. Wouldn't give her name,' she said over the intercom. 'Do you want to take it?'

'Sure,' I said. I pressed the blinking button on my telephone console and said, 'Brady Coyne.'

'Mr Coyne,' came a female voice. 'One moment, please.'

78

I heard a click and a few seconds of static, and then a man's voice began to speak. It sounded unnaturally deep and slow, as if it had been recorded at forty-five and was being played back at thirty-three. Something like that, I quickly realized, was what in fact had been done.

'This is the only communication you will receive from us, Mr Coyne,' growled the voice. 'For the sake of the boy, please listen carefully and follow precisely the instructions I will give you. Please note down what I am about to say. The details are important. I will repeat it only once. I will now allow you one minute to assemble paper and pen.'

I buzzed Julie, who picked up the line. 'Julie, listen to this and make notes, please.'

'What . . . ?'

'I'll explain later.'

'All right, then, Mr Coyne,' came the voice again. 'I trust you are ready. First, please be assured that the boy is with us and that he is fine. He will be returned unharmed once our transaction is satisfactorily completed. This will assure you that I am telling you the truth.' There was a click, and then I heard E.J. Donagan's voice. It was unmistakably his. 'This is E.J. I'm fine. The Red Sox won today. Dwight Evans hit a homer. I miss my mother.'

I heard Julie breathe, 'Oh, my God!'

'We choose to deal with you, Mr Coyne,' resumed that deep, slow voice, 'because you have the reputation for being sensible and discreet. For the sake of the boy, we trust that is true. We will want one hundred and fifty thousand dollars in used bills as follows. Please note this down carefully. First, one thousand hundreds. Second, six hundred fifties. Third, one thousand twenties. We will examine these bills to verify that they have been marked in no way and that they do not have consecutive serial numbers. These bills must be tied into ten-thousand-dollar bundles and put into a large green plastic trash bag. Knot the top securely. Lock it into the trunk of your white BMW. Drive to the bowling alleys on Route 2 in Cambridge tomorrow night. That's Tuesday night. Be there at nine o'clock. Wear a suit and tie. Go upstairs to the lounge. Sit at the bar. Order Wild Turkey on the rocks with two olives. Wait for instructions. Be alone. We will know what's going on. If there are any police around, if there's any effort to follow you, or to interfere in this transaction, you will not see the boy again. Please believe me.

'This message will now be repeated in its entirety one time. Make sure every detail is followed. You will not hear from us again.'

There was a click, a moment of static, and again the voice began, 'This is the only communication you will receive from us, Mr Coyne.' I listened to it all again. When it was over, I said into the telephone, 'Julie?'

'I'm here,' she said. 'Is that what it sounds like, Brady?'

'I'm afraid so. Did you get all of it?'

'Of course. It's in shorthand.'

'Bring it in here, then, so we can check the details.'

A moment later she came into my office, and except for the horror on her face she was still the green-eyed Irish beauty I had hired twelve years earlier. She sank on to the sofa. I moved from behind my desk to sit beside her.

'You never told me . . .'

'I would have, Julie. I'm sorry. I didn't know I was going to get this call.'

'What has happened?'

As I recounted the story, Julie's eyes filled with tears. She had a two-year-old daughter. It wasn't hard to imagine what was going through her mind. My own sons were in college, and I had no trouble identifying with Jan and Eddie Donagan.

When I finished, Julie said, 'So what now?'

'I want you to get Sam Farina on the phone for me. Then type up the transcript of that telephone call.'

81

She nodded.

'Tell me,' I said. 'What exactly did the woman who called say? Can you remember her exact words?'

'She just asked for you. She said, "May I speak with Mr Coyne, please?" I said, "May I ask who's calling?", of course, and she said, "This is urgent. I must speak with Mr Coyne." So I buzzed you.'

'Did you notice anything about her voice? Any accent? Young, old, or what?'

Julie frowned. 'Youngish, I'd say. Mature, you know, but young. Kind of a low voice. You'd probably call it sexy.'

'From the little she said to me, yes, I'd call it sexy. Anything else about it?'

'Well, maybe a hint of a Boston accent. When she said, "Mr Coyne" to me it came out "Mistah". The way we all talk around here.'

I smiled and nodded. 'Anything else?'

She shrugged. 'No. She didn't say that much.' Julie frowned and shook her head slowly. 'Oh, those poor people. What's going to happen?'

'I don't know. I just don't know.'

*　　*　　*

There were eight of us in Sam Farina's living-room that afternoon. Besides Sam, Jan, Josie and me, Eddie was there, perched uncomfortably on the edge of one of the kitchen chairs that had been dragged out to accommodate us all. The Winchester cop, Basile, was flanked by two other men. One was a sturdy, white-haired guy who looked like he pressed weights. Basile introduced him as Inspector Bill Travers of the State Police. The other was a skinny little olive-skinned FBI agent with a face like a tomahawk named Marty Stern. Stern wore heavy horn-rimmed glasses, which he would nervously grab from his face and wave around in the air when he talked. Stern seemed to be running the show. He spat out questions like a prosecutor.

'How'd they know you drove a BMW?' he said to me, after he had read over the transcript of the telephone conversation I had handed to him.

'I don't know.'

'You drink Wild Turkey usually?'

'Whatever.'

'What's that supposed to mean?'

'It means I drink whatever there is. I do prefer bourbon.'

'With olives in it?'

'Never.'

'Why you figure they called you?'

'It's no secret Brady's my lawyer,' said Sam.

83

'I asked him,' said Stern, whipping the glasses off his nose and stabbing at me with them.

'It's no secret I'm Sam's lawyer,' I said with a smirk. 'Where are you headed with this, anyway?'

Stern sighed. 'Be kinda nice to know who called you, huh?'

'Sure.'

'That's where I'm headed.' He sighed again. 'It's gotta be somebody who knows you all, who knows that Coyne was here Saturday, is how I figure it. Dontcha think?'

He looked around at all of us. Then he answered his own question. 'The answer is, I'm right.' He jammed his glasses back on to his face, pushing them on to the bridge of his nose with his forefinger. He studied the transcript I had given him. 'Okay,' he said after a minute. 'Two things. First, we get the boy back. First priority. We do nothing to screw that up. Second, we catch them.' He peered at Sam. 'Can you raise this kind of money?'

Sam nodded. 'Just about. A hundred and fifty grand is just about what I can raise in twenty-four hours.'

'Like they knew that, too, huh?'

Suddenly Eddie pounded his knee with his fist. 'Jesus Christ! Can we just get on with it, huh? Brady didn't kidnap E.J. Neither did Sam. Why don't you cut the bullshit? This is ridiculous.' He got up from his chair and glared down at the diminutive FBI agent. 'How the hell are we gonna get E.J. back? Ain't that what we're supposed to be doing here? Let's get him back first. Then we can worry about catching these guys.'

Stern slowly removed his glasses. 'Sit down, Mr Donagan. Please. Sit down.' He leaned forward and stared at Eddie through narrowed eyes. Eddie returned his stare for a moment, then slowly took his seat. 'Just let me worry about this.'

'Why should you worry?' muttered Eddie. 'E.J. ain't your kid.'

'Because I've been through this before and you haven't, that's why. Because if we don't think about catching them then every crazy out there will think kidnapping is a neat way to make a quick couple of bills. Better 'n megabucks, huh? So I'm worried about E.J., yes. And all the rest of the kids out there.'

'We've only got until tomorrow night.'

Stern nodded. 'Right. So here's what we do. We'll put a man in the bar at the bowling alley. We'll have someone follow Coyne, keep track of the bag of money. We'll tap into all the phones at the bowling alley. Also,' he added, glancing at me, 'your office phone.

And here, too. Some point they've gotta tell you what to do next. And some point, you gotta transfer that bag of money. We find out what we can, try to keep tabs on 'em, and as soon as we get the boy back we move in.' He poked his glasses at Travers, the State Policeman. 'Can you give me some men?'

Travers nodded. 'Sure. No problem.'

'Okay. One in the bar. One in a car in the parking lot. Another one to tail him when he leaves the alleys, assuming they make the transaction somewhere else. Okay?'

'Okay,' said Travers.

'Get 'em together. We'll brief 'em tomorrow. We'll put a woman in the bar. They won't expect a woman.'

'I don't know,' I said. 'The guy who called was pretty specific about me not being followed. If they pick up on it—'

'I agree,' said Eddie. 'I don't want to risk—'

'Trust me,' said Stern.

'Why?' said Eddie. 'Why the fuck should we trust you?'

Stern turned his head to look at Eddie. His smile resembled that of a coral snake. 'Because, Mr Donagan, I'm in charge and I know what I'm doing. And you don't have any idea what you're talking about.' He turned to look at Jan, and his tone softened. 'I know you're scared and worried. Believe me, I

86

understand how it is. I've been through it. I promise you we'll do nothing to jeopardize the safe return of your son. But once we get him back, we want to do everything we can to catch the lousy bastards who are doing this. You want that, don't you?'

'I just want him back,' whispered Jan.

'Me too,' said Eddie, 'and I think all this is just going to screw it up. It's too risky. Let's just give them their money. If they think we're not doing what they said . . .'

'They're pros,' said Basile, speaking for the first time. 'But so are we.'

'It ain't a goddam game,' Eddie answered, his voice rising. 'Christ! You talk like this was some kind of a game you wanna see if you can win. This is my kid you're playing with.'

'Leave it to us, will you?' Stern glanced at Travers and Basile, who nodded.

'Yeah, okay. We'll leave it to you pros. But I'm warning you . . .'

'Don't,' said Travers. 'Don't warn me, Mr Donagan.'

'Eddie,' said Jan. 'Please.'

Eddie suddenly shoved his chair back and stood up. 'Fine,' he said loudly. 'Good. Okay. You take care of it. I'm getting out of here. I'm gone. Just remember,' he added, sweeping his hand to include all of us, 'if anything goes wrong you've all got it on your consciences. All of you.'

Eddie left the room and a moment later we heard the front door slam.

'He's very upset,' said Jan. She got up and moved to follow him.

'Let him go,' said Sam. But Jan disappeared out the door.

'It doesn't matter,' said Stern. 'That's about it for now, anyway. Okay?'

He looked from one to the other, and we all nodded. We started to stand, in preparation to leaving, when Jan came back into the room. Eddie was with her, scowling. He looked directly at me. 'I'm gonna stick it out,' he said. He glanced at Stern. 'But I don't like it.'

Stern twitched his shoulders, indicating exactly how much he cared what Eddie thought, and said, 'All right, then. You get the money, Mr Farina, and we'll all meet back here at six tomorrow.'

CHAPTER SEVEN

I arrived at the Route 2 bowling alleys a little after eight-thirty. The green plastic trash bag, heavy with stacks of bills, was locked in the trunk of my BMW. I circled the building a couple of times, searching fruitlessly for a place to leave the car. I finally found a spot next door in front of an abandoned gas station. I hoped that the State Police officer who was stationed somewhere outside had seen me.

I locked up and went inside. The summer leagues were in full swing. The place echoed with the din and clatter of bowling balls rumbling down the wooden lanes and crashing against the pins, the lusty shouts of the bowlers, and the clank and whirr of the automatic pinsetting machines.

I found the bar upstairs. The Kegler's Eleventh Frame Lounge. It was dimly lit, with deep maroon carpeting and heavy dark wood panelling and furniture. Against the far wall was an L-shaped bar. A giant-screen TV over the bar showed in silent pantomime the Red Sox tilting, as the sportswriters liked to say, against the Orioles. When I stepped into the room the bowling noises behind me subsided into a low hum.

I found a seat at the bar and looked around. One of the couple of dozen people in pastel bowling shirts sitting around drinking draught beer was supposed to be a State Police officer. I didn't know which one. A woman, I assumed. I felt out of place in my suit and tie. I didn't know what I was getting into, and I desperately wanted the reassurance that I was not alone in this caper. At a corner table a chunky grey-haired woman sat alone. As my gaze settled on her I sensed that she had been watching me. Her eyes seemed to deflect off me to the television. I stared at her for a minute, hoping to catch her eye, to promote a quick wink or slight nod that would confirm what I hoped was true. She seemed intent on the efforts of Oil Can Boyd to extricate himself from a nasty bases-loaded situation. It occurred to me that if things had worked out differently, it could have been Eddie Donagan out there on the Fenway Park mound getting shelled by the Orioles on a muggy summer evening.

The bartender had a florid face and a receding hairline. He ceremoniously passed a rag over the bar in front of me. I lifted my elbows for him.

'What'll ya have?'

'A Wild Turkey on the rocks. With, ah, two olives.'

'You shitting me.'

'What do you mean?'

'Two olives?'

'Yeah. Of course. Two olives.'

He rolled his eyes and moved to the other end of the bar. I saw him whisper something to one of the men sitting there. They both looked my way, grinning.

On the television Eddie Murray lined a hit

into centre field. I swivelled around to check the grey-haired police lady. Her table was empty.

'Here ya go. Wild Turkey. On the rocks. Two olives. You want a little cocktail onion, maybe, in there too? How's about a Maraschino cherry? Twist of lemon? Wedge of lime?'

'Just the olives. Thank you.'

He shrugged and moved down the bar to resume his conversation. There was a constant movement of people in and out of the lounge. They seemed to come in, order a beer, wait for their turn to bowl, leave with half-empty glasses on the tables, then return several minutes later to resume their places. I couldn't figure out how they remembered which were their own beers.

I sat there on the stool, one elbow on the bar, my Wild Turkey in my hand, half turned so that I could watch the room. I was waiting. I didn't know what for. The grey-haired lady came back in, accompanied by two other women. One of them was slender and blonde and wore jeans so tight as to defy all the logical possibilities of bending and stretching to roll a bowling ball. I thought it would be interesting to watch her try. The other lugged around a bosom that must have made her bowling technique unusual. All three women glanced my way and seemed to smile at me. I wondered if they knew that I had two olives in my bourbon.

The Red Sox changed pitchers. I smoked a Winston and sipped my drink. It was five of nine. Nothing was happening. It occurred to me that maybe the kidnappers had discovered that I had allies in there with me and that the phones were tapped, and had decided to change their plans. There was nothing I could do but wait.

I finished my drink and swivelled back to the bar. The red-faced bartender said, ''Nother?'

'Please.'

'Two olives, right?'

'Of course.'

A group of half a dozen men entered the lounge and bore down on the bar. They stopped beside me, and one of them said, 'You mind moving down a couple?'

I shrugged and slid over to an empty stool near the end of the bar. The men crowded around me, one sitting on the stool beside me and two standing close behind me. I had to keep my elbows close to my body to avoid contact with them. I cradled my drink and crooked my neck to watch the television.

'Goddam splits,' one of the guys said loudly. 'I'm in the pocket all night, nothin' but splits.'

'Ahh, it's the damn lanes. You oughta move over maybe two boards. You're comin' in too high on the head pin.'

'Nah. I tried that. Ball don't feel right any more. Maybe get it redrilled.'

'Hey, let's go, Pete, willya? Miller Lites all around, okay?'

The Red Sox had finally taken their turn at bat. The Baltimore right fielder made a nice over-the-shoulder catch sprinting towards the bullpen. I tried to peer around the men standing near me to see if the grey-haired lady was at her seat. She was gone, but the blonde and the big-breasted girl were there. I wondered how many gutter balls were rolled by the time the third string came along, the way these people consumed beer.

I turned back to the bar. A long envelope lay on top of my napkin. Nothing was written on it. I tore it open. Inside was a greeting card, with a picture of Snoopy lying on his back atop his doghouse staring at the sky through big dark sunglasses. Snoopy was saying, 'I'm not moving until you do.'

Beneath that, printed in all capital letters with a black felt-tip pen, was written, 'Go to the phone downstairs.'

I caught the bartender's eye, and he came over, prepared to wield his rag and take my order. 'Ready for another two-olive special?'

'No. Let me have my bill. And did you happen to see who left this?' I held up the envelope.

'Nope. Hang on a minute, I'll get you the bill.'

I glanced around at the bowlers who were crowded against me. They were engaged in an animated debate on the relative merits of the four-step versus the five-step approach. They seemed to take their bowling nearly as seriously as their beer drinking. None of them met my eye. I hoped that the State Police person, whoever and wherever he or she was in the lounge, noticed where the envelope had come from.

The bartender was pouring beer from the spigots. He seemed to have forgotten my bill. I extracted a five-dollar bill from my wallet, slid it under my glass, and elbowed my way out of the lounge. The racket outside assaulted me. It seemed to have been lubricated by all that beer I had seen consumed. The yells and laughter seemed pitched higher, the crash of colliding pins seemed to echo louder, and the whine of the machinery seemed to penetrate my brain deeper, than they had when I had entered the building.

The downstairs alleys were rigged for

candlepins, that bowling variation peculiar to New England. The balls are smaller, about the size of a softball, and the pins are tall and slender. When I reached the foot of the stairs I noticed that the pitch of the din was set an octave or so higher than that of the ten-pin lanes upstairs.

The people were just as boisterous.

The pay phone was set against the wall at the far end of the alleys. A woman with 'Prime Time Players' stitched in script across the back of her bowling shirt was talking into it. I moved to stand near her. She glanced up at me, her black eyes crackling with what appeared to be anger. 'Molly' was written on the pocket over her left breast.

'Look,' she was saying into the phone, her eyes appealing to the ceiling for patience, 'I really gotta go. That's just your problem and you're gonna hafta take care of it ... There's some guy standing here waiting for the phone, and I don't wanna talk about it anyway. In case you forgot, I am married, you know?'

She glowered at me, shifted her eyes to the receiver she held in her hand, then said softly, 'Yeah, me too, honey. Yeah, it sounds nice. But I really do. I really gotta go.'

She held the phone away from her ear and stared at it as if she might embrace it, then set it gently on its cradle. She cocked her head at

95

me, showed me the pink tip of her tongue, and tossed her hair. I watched her walk away.

The jangle of the telephone was almost lost in the general din of the place. I picked it up before it could ring a second time.

'Hello?' I said.

'Mr Coyne?' I could barely hear her, but I was certain it was the same female voice I had heard over my office phone the previous day.

'Yes. You'll have to speak louder.'

She said something I didn't catch. I felt an instant of panic. I could botch the whole thing up by misunderstanding the message.

'Please,' I said loudly, cupping one ear with my hand and pressing the receiver against my other ear. 'It's deafening in here.'

'I have your instructions,' I heard her say. 'Can you hear me now?'

'Barely. Yes.'

'Okay. Get on to Route 2 heading west. In Lexington you'll see a sign for Waltham Street. The first exit goes to Lexington Center. Pass that and stop on the overpass. Drop the parcel over the bridge. Do you understand?'

'Drop it over the bridge to Waltham Street. Yes.'

'What time do you have?'

I looked at my watch. 'Nine-eleven.'

'You're two minutes slow. All right. Drop

96

the parcel off the bridge at exactly nine forty-three by your watch. Do you have that?'

'Nine forty-three. Okay.'

'Go, now, then.'

'Wait a minute,' I said. 'Will—?'

I heard a click on the other end. I replaced the telephone and glanced quickly around. The grey-haired lady was nowhere to be seen, nor did anybody else seem to be paying any attention to me. Outside, the only noise was the swish of the traffic on Route 2 and the distant grumble of thunder. I could see lightning playing across the western horizon.

I unlocked my car and climbed in, resisting the temptation to open the trunk to check that the bag of money was still there. I wanted to proceed with total caution, and I didn't want to keep anybody waiting. I was acutely aware that it was E.J. Donagan's life riding in my car with me.

I nosed into the traffic and merged with the left lane so I could negotiate the traffic circle and reverse my direction on the divided highway and get on to the west-bound lane. I took it carefully. I had no desire to scrape fenders with some drunken bowler on his way home after a bad night.

My little BMW purred up a long hill. Traffic was sparse, and straight ahead of me the thunderclouds hung low over the highway where it bisected a residential section of Arlington. The lights of the homes clustered on both sides of the road blinked warm orange. Everyone safe and snug in their living-rooms. Over in Winchester, I knew, E.J. Donagan's family huddled with an assortment of FBI agents and other cops waiting for my report. I doubted that they were feeling snug and secure.

A few minutes later I pulled over to the side and stopped on the overpass. I left the engine running and the lights on. The last thing I wanted was for some well-meaning citizen—or, worse yet, a policeman—to pull up behind me to offer assistance. I got out and went to the trunk before I remembered the keys were still in the ignition. I went back to fetch them. I left the parking lights on.

The bag of money was heavy. I needed both arms to hoist it up on to the rail of the bridge. It occurred to me that I had heard the directions wrong. This was Waltham Street. Did she say the one *after* Waltham Street? She did say to drop it over the side. Didn't she?

I imagined a pedestrian or jogger or dog-walker hearing the thump of falling money. I imagined the kidnappers waiting somewhere else for it.

I imagined myself screwing it all up and E.J. Donagan dying because of it.

I looked at my watch. It read nine forty-one. Two minutes. I held the bag of money balanced on the rail. The drumroll of thunder sounded closer, and a freshening breeze carried with it the sharp smell of ozone. A few cars passed close by me. One slowed down as it went by, and I saw the brake lights flash on. I willed it not to stop. It took the exit over the bridge.

Nine forty-two. I leaned over the bridge to peer down. I could neither see nor hear a thing down there. I thought of the hundreds of ways the exchange could fail. Even if it wasn't my fault, I feared that wouldn't matter. E.J. Donagan's life depended on my delivering that money.

The two changed into a three on my digital watch.

I stood there, alone on the dark highway, and with a little grunt pushed the bag over the edge. I heard it hit the ground below with a hollow plop, the same sound you get when you punch a half-inflated beach ball. I waited for a moment, peering over the rail, waiting for the beam of a flashlight, or the sudden glow of headlights cutting through the blackness, or the growl of a car's engine starting up. Then I thought better of it. I climbed into my car and drove away as fast as I could safely go.

I pulled into the first gas station I came to. There was a pay phone in an open stall outside. I deposited a quarter and punched out Sam Farina's phone number.

Sam answered on the first ring. 'It's done,' I said.

'You gave them the money?'

'I dropped it over a bridge. Who's there?'

'Me, Jan, Josie. Stern and Basile.'

'Eddie?'

'He's here. Not saying much, but he's here.'

'Okay. I better talk to Stern.'

A moment later the FBI man came on to the line. I recounted for him what had happened. He said, 'Damn!'

'What?'

'We missed whoever gave you that envelope.'

'There was someone there?'

'Yeah. Travers' man. State cop. I should have put one of my own guys there. He called after you left. He didn't see anything.'

'Did somebody follow me in the car?'

'Yes. Had to keep going when you stopped on the bridge.'

'So we're no better off than we were.'

'So far they've had it all their way. Hopefully now we'll hear from them and get the boy back. You think the woman who called was the same one?'

'Couldn't swear to it, but, yes, I think so.' A raindrop about the size of a grapefruit landed on my hand. 'It's starting to rain,' I said to Stern. 'I'm at an outside phone. What do you want me to do now?'

'Go home. Stick close to your phone. They seem to want to deal with you. Maybe they'll call you at home, maybe in your office. About all we can do now is wait. They've got what they wanted.'

'We wait for them to call.'

'Yes. We hope they'll call.'

'What about the phone call at the alleys? Can you trace it?'

'Sure. It was from a booth somewhere, no doubt. We'll have it recorded, too, though not much chance that'll help us. You still have that note, I hope.'

I patted my pocket. 'Yes. It's right here, in my pocket.'

'We'll want it.'

'Fingerprints and so forth.'

Stern's laugh was ironic. 'Sure. All the up-to-the-minute technology of the Bureau's at our disposal. We've got buildings full of computers. Scientists hunched over test tubes and electron microscopes.' His voice was low and conspiratorial. 'Listen. We hope to hell they call again, okay? We hope they decide to

101

give us back the boy. Because so far they've done everything right, you know? And we're sitting around with our thumbs up our fannies while they call all the shots. So don't get too optimistic, okay?'

'That's really encouraging,' I said.

'You're a big boy. You should know how it is.' He paused. 'Hang on a minute, will you?' he said. I could hear Stern talking with somebody. A sudden gust of wind blew a cool mist on my face. Then Sam Farina's voice came on the phone.

'Hey, Brady?'

'Yes, Sam?'

'Look, thanks, huh? For what you've done.'

'What I did was easy. You've got the hard part.'

'Yeah,' he said softly. 'Yeah. This is hard. Still, thanks.'

'Gotta go,' I said. 'It's raining. We'll be in touch.'

'Jan needs you, my friend.'

'Right.'

I replaced the phone and dashed for my car. The wind was bouncing the branches of the big oak trees behind the gas station, and fat raindrops rattled off the hood of my BMW. When I pulled out into the eastbound lane of Route 2, the rain came driving in hard, angled sheets, and even with the wipers on high speed the headlights barely cut twenty feet through the downpour.

I wondered if E.J. Donagan, wherever he was, was afraid of the thunder.

★   ★   ★

When I got back to my apartment, I kicked my shoes into a corner, dropped my jacket and tie on to the sofa, and found a can of Molson's in the refrigerator. I padded over to the glass doors that overlook the harbour and slid them open to let in the clean smell of ocean and rain. I stood out on my balcony for a few minutes, sipping my ale and breathing deeply. I waited for the knot in my solar plexus to unravel.

I couldn't get E.J. Donagan's freckled smile out of my mind. I remembered the bright July day the previous summer when I had taken E.J. and Jan with me for a day on the ocean. Charlie McDevitt, my old Yale Law School chum, kept a boat moored in Gloucester. Charlie navigated and E.J. and I trolled for bluefish while Jan stripped to her bikini and sunned herself on the forward bulkhead. Charlie chased the humpback and finback whales that basked near the surface eight miles out on Stellwagen, and out there where

103

the sky formed a big bowl over the ocean we circled the Moonie tuna fleet that lay at anchor. Clouds of gulls swirled and darted in their chumline. E.J. climbed up into the tower and played at being a pirate. 'Land, ho!' he called out, and Charlie yelled back, 'Avast, me hearty.' 'Yo, ho, ho and a bottle of rum,' laughed the boy.

On the way in E.J. hooked a blue. The powerful fish threatened to drag the skinny little kid over the side, but he hung on stubbornly while I clung to his belt. Charlie threw the twin motors into neutral, and we rolled and pitched on the deep swells. E.J. pumped the rod, reeling when he could and giving line when the fish insisted, gaining more than he lost. When he finally had the fish alongside, I said, 'Oh, he's a beauty. Twelve pounds easy.' I reached for the gaff.

'No, don't,' said E.J.

'It's the only way,' I answered. 'You can't bring them aboard any other way. Likely to throw the plug into your face. They have teeth that'll slice your finger right off.'

'I want to let him go.'

By now Jan was standing with us. She leaned close against me, one arm thrown carelessly around my waist, looking into the water at the fish. Her skin felt warm and moist against my arm.

104

'We can bring him home for your grandmother to cook,' she said to her son.

'No. Let him go.'

'Okay,' I said. I leaned over the side, holding the line in my left hand, and I cut it free with my pocketknife. The bluefish lay motionless beside the boat for a moment. Then with a sudden movement it was gone.

'He was a brave fish,' E.J. said.

'You were a brave fisherman.'

When I dropped E.J. and Jan off at Sam's house that afternoon, E.J. shook my hand solemnly at the front door. 'Thank you, Uncle Brady,' he said.

'You're a good man, Charlie Brown,' I told him.

He darted into the house. Jan touched my arm. 'Come in for a beer?'

'Nope. Thanks.'

'It was a nice day.'

I nodded.

'I haven't seen E.J. so happy since . . .'

'Since Eddie left?'

'Yes.'

'We'll do it again some time.'

We exchanged self-consciously chaste kisses on the cheek and I retreated to my car. As I started it up I glanced back. Jan was still standing by the door watching me, her hand raised in a motionless wave. I could only read sadness on her face.

That was a year earlier. Since that time E.J. and Jan and I climbed Mount Monadnock, watched the Celtics beat the Chicago Bulls, and celebrated E.J.'s tenth birthday at Mama Maria's in the North End. I remained uncomfortable in the role of surrogate father which Jan seemed eager to thrust upon me. I felt that I had to struggle to keep my relationship with her on a casually friendly basis. I was committed to George Washington's precept: no entangling alliances.

But I also found myself growing fond of both of them. E.J. was a shy, enthusiastic kid, a lot like my own son Joey had been at that age. Jan was warm and sexy.

But they were Eddie's family. Not mine.

I went back into my apartment, leaving the sliders open. I tossed the empty Molson's can into the basket, decided against cracking another, and went to the phone. I dialled Eddie's number. I let it ring twelve times before I hung up.

I found an FM station that was playing Oscar Peterson. I smoked a cigarette. I found myself pacing aimlessly around my living-room. Then I went back to the telephone and dialled a familiar number.

It rang only once before I heard the phone

lifted from the receiver. I knew Gloria kept it beside the bed. 'Hello?' she mumbled in a blurry voice, the same voice she used to use when one of the boys would wake her up with their crying when we were all younger.

I cleared my throat. 'It's me.'

'Wait a minute,' she said. Then she said, 'What time is it, anyway?'

'Eleven-thirty. A little after. I'm sorry . . .'

'It's okay. What's the matter?' I pictured her hitching herself into a sitting position in her bed, her hair tangled and loose around her face and those little frown lines etched between her eyebrows.

'Nothing's the matter. I was just wondering. How are the boys?'

'You called me at this hour just to see how the boys are?' Her voice lost its fuzziness. 'Brady, what *is* it?'

'It's—nothing. Really. I was just thinking of Billy and Joey. And you. Are they okay?'

Her sigh hissed in the telephone. 'Of course they're all right. Do you want to talk to them? I think they're both asleep. They've both got summer jobs, you know. They have to get up early. We were *all* asleep.'

'I'm sorry,' I said again. 'No, let them sleep.' I fumbled for a cigarette. 'Remember how we used to go in and check on them when they were sleeping? To make sure they were still breathing?'

'*You* did that. What is this all about, anyway?'

I found my Zippo in my pants pocket and lit my Winston. 'E.J. Donagan has been kidnapped. I delivered the ransom money a little while ago.'

'Oh, Jesus!' Gloria was silent for a long time. Then she said, 'Do you want to come over? It would be all right.'

My brain screamed, 'Yes!' I wanted to go back to my colonial house in Wellesley. I wanted my two boys to be young again, and me and Gloria, too, and I wanted to pull the covers up to their chins while they slept in their beds, and then crawl in beside Gloria and hold her until I slept, too.

'No,' I said to her. 'No, that's all right. Say hi to them for me. Sorry I woke you up.'

'Brady, really—'

'Go to sleep, Gloria. I'm sorry I disturbed you.' After all those years I still was apologizing to my former wife.

'How's Jan?' she asked.

'Bad. As you might expect. Look. I'll keep you posted. I shouldn't have called. It was just . . .'

'I know.' Her voice was fuzzy again.

'Hug them for me.'

'Sure. G'night.'

The man was right. You can't go back. Not ever.

CHAPTER EIGHT

I stayed close to my desk all day Wednesday, waiting. Several times I called Sam's number. They were waiting, too. Thursday came and went. Sam wanted me to go to his house for dinner, but Stern vetoed the idea. 'Stick by your phone,' he said. 'You're the one they'll contact.'

I kept asking to talk to Jan. Sam said she couldn't come to the phone. He meant, I thought, that she wouldn't. I imagined that she was blaming me for it all, and while it made no sense to me, I couldn't shake the feeling that somehow she was right.

I was eating ham and Swiss cheese on rye off waxed paper at my desk Friday noon when Julie buzzed me.

'Umph,' I mumbled into the phone.

'Swallow it,' Julie said. 'It's her on the phone. The same one.'

I gulped down a big glob of half-chewed sandwich and took a swig of my chocolate frappe. 'Jesus,' I said, failing to stifle a belch.

'Excuse me. Okay. Put her on. You listen in. Take down everything.'

It was the same female voice. 'Listen carefully, Mr Coyne,' she said. Then I heard the deep, slow, recorded male voice. His directions were detailed and precise, the threat in his message unmistakable. This time he did not repeat it.

When I heard the click that terminated the recording, Julie said, 'I got it.'

'Okay. See if you can reach Stern.'

I lit a cigarette and waited. I had stubbed it out when Julie buzzed me again.

'Okay. Put him on.'

When I told Stern about the phone call he said, 'Tomorrow at noon, huh? Well, do it then.'

'What about—?'

'We'll take care of our part. You just do yours. Just like the man said.'

'But—'

'It's called division of labour. Okay? Like an assembly line. Everybody does his little part, and in the end the whole job gets done. That's all you need to know. You go to the place and wait. And hope to hell there's a little boy waiting for you there.'

'All things being equal,' I said to Stern, 'I doubt if you and I would turn out to be real pals, you know?'

'That's one thing we see eye to eye on, Mr Coyne.'

*   *   *

I studied the directions until I had them memorized. I followed Route 3 past Route 495, heading north towards New Hampshire. I found the numbered route that took me across the Merrimack River, then the dusty side road that led me into the countryside. Precisely four-point-seven miles beyond the sawmill I pulled to the side of the road and stopped. I found the old roadway hidden by overgrown brush and the two stone pillars at the end of it joined by a rusted chain. I checked my watch. High noon. The sun smouldered through a thin summer haze. I started walking.

The road sloped gently upward. After a hundred yards of clawing through the alder and poplar growth that crowded against it, it levelled off and I stepped into an abandoned quarry. I was standing in a kind of dusty amphitheatre that had been carved out of the hill. At the far end a curved wall of sheer granite rose about a hundred feet straight up into the sky. Great slabs of rock lay tumbled all around as if a giant had scattered a couple of basketfuls of twenty-foot dominoes. It looked like a vandalized graveyard. Stunted

111

birch and pine struggled to send their roots into the crevices among the stones. Weeds and grass sprouted against them. The humid noontime air was trapped in there like a steaming bowl of soup. My shirt was pasted to my back.

In the shadow of the cliff lay a dark pool of water, cut roughly square and as big as a basketball court. Beside the pool nestled against the rock wall stood an old wood and tarpaper shack with a rusted corrugated tin roof. I picked my way among the slabs of stone until I stood in front of the shack. The wooden door hung open a slit. Through the crack I could see darkness inside, broken by a narrow beam of sunlight where dust motes hung suspended.

I hesitated. My instructions had been to wait. I stepped close to the door and whispered, 'E.J.?'

There was no answer. I pulled on the door until it groaned open. I stepped into the doorway and waited for my eyes to adjust to the dim light. I looked around. Nobody was there. 'E.J.,' I called again. 'Are you here?' My voice echoed hollowly in the empty room.

I moved away from the shack and picked my way among the rubble along the base of the blasted rock cliff. I stopped beside the pool, squatted on my heels, and lit a cigarette.

112

I'd wait, then.

I stared into the water. It was faintly tinted, the pale amber of bourbon, but it looked cool and potable. Despite the discolouration, the water was clean and clear, and I peered down into it as far as the refracted light would allow. The green sides of the pool descended straight down. I picked up a slice of shale the size of a silver dollar and dropped it into the pool. It sank slowly, tilting from side to side. I watched it for a long time before it disappeared without having reached bottom.

I was intensely aware of the gathered summer heat that had collected, unrelieved by any breeze, in the granite bowl. I edged into the shadow against the cliff and rested my back against it. The rock felt cool through my damp shirt. I watched a chipmunk scurry among the weeds and rocks. In the high branches of the trees beyond the edge of the quarry half a dozen crows settled, and I could hear them arguing.

It was a desolate, godforsaken place. As the perspiration on my back dried I shivered. I glanced at my watch. I didn't know how long I was supposed to wait. I settled myself as well as I could into my position beside the pool and prepared to exercise patience—not normally my strong suit.

I waited exactly an hour there, smoking

several Winstons and scanning the perimeter of the rock-strewn quarry. The only life I saw belonged to the chipmunks and birds that lived there.

I gave it an extra fifteen minutes, then I decided no one was coming. I stood, groaning at the stiffness in my legs and back, and walked over to the shack. I hesitated a moment, then stepped inside. The air tasted cool and musty and smelled of wet earth. I paused once again to allow my eyes to adjust to the dim light. Black shapes gradually took form. Against one wall stood a row of fifty-gallon drums. Four wooden boxes were set out in the middle of the single room as if they had once served as table and chairs.

'E.J.? Are you in here?'

There was no answer. I went over to the barrels and peered behind them. I kicked one and it pinged hollowly. In the corner I saw several six-packs of rusting beer cans. Another object caught my eye. I picked it up and carried it outside to examine it in the daylight.

It was a sneaker. A small, leather Nike. With a red stripe.

'Oh, Christ,' I whispered. I wandered back to my seat by the pool and sank to the ground. I didn't like what I was thinking. I held the little sneaker—Eddie had called them 'running shoes', I remembered—and pictured

E.J. Donagan's grin.

I lit a cigarette and willed my hands to stop trembling. I assumed the sneaker had been left for me to find. They had been too careful, too precise, for it to have been an accident. But what did it mean? It was a message.

I hoped I misread it.

I stepped on my cigarette butt and made my way back to my car, E.J.'s sneaker clutched in my hand. I drove to a gas station I had passed on my way, dropped a quarter into the slot of the pay phone I found there, and punched out the number Stern had given to me, where he was waiting close by for my report.

'Yeah, Stern,' he answered.

'He wasn't there. Nobody was there. But— I found his sneaker.'

'Slow down,' said Stern. His voice was low and calm. 'Start over.'

'E.J. wasn't there. I went and waited. Like they said. I found a sneaker in the shack. It's his. I'm sure it's his.'

'Nothing else?'

'No.' His businesslike patience was annoying me.

'Look. There's this deep pool of water. It looks bottomless. It—'

'You're jumping to conclusions.'

'You know what I'm saying, then?'

I heard him sigh. 'Yes, I know what you're

saying. Look, okay. We'll get up there. You go home.'

'Divers?'

'Yes. We'll bring divers.'

There was a heavy lump in my chest. 'That's what I was thinking,' I said.

'Just go home, Mr Coyne. You did fine.'

'What about the sneaker?'

'Bring it with you. We'll have to show it to Mrs Donagan. Unless you want to do that.'

'No. No, I don't want to do that. And I'm not ready to go home. I'll meet you there.'

'You've done your part. You'll just be in the way. Division of labour, remember?'

'Up yours,' I said, and I hung up.

Stern arrived at the roadway a few minutes after I did, followed in short order by several more vehicles, including two State Police cruisers, each manned by two uniformed officers, and a panel truck containing two hefty guys with diving gear. I gave Stern E.J.'s sneaker, which he dropped into a Baggie and locked in the trunk of his car.

We trekked up the road to the quarry, then made our way among the tumbled granite slabs to the shack beside the pool. There the men gathered around Stern, who spat out his orders. Most of the men, including the state cops, he directed to explore the floor of the quarry to search for footprints, tyre tracks, anything. The two divers moved towards the pool. I took Stern into the shack.

He flicked on the big flashlight he was carrying and probed methodically through the darkness into the corners of the room. 'I suppose you've touched everything,' he muttered.

'Not really. As soon as I found the sneaker I went outside.'

'Humph.'

The dirt floor was caked too hard for footprints to show, but Stern nevertheless knelt down and studied it closely. Then he examined the heap of empty beer cans near where I told him I had found the sneaker. After a few minutes we went back outside and Stern called to one of his men who was heavily armed with camera gear.

'In there, Soderstrom. Get everything.' He turned to me. 'I couldn't see anything in there.'

We walked over to the pool. One of the divers, wearing the top of a wet suit, bathing trunks, a facemask, and a pair of big metal tanks strapped to his back, was just lowering himself in. He carried a big square waterproof flashlight, and had a rope tied under his arms. The other man knelt beside the pool, holding the rope.

'What's going on?' said Stern.

'No purchase. The sides are pure vertical and slick as a whore's thighs. Algae growing all over them. Nothing to hang on to. I'm gonna lower him down. It looks deep and dark. No fun.'

Stern nodded. He and I squatted beside the pool and watched the diver sink slowly down. The man beside us paid out the rope a foot at a time. We could still make out the fuzzy image of the diver when his partner muttered, 'Fifteen feet.'

One of the uniformed State Police officers approached. 'Sir?'

'What is it?' said Stern.

'We found these.' He handed Stern a plastic bag. 'Cigarette butts. Fresh, from the smell.'

'They're mine,' I said.

'Jesus Christ,' Stern muttered. 'Okay. Keep looking,' he said to the policeman.

'Twenty-five feet,' announced the man holding the rope. From the depths of the water I could see the shimmering rays of the light. The diver had disappeared from sight. 'Thirty feet.'

At fifty feet he turned to us. 'He's coming up.' He began to haul slowly on the rope. After several minutes the diver hoisted himself out of the water. His partner helped him take off the tanks, and he pulled his mask off.

'Man, it's cold down there,' he breathed. He towelled his face and legs with a balled up sweatshirt.

'See anything?' said Stern.

'Nothing. I didn't hit bottom. About thirty feet down there's an opening that goes back under. Looks like a big cave. There's current under there, it feels like. About fifty feet there's another big hole in the side. Looks like a tunnel that curves in and back. I looked down with the light and all I could see was more water and a lot more of those ledges and caves. I figure somewhere down there there's an underground river. We'll need better gear if you want us to really explore it.' He raised his eyebrows at Stern.

'No signs of anything, then?'

'Nope. Anything that fell in there could get sucked into one of those tunnels. Or maybe just go straight down, God knows how far.'

'These quarry pools,' the other man said. 'Kid drowned in one in Quincy couple of years ago. We went down, found some old auto bodies. Couldn't find the kid. Finally they drained it. Still couldn't find him.' He shrugged. 'Something about these quarry pools.'

Stern nodded. 'We'll get the proper equipment in and try to do it right.' He turned to me. 'Look, Mr Coyne. You're in the way, okay? It's going to be a long, boring afternoon, and I doubt we're gonna find anything very dramatic. You're thinking the boy's body is down there. Well, if it is we may not find it. Okay?' He snatched his dark-framed glasses from his face and jabbed at me with them. 'So why don't you go home and do whatever it is you do to make a living, and let us do what we do?'

I stared at him for a moment, then nodded. 'You'll let me know?'

'Sure. You're involved, okay? You're an important part of this investigation. I'll keep in touch. Don't call me. I'll call you. So run along, now, huh?'

I stood up. 'Let me know if you ever decide to run for public office, will you, Stern?'

I walked back to my car and drove home. I needed a shower.

CHAPTER NINE

Jan was lying on her stomach on a big beach towel spread out on the concrete apron by the pool. By her head a paperback book sat on its open pages. The white bikini she wore contrasted with the deep bronze of her skin. It looked as if she had been investing considerable time—and whatever sort of energy it took—into acquiring her tan.

I dragged an aluminium folding chair close to her and sat in it. Her face rested on her left cheek, turned away from me.

'Watch the rays, will you?' she said without moving her head.

'Sorry.' I moved back. 'How are you?'

'How do you like my tan?' she mumbled into the towel.

'Real nice, Jan. It's a good one.'

'They said you were coming. I told them you shouldn't bother. I had to put a top on because you were coming. Now I'll get lines.'

'Lines?'

'On my back. Oh, hell. You don't mind if I take this off, do you? I really don't want to get lines.'

She reached around and unsnapped the top of her bathing suit. It fell away and she lay spread out in front of me naked except for the little patch of white cloth across her rump.

'You should see my breasts. No lines at all. I had a little problem with them at first. The nipples get burned, you know? They're very sensitive. I had to put a lot of lotion on them. Rub it in thick. This is the best tan I ever had.'

'Jan—'

'Let's have a drink. There's a cooler over

121

there in the shade. Vodka and tonic. All mixed. We'll have to share. Only one glass. You don't mind sharing a glass with me, do you?'

I took the glass over to the cooler and filled it. I took a sip. It was mostly vodka. I put it down beside her, and she lifted herself up on her elbows to take a drink. Her breasts, I noticed, were indeed well tanned.

'Jan, we have to talk.'

'Rub a little lotion on my back, will you? I'm afraid I might have gotten a line where I was wearing the top.' She lay down again. This time she turned her head so that she was facing me. Her eyes were closed. I could see the edge of one breast flattened out under her.

'Don't try to seduce me, Jan. We have to talk about E.J.'

'Lotion, Brady.'

I squeezed a little worm of the white grease on to my palm and rubbed my hands together. Then I knelt beside her and began to apply it to her back. There was a moist sheen on her dark skin. It was smooth and alive under my fingers as I massaged the flesh of her shoulders and back.

'The legs, too,' she mumbled.

I moved over the backs of her thighs. The sun baked down on the concrete, unrelieved by any breeze. It reflected off the pool, and as

I worked over Jan's body sweat burned in my eyes and gathered under the polo shirt I wore.

'Umm. That feels good. Up the sides, now, please.'

My hands spread the grease over her hips, up her waist, then along her ribcage, steering carefully around her breasts. I heard her chuckle.

'Good ol' Brady. Good ol' proper attorney. Never fool around with the clients' wives. Or the clients' daughters. Never even fool around with the clients.' She sighed. 'That's fine. That's good enough. Thank you.'

I sat back on my heels. She rolled over, propped herself up on her elbows, and squinted at me. 'Don't you like what you see?'

'I like it very much,' I said. 'Cover yourself up, will you?'

She tilted her head and smiled briefly. Then she shrugged and sat up to pull on a tee-shirt. It was much too big for her, and it fell below her hips, giving the illusion that it was all she was wearing. It made her look much sexier.

She picked up the glass and took a long drink. She handed it to me. I sipped then put it down.

'So you're here on business, then.'

'Yes.'

'You're not here to comfort the grieving mother.'

'You shouldn't be grieving, Jan.'

'No?'

'No. You should be helping. You should insist on helping. If we're going to find E.J....'

She snorted. 'Find him? You mean find his body, don't you? Am I supposed to be out looking for my little boy's body?'

'We don't know that he's dead, Jan. There's no reason not to assume he's alive. There are things we can do.'

'The FBI, that guy, Stern, he thinks he's dead. Right? They've given up, haven't they? And the police, they're not exactly conducting an all-out hunt for my boy. So what am I supposed to do?'

'Jan—'

'I'll tell you what I'm doing. I'm getting the best goddam tan I've ever had, that's what I'm doing. I'm working hard at it, concentrating. And I'm acquiring a real taste for vodka and tonic. And I figure I'm doing as much as anybody.'

'Every policeman in the country has a picture of E.J. Every FBI office has his picture. No one has given up.'

Jan lifted her glass and took a quick swallow. Then she leaned towards me and gripped my leg. 'Well, *I* have,' she hissed. 'I've spent the last week lying here giving up.

124

It wasn't easy. But I did it. I gave up. I got it through my dumb Eyetalian skull that my boy is gone, and that you and Stern and all the rest of you guys have gone back to your jobs, and that Eddie's no help at all, and that it's all over, and that I've got to accept all that.' She hitched herself forward until her face was close to mine. Her dark eyes were shining, and her voice went soft. 'So don't come around here trying to give me hope, Brady Coyne. Please don't do that. It would be an unwelcome gift. I don't want hope now. I want it over. I just want to forget it all. Help me do that, will you?'

Her hand went to the back of my neck and her mouth found mine. Her lips were soft and I could feel her breasts press against my chest, and in spite of myself I found myself responding to her. A little moan came from her throat. Her mouth moved on mine. Our tongues touched briefly, and then hers flicked and darted, inviting mine to follow. I reached up to hold her face in both of my hands and pulled back from her kiss. Her eyes were wide and dry and staring into mine. I kissed her softly on her lips, then hugged her to me. She buried her face in my shoulder and her arms went around my neck. I held her while she rocked and shuddered in my arms.

I wondered if Sam or Josie were watching

from the windows of the house, and if they were, what they were thinking. 'Jan, listen to me,' I said into her ear.

'Don't. Please. Just hold me.'

I pushed her gently away. I had thought she was crying, but her eyes were dry. They were scowling at me. 'Okay,' she said. 'What, then? Damn you, what do you want from me?'

I stood up and held my hands to her. 'Come on. Get up,' I said to her. She staggered a little.

'Let's sit in the shade. The sun makes me dizzy,' she said.

We moved to a pair of patio chairs by a round table with a pole through the middle and a big flowered umbrella on top. I reached across to take Jan's hands in mine. She sat there passively and let me hold them. They were lifeless, like her eyes.

'I want you to go on television.'

'Is this that Stern's idea?'

'No,' I said. 'It's mine.'

'Does the big FBI agent approve?'

'I don't know. I didn't talk with him about it.'

'What do you have in mind?'

'I know a news director at Channel 5. He'll get a reporter out here to interview you. Get E.J.'s picture on the television, tell your story. Maybe somebody has seen him.'

Jan studied our hands where they lay together in the middle of the table. 'I don't think I could handle that. It might give me hope again.' She peered up at me. 'That would be cruel. Don't you see?'

'I don't mean to be cruel. I think you *should* have hope. I think it's reasonable to have hope. I think E.J.'s alive. I really do. I think his sneaker meant just that. That he's alive somewhere, and that he'll be coming back to you. But you've got to do something, too.'

'But the FBI is looking for his body. Not him. Not E.J. alive, but his dead body. Isn't that right?'

I shrugged. 'They don't know what they're looking for. But they haven't given up. I know that.'

She smiled sadly. 'I wish Eddie were here.'

'You haven't heard from him either?'

'Eddie's gone. Remember what he said? "I'm gone."'

'I tried to reach him at work,' I told her. 'They haven't seen him, either. But you know Eddie. He'll probably call. He always has.'

Jan sighed. 'Oh, yes. I know Eddie. He runs away from things. He ran away from baseball. He ran away from me and E.J. Now he's run away from all this. He always talked about Alaska. No, Eddie's gone. That's what he does when he stops hoping. I work on my

tan and drink vodka tonics. Eddie runs away.'
She squeezed my hands and then pulled hers
away and leaned back in her chair. 'It's all the
same, I guess.'

'Go on television, Jan. Do it.'

'No. I can't.'

I nodded. 'Okay.' I stood up. 'I guess I'll
give up, too, then.' I turned to leave.

'Brady, wait.'

I stopped but did not turn to face her.

'Don't you understand how hard that would
be for me?'

I shrugged. 'Sure. So give up, then.'

I felt her standing behind me. Her hand
touched my shoulder. 'You're right, of
course,' she said softly. 'I've been trying to
give up. I don't want to hope. It hurts too
much. I try to tell myself that it's over, that
he's gone forever, and sometimes it works and
I can just be numb. But then when I'm not
careful it creeps up on me and I see him
smiling and I know I'll never stop hoping and
crying for him.'

I turned to face her. She leaned against me
and put her arms around my waist. She tilted
back a little so she could look up at me. 'Last
night I was getting ready for bed,' she said,
'and I went to brush my teeth. And there in
the holder was his toothbrush. It's a little
green kid-sized toothbrush, and it has old

128

toothpaste all gunked in the bristles. He always hated brushing his teeth. I mean, I see him every day. His room, the furniture he used to sit on. There are pictures of him. His toys are under the sofa. And I don't think of him as being dead. I should. I think I should. I try to. I try to imagine it. I pretend it's as if he had never been born. If he'd never been born, I wouldn't miss him now, see? But it doesn't work. I can't make it work. I can't trick myself that way. So, yeah, I'll go on television, if you want me to. Just tell me I must. Tell me I have no choice, that you're making me, that it's not my decision.'

I kissed her forehead. 'You must. I have decided. I'll arrange it right away.'

★　　★　　★

Sylvie Szabo and I sprawled side by side on my sofa, our bare feet propped up on a stack of old newspapers atop the coffee table. We were sipping white wine and, like untold millions of other Americans, staring at the six o'clock news on the television. After a brief introductory lesson on feminine hygiene, featuring the relative benefits of pads versus tampons, the anchor people came on and told us all we'd ever need to know about Arthur, the season's first tropical storm gathering steam two hundred miles southeast of Cuba, the President's newest tax reform scheme, hostilities in the Mid-East, and a cocaine bust in New Orleans starring a well-known professional football player.

'He was always considered a shifty one,' smirked the anchorman.

'That's right, Frank,' replied the anchorwoman. 'Heh, heh.' She turned to face a different camera. 'And now on the local scene, we have this story from Winchester.'

I sat up. 'This is it,' I said to Sylvie. She gripped my hand.

On the screen appeared Sam Farina's house. It looked more opulent on television than it did to the eye, if that was possible, as the camera panned across the broad emerald lawn and lingered meaningfully on Sam's putting green and then switched to the kidney-shaped swimming pool out back. The reporter, in voice-over, was saying, 'This is the home of Salvatore Farina, owner of the Farina Liquor chain. Farina lives in this custom-built seven-bedroom home on the exclusive west side of Winchester with his wife and daughter and, until almost two weeks ago, his ten-year-old grandson. But tragedy now haunts this home. One week ago last Saturday little E.J. Donagan failed to return home from his paper route. He has not been seen since.'

At this point a photograph of E.J. flashed on the screen. The reporter continued, 'Little E.J. was kidnapped. The family, working with the Winchester police, the State Police, and the FBI, delivered one hundred and fifty thousand dollars in ransom money. E.J. Donagan, whose father is the former Red Sox pitcher, Eddie Donagan, has not been returned to the family. I talked with Janet Donagan, E.J.'s mother, this afternoon.'

Jan appeared on the screen, sitting on Sam's living-room sofa. The reporter, a young blonde, sat on a chair facing her.

'She looks so sad,' whispered Sylvie.

'Mrs Donagan,' began the reporter, 'what is being done to find your son?'

'I don't know,' said Jan with a shrug. 'We—for a while, they—the FBI, the police— they were here all the time. But now—lately— we don't see them. I don't know. I guess they're looking. I don't know.'

'You are still hopeful?' The reporter's voice was soft and spread thickly with sympathy, like honey on toast.

The camera zoomed in on Jan's face in time to catch the sparkle of panic in her eyes. 'Hopeful?' she repeated. 'Oh, Jesus! Yes, I'm—we're trying. I can't believe . . .'

E.J.'s picture appeared again. 'The FBI and

the other authorities declined to be interviewed,' said the reporter, 'but the family's attorney told this reporter that they are prepared to offer a ten-thousand dollar reward for information leading to the return of E.J. Donagan. Or,' she went on after a pause, her voice low and dramatic, 'the boy's body. Call this number if you have seen, or know anything of, E.J. Donagan.' And the phone number of the Winchester police appeared on the screen under E.J.'s picture. After a moment's silence, the reporter said, 'And now back to you, Dorothy and Frank.'

I got up and snapped off the television, then returned to my place beside Sylvie. She snuggled close to me. I turned to her and saw tears glittering in her eyes. 'Oh, that is so sad,' she murmured.

I grunted.

'Will they find him?'

'I don't know. We hope somebody has seen him. It's been two weeks. He could be anywhere.'

'Oh, Brady ...'

I put my arm around Sylvie's shoulders and stared at the blank television screen. What else could we do now? The news story, as brief and as superficial as it had been, was touching. Jan and I, in talking to the reporter off camera, had refused to discuss the details

132

of the ransom payment or the aborted meeting in the quarry, hoping to allow the kidnappers no opportunity to feel trapped or pursued. We wanted only to get E.J.'s picture on the screen. And while the reporter had been unable to resist the attraction of the tragedy-befalls-the-wealthy aspects of the story, much as they insist on squeezing the most out of every Kennedy catastrophe, she had accomplished what we wanted. I hoped it wouldn't backfire. The story was out, and there was no way to pull it back.

I was startled by the jangling of my telephone. I went into the kitchen and answered it.

'Helluva show,' came Stern's sarcastic voice. 'Damn nice.'

'Glad you approve.'

'You know what you've done, Coyne? You've just sealed that boy's death warrant is what you've done. You think if those people still have him they'll keep him alive now that everybody in the state is drooling over that ten K reward? And are those folks in Winchester prepared to have *People* magazine crawling through their peony beds and taking pictures through telephoto lenses, and having every crackpot after that reward? You just shit the bed, Coyne.'

'I can't see that what you've been doing has

133

accomplished much,' I said lamely.

'You're not supposed to see it. You're supposed to go back to your lawbooks and make out some wills or whatever the hell it is you do for a living, and keep your goddam nose out of places where it's gonna get all bloody. This was the stupidest, most destructive thing you could've done.'

'I see,' I said. 'Division of labour.'

'Hey, you've gotta face them. You've gotta live with it. Good luck to you.'

'Look, Stern. I hope—'

'You better hope, Coyne. You better hope and pray and meditate and every other damn thing you can think of.'

I heard him replace the receiver. He did not do it gently.

I hung up and wandered out on to my little balcony. Sylvie followed me. She handed me my wineglass and we stood side by side staring out towards the horizon, where the sky was the same grey as the water and they merged together so that you couldn't tell where heaven and earth joined.

'Are you all right?' murmured Sylvie.

I hugged her against me. 'No, dear, I'm not all right. I may just have done a very stupid thing.'

She nuzzled against my throat. 'Would you like to make love?'

'It probably won't help,' I said. 'But we could try it.'

PART THREE

ANNIE

CHAPTER TEN

A sultry Friday afternoon in July, a week after Jan's appearance on television. Julie had the day off. I don't exactly give her days off. We don't work that way. She'll say to me, 'Any problem if I take Friday?' and I'll say yea or nay and we work it out. The other side of that particular coin is when I say to her, 'How about Saturday morning?' It all balances out.

This time she was off with her Edward and little Megan for a long weekend in Ogunquit. Overdue and well deserved.

I spent the day talking to other lawyers, all of us trying to find alternatives to going to court. We attorneys spend most of our time looking for ways to avoid practising law. So far as I know, no one has come up with anything better than a leisurely luncheon at Locke-Obers. On any given day, more legal disputes are resolved in the mirrored downstairs Men's Bar, Hizzoner the distinguished maître d' in his black tie presiding, than in all the courtrooms in Suffolk County.

I mended a fence here, created a strategic gap in one there, cajoled the odd client, the telephone suctioned to my ear for most of the day. Real Perry Mason stuff. When the phone jangled about three o'clock, it interrupted the daydream I was indulging in, in which I packed my waders and seven-foot Orvis fly rod into the car and drove to the Deerfield River in time for the evening stonefly hatch.

'Mr Coyne?' The voice was low and tentative. I recognized it immediately. I had heard it three previous times, once over the crash and clatter of pins being struck by bowling balls.

'Yes,' I said. 'Do you have another recorded message for me?'

'No. I want to talk to you.'

'You have news of E.J. Donagan?'

'I don't want to talk on the phone.' She hesitated. 'Can I trust you?'

'Yes,' I said immediately. 'Yes, you can trust me.'

'You're a lawyer. You're supposed to . . .'

'I promise you client privilege, yes. You're in trouble.'

I heard her exhale abruptly. 'You know I am. But you mustn't ask me any questions. You have to promise not to ask me anything.

I—I have to do this my own way. If you go to the police or something you'll never hear from me again.'

'You need an attorney.'

'Okay. Let's put it that way. You're my attorney.'

'I'll have to know your name.'

'No. No questions. Please.'

'This isn't—'

'It has to be my way, Mr Coyne. I want to trust you. I don't know if I can. I think you can understand that.'

'Sure. Okay.'

'Can you meet me in an hour?'

'Where?'

'The Aquarium. Be there at four. Okay?'

'Yes. How will I recognize you?'

'You won't. I'll recognize you. What do you look like?'

'Well, I'm wearing a brownish glen plaid suit, a bit rumpled, yellow shirt, dark green tie. I'm six-one, just the beginnings of a pot belly that you'd never notice, black hair with a little more grey in it than there was yesterday. Bluish-grey eyes.'

'Okay,' she said. 'Carry your jacket over your shoulder. Look at the fish. I'll find you.'

She hung up. I found my pulse beating hard in my temples and a kink in my stomach. I leaned back in my chair, sighed deeply, and lit

138

a Winston. I contemplated calling Stern, then quickly discarded the idea. He wouldn't like it, but I had the feeling that he wouldn't want me to handle this alone, and that this woman was too cautious for me to handle it any other way. I decided to go along, do it exactly her way. The worst that could happen would be nothing, and then we'd be no worse off than we had been. At best I might learn something about the disappearance of E.J. Donagan.

★   ★   ★

Every summer camp and recreation programme in the city had decided to bring the kids to the New England Aquarium to escape the oppressive heat of the afternoon. It was a good choice. Inside the big concrete structure down on the waterfront it was dark and cool.

I worked my way through the clusters of small children along the spiral ramp that encircled the great tank in the core of the building. I found a spot by a thick glass window so I could watch the fish fin past in their slow, endless circles. Some of them I could identify—the striped bass, the big sawfish, the primitive gars, turtles the size of the Plymouth Rock, and the stolid sharks, whose dead little marble eyes seemed to lock on to mine each time they glided past my window. Then there were the exotic species that most of us see only in aquariums. There was a hypnotic rhythm to the monotonous, ordered movement of this community of fishes. They swam effortlessly, round and round, all at the same speed, their tails and fins barely moving. Once in a while one fish would dart forward, but then it would fall back into the pace. They reminded me of joggers on a circular track, moving for the sake of moving, going nowhere, passing the time, hour after hour, day after day, for a lifetime. I imagined one of the fish dying. I supposed it would just sink to the bottom, and none of the others would notice. They'd continue to move in their drugged orbits, waiting for their own turn to die. Each seemed to know its place, and I wondered what happened to procreation and hunger and aggression and territoriality in this artificially sterile little ecosystem.

'Do you know why they all swim in the same direction?'

I jerked my head around. She was tall, nearly my height, with sleek ebony hair and olive skin and dark almond eyes. She wore open-toed sandals, blue jeans, and a pale yellow silk blouse buttoned tight to her slim throat. I thought she was the most beautiful

Oriental woman I had ever seen.

'I never really thought about it,' I answered.

'They follow the sharks,' she said, in a voice that sounded like a mountain stream bubbling over white stones.

'I would've thought it was for the same reason the water swirls down the bathtub drain counterclockwise in the northern hemisphere,' I said, smiling. 'Or maybe it's just the currents in the tank.'

She didn't return my smile. 'Maybe that's it.' She looked me up and down quickly. 'You are Mr Coyne?'

I nodded. 'And you? What's your name?'

She frowned. 'I told you. No questions. Please, I'm not—'

'And I told you. You can trust me.'

'I don't know that,' she said. She moved closer to me. 'I'm Annie. I—I saw the mother on television.' We watched the fish for a minute. 'I decided I had to help. I don't know. I think it was a mistake.' She glanced back over her shoulder. 'I should leave. I should never have come here.'

'Don't be afraid.' I touched her shoulder.

'But I *am* afraid. This was stupid.'

'Are you interested in the reward? Is that it?'

She drew away from me and shook her

head. 'No. Of course not. It—it's my conscience, don't you see?'

I nodded. 'Then let me help you.'

She stared into my eyes. 'You can't help me. It's too late for that. I know what you're thinking, but I've got to take care of myself now.' She put her hand on my wrist. 'Mr Coyne, listen. I'm going to trust you. I'm involved in this. You know that. I didn't know—never mind. I have to do something now. I can't just follow the sharks. If they knew what I was doing, if they ever found out that I was here with you . . .'

'Annie . . .'

'Don't,' she said. Her hand found mine and I felt her pass me a scrap of paper. She gave my hand a quick squeeze then pulled it away. 'Don't look at it now. Put it into your pocket. I'm going to leave. Please stay here for fifteen more minutes. Don't even turn around when I go. Don't try to follow me or anything. If— when I'm certain I can trust you, I'll get in touch again.'

'Does this . . . ?'

'This doesn't give you all the answers you want to know. It's—it's something. For now it's all I dare.'

'Annie,' I whispered. 'Just tell me. Is E.J. . . .'

But she was gone, as abruptly as she had

142

appeared. I remained standing there, watching the fish follow the sharks in their slow eternal circles and feeling the scrap of paper in my pocket weighing there like a ton of guilt.

A quarter of an hour later I turned and walked out into the liquid heat of the city.

★   ★   ★

I was seated at a tiny metal table at the Café Florian on the sidewalk of Newbury Street. The breeze that was funnelled down the street ruffled the linen tablecloth but failed to relieve the city heat. I sipped iced chocolate and nibbled at a rich chocolaty Sachertorte and wondered if I'd done the right thing. I probably shouldn't have called Stern. He'd bitch and bluster and insist on trying to find Annie. But a glance at the paper she'd given me persuaded me that I needed his help. My first obligation was to E.J. Donagan, not the Oriental woman who called herself Annie, and who, after all, had participated in kidnapping him.

On the other hand, Stern could screw it up, and then we'd be back where we started.

I took the sheet of paper from my jacket pocket, unfolded it, and smoothed it on the table. I don't know what I had expected it to

143

say. Annie had made it clear that she wasn't ready to tell me where to find E.J., or who had kidnapped him, or even if he were still alive. But I had hoped for something more, something less oblique, something that made sense.

She was cautious, and she had given me a puzzle. Five names. The names of five baseball players. So her message concerned Eddie. That was as far as I could take it.

I glanced up and saw Stern coming down the sidewalk towards me. I refolded the paper and shoved it back into my pocket. Stern walked with a cocky, elbows-out swagger that reminded me of a rooster. His hatchet-shaped face and big dark-rimmed glasses completed the picture.

He didn't look too happy.

He sat down opposite me and flourished his handkerchief. He was sweating profusely. 'Damn this humidity,' he muttered. 'No relief in the whole damn city.'

'Have some iced chocolate,' I said. 'Cools you right down.'

He took off his glasses and mopped his face. 'I could use a beer.'

'They don't sell beer here.'

'I could use my air-conditioned office, is what I could use. So whyn't you just tell me what the hell you've got, huh?'

144

'Take it easy. Relax. We've got to have some understandings first. Okay?'

Stern narrowed his eyes. 'What kind of understandings?'

I ate a hunk of my torte. Stern watched me, his eyebrows lifted expectantly. 'I think I've got a source of information,' I said. 'I have agreed to certain things. In return, I think we may get some help in solving this case.'

Stern jabbed at me with his glasses. 'You've agreed to certain things, huh? Like what? You know this is a federal case, don't you? If you plan to withhold information material to a federal case, Coyne—'

'Don't, for Christ's sake, try to tell me the law. This person came to me because I'm a lawyer, okay? You'll notice she didn't go to you.'

'She?'

I nodded. 'The person. My source.'

'It's a woman, huh?'

'Look,' I said. 'We can terminate this right now. I do want your advice, but I've made certain commitments.'

'Client privilege. Sure. Figures. This woman is your client.'

'Right.'

'Coyne, I can get a subpoena, you know.'

'Oh, don't try to bully me. Just shut up and listen. Okay?'

He shoved his glasses back on and frowned. 'Go ahead,' he said.

'She called me this afternoon. She said she wanted to talk to me. I recognized her voice.'

'The same one?'

'Yes. I met her at the Aquarium. She gave me something. Said there'd be more, implying that it depended on my handling it discreetly. Talking to you now isn't particularly discreet. So I've taken a risk. But I figured you should know what's going on.'

He nodded. 'What did she give you?'

I removed the paper from my pocket, unfolded it, and spread it out on the table for him to see.

He glanced at it and frowned. 'There's just five names here.'

'Yes.'

'Who are these people, do you know?'

'They're baseball players. Or they were. None of them is still active.'

'You think they're the ones who kidnapped the boy?'

'No,' I said. 'I'm afraid it's not that simple. Two of these men aren't even alive. This one—' I pointed to one of the names—'this Gus Geralchik died of cancer two years ago. And Bobo Halley, here, drove his car into a bridge abutment or something back in eighty-three.'

Without warning Stern's fist came down on the table. I grabbed at my glass of iced chocolate and saved it from tipping over. 'Damn it, Coyne!' he growled. 'You're telling me you had this—this woman, who helped to kidnap E.J. Donagan, and all you got out of her is *this*? The names of five goddam *baseball* players, for Christ's sake? Listen. Did you *ask* her who did it? Did you ask her who snatched the boy? Did you?'

I took a sip of my chocolate. I could tell that my refusal to allow him to ruffle me infuriated him. I put down my glass and dabbed my mouth with a napkin. 'No. No, I didn't.'

'Did you threaten to bring her in?'

'Of course not. And I didn't hint at thumb screws or water torture, either. Calm down for a minute and listen to me. She called me. Of her own free will. She's very scared. I gave her my word that I would ask no questions, that I'd take what she had to give. And this is what she gave me. She said maybe there'd be more.' I shrugged.

'Terrific,' he mumbled. 'Just terrific. So she wants us to play a fucking game of Clue with her.' He shook his head sadly and peered up at me. 'Okay. So tell me about these baseball players, then. You checked 'em all out, right?'

'I looked 'em up in the *Baseball*
147

Encyclopedia at the library, and then I called a sportswriter I know at the *Globe*. Can't say I really learned a hell of a lot. This one here, Pete Bello, is managing in the minor leagues in the Pittsburgh chain. Arnie Bloom is selling life insurance out in Sacramento. And Johnny Warrick has a hog farm in Alabama.'

Stern stared at the list of names, neatly printed on the single sheet of plain white paper. 'What do you make of it?' he said.

'I don't know,' I said slowly. 'Obviously it makes you think of Eddie. But they couldn't have been his teammates. These guys weren't even each other's contemporaries. Geralchik played in the late fifties, and Bello had a couple of years in the big leagues in the mid-seventies. Halley pitched for the Tigers a couple of seasons back in the sixties. Three of them played for the Red Sox. Bello had eleven games with them at the tail end of seventy-three, after Donagan had left, and Bloom was with them four seasons before they traded him to the Twins. Warrick, you may remember, played his entire undistinguished career with them.'

'Reserve outfielder, right? I remember, now.'

'Yes. Bloom and Geralchik were pretty decent players. The other three were journeymen.'

'So,' said Stern, tapping the paper with his eyeglasses. 'They played for different teams at different times. Some were good, some not so good. Different positions. And some are alive and some aren't. Not much, is it?'

'There has to be something. The names must mean something. Anyhow, the girl said she'd get back to me. I assume to give me more information. Maybe we'll learn more then.'

'What do you figure her game is?' said Stern.

'It's pretty obvious. I think she wants to help us find the guys who kidnapped E.J. Donagan. I think she wants to do that without them knowing she helped. She's scared and she feels guilty, and as long as we don't mess it up she'll keep feeding us information. That's the way it seems to me.'

He nodded. 'Yeah. That's possible. Or it could be nothing. A ruse, a smokescreen, a joke, for Christ's sake.' He reached across the table, took a sip of my iced chocolate, and grimaced. 'Anyway, what can you tell me about the girl?'

I stared at him. 'I can tell you what she looks like. But I don't think I will.'

He laid his forearms on the table and leaned towards me. His hands were clenched into fists. 'Look,' he said, his voice tense. 'I know about you.'

I leaned back and folded my arms. 'Oh?'

'Yes. I know you like to interfere. You've got some sort of Wyatt Earp complex. You like to ride into town with your guns blazing.'

'You mean having Jan go on television, for example.'

'For example, yeah.'

'You checked me out, too, huh?'

'I did. Right. You don't think much of the police, do you?'

I shrugged. 'I'm a lawyer. I just do my job.'

Stern smiled sarcastically. 'You're not that kind of lawyer. You're out of your element, now. Way out. You've been there before, and you've gotten yourself in trouble. I understand you tend to wind up in the hospital.'

'If I didn't know better, I might think you disapproved of me.'

'Funny thing, Coyne. You might be surprised. Fact is, I don't necessarily disapprove. You've got the right idea. Too goddam many citizens are afraid to get involved. They refuse to come forward, they refuse to cooperate. They never see anything. They say, "Not my problem." Right? Look, don't get me wrong. I don't care for your methods. You should be working with us. This shouldn't be an adversary relationship,

150

you know. Listen. We haven't given up on this case, and just because we don't give you a blow-by-blow of what we're doing doesn't mean we're sitting around sucking our fingers. But we can use help. Any help.' He cocked his eyebrow at me. 'Even your help.'

I stared at him for a moment. 'You think we can work together?'

'Yes. I do.' He fiddled with his glasses but didn't take them off. 'Look,' he said, 'I happen to think we can agree on how to handle this. I think you did the right thing to call me, and I'm willing to try not to do anything that doesn't feel right to both of us. Okay? I know, you're afraid I'll try to catch up with that girl, and that we'll lose out on what she's going to give us. Well, I won't do that. At least not for now. Not as long as there's a chance of her helping us. So here's what I think. I think I'll agree not to go after her unless you and I discuss it. But I think you should help me get a line on her. See if we can't figure out who she might be. Do the research. Be ready. The more we know, the better off we are. What do you think?'

I took a bite of my torte, and stared at the people passing along the sidewalk while I chewed it. Then I looked at Stern. 'You wouldn't interfere?'

'No. I'd just like to be ready to act when the

time comes. It would be nice to know who she is.'

I swirled the dark remains of my iced chocolate in the bottom of my glass. Then I nodded. 'Okay. Her name is Annie. She's tall. Maybe five-ten or eleven. Mid-twenties. Black hair, black eyes. Slim. Oriental. Japanese, maybe. No scars or tattoos that I could see. Pretty well educated, I'd say, from her diction. New Englander, from the way she drops her R's.'

Stern had taken out a little notebook and was making notes. When I finished he looked up. 'That's not much.'

'Did I say how beautiful she was? And how her voice sounds like rain falling in a pond? And that she smells like hyacinths?'

'Jesus!' said Stern, grinning. 'Are you in love with her?'

'Wouldn't be difficult, believe me.'

'What else?'

I thought for a minute, then shrugged. 'That's about it. I was only with her a couple of minutes.'

He shoved the notebook back in his pocket. 'Guess I'll go get some real food, then,' he said. 'There's a good cue over Kenmore Square.'

'Cue?'

'You know,' said Stern. 'Bones. Ribs.'

'Oh. *Bar*becue. You fooled me. You don't strike me as the barbecue type.'

'Well, you don't strike me as the iced chocolate type, either,' he said. 'I spent six years in an office in El Paso. Rib joints and whore houses is what they've mainly got in El Paso. You learn to adapt. Pros and bones. That's about it in El Paso.' He pushed himself away from the table and stood up. 'Why don't you let me take that paper with me. We can run it through the lab, for whatever that might be worth. And we can do a rundown on these baseball players, too.'

I hesitated, then took my hand off the paper with the list of names on it. 'We have an understanding?' I said.

He picked up the paper. 'We do.' He extended his hand and we shook. His mitt was small and bony, but his grip was surprisingly hard. 'Keep in touch,' he said.

I gave him a half salute. 'Roger.'

He turned with a little nod and I watched him swagger away. He had surprised me. He didn't seem to be such a bad guy.

CHAPTER ELEVEN

The Prudential Building was Boston's first legitimate skyscraper. For many years the Pru stuck up from the middle of the city all by itself, all fifty-two storeys of it. Charlie McDevitt used to liken it to an upthrust middle digit, giving the finger to an otherwise distinctive skyline of church spires and low-slung office buildings. Then, not to be outdone, the John Hancock Insurance folks built their own tower practically next door, and the Pru lost whatever distinction it may have held.

The restaurant on the fifty-second floor of the Pru is called The Top of the Hub. It has pretty decent seafood, a panoramic view of the city, and prices geared to business luncheons on company credit cards. That's where Farley Vaughn insisted on meeting me for lunch. 'On the Red Sox,' he said over the phone, which was okay with me.

When I was deposited in the lobby of the restaurant after an ear-cracking ride on the express elevator, I whispered Vaughn's name into the ear of the hostess who greeted me. 'Oh, yes, sir,' she said, in a tone that suggested she and I shared an important secret. 'Mr Vaughn is expecting you.'

Vaughn was seated at a small table against the window that was wrapped all the way around the restaurant. He was gazing off towards the eastern horizon where every few seconds an airliner descended from its holding pattern towards the runway over at Logan. He was toying absent-mindedly with a wineglass containing an unnaturally brilliant coloured rosé. He stood and extended his hand when I arrived at the table.

Farley Vaughn looked like a guy who worked hard at his conditioning, one of those compulsive joggers with stringy forearms and a leathery face and pale narrow eyes. About one per cent body fat. He was some kind of vice president for the Red Sox, responsible for the various operations that make professional baseball indistinguishable from any other big business.

The Red Sox, at the time, were playing lousy baseball again, much to the glee of the local sportswriters, and their perennial front-office feuds had superseded news of the games as lead stories on the sports pages. So I intended a touch of irony when I asked Farley how business was.

'Oh, good, good,' he said, his eyes twinkling to let me know he caught my sarcasm. 'Turnstiles are well oiled. God bless the Boston fans. They'd just as soon come out to boo as to cheer.'

'Nothing a good reliever wouldn't cure, anyway,' I said. 'Sorry I'm late,' I added, taking my seat across from him. 'Couple of appointments got backed up. Time. The enemy of us all.'

'Time is our ally, Brady,' said Vaughn earnestly. 'Time is what prevents everything from happening at once.'

'Well, time is what made me late,' I smiled. 'What are you drinking?'

'Cranberry juice. Good for the kidneys. Hardly any calories. Have some?'

He crooked a finger and a waitress appeared. 'Cocktail, sir?' she said to me.

'Bourbon old-fashioned,' I said. 'No soda. Extra hunk of orange. My kidneys are in great shape.'

She frowned, then shrugged and went away to fetch my drink.

'So what's up?' said Vaughn. 'You said you wanted to pick my brain. Such as it is, pick away.'

'You have the reputation of knowing more about the players than just about anybody in the game. I've got some names I'd like to try out on you.'

He sipped his cranberry juice and nodded. 'Okay. Shoot.'

'Pete Bello.'

Vaughn steepled his fingers. 'He's doing a nice job for Pittsburgh, I hear. Managing in A ball. We signed him out of Holy Cross in seventy, I think it was. He was a shortstop then. Nice, soft hands, good arm, contact type of hitter. Limited range, though, and no power and only average speed. We brought him up for a few games in September in seventy-three or four, then traded him to the Pirates. He hung on a few years with them. Smart. College kid. He saw the handwriting, and was happy to take a job in the bushes for them. Pete Bello is a pretty nice guy, and they're high on him. Why're you asking about Pete Bello?'

I spread my palms. 'It's a long story, Farley.'

'Something to do with Eddie? I heard about his boy. Is that . . . ?'

'He's still missing.'

Vaughn shook his head. 'What a shame.'

I nodded.

'And you think Pete Bello is connected to that?'

I shook my head. 'I don't know. I really don't want to go into it.'

'Because I seriously doubt it. Not Pete Bello.'

'Like I said, I can't speculate.'

157

He shrugged. 'Okay. That's okay.'

The waitress slid my drink in front of me. I took a long sip and stared out the window at the grids of the city streets for a moment. From the fifty-second floor it looked like a big contour map laid out below us.

I looked back at Farley Vaughn. 'Anything, ah, funny about him? Anything unusual?'

'Bello?' He frowned. 'Well, he had this hitch in his swing. We never could do anything with it. Had the damnedest time pulling the ball. Dead opposite field hitter. That's probably not what you're after, huh?'

'No. I mean as a person, not ballplayer. Anything in his personal life?'

He stared at me out of those washed-out blue eyes. 'He was divorced. But I guess that's not unusual.'

'No, it's not. When did it happen?'

'Before he got to the big league. I recall, they had a couple of little kids. He was married when he was in college. One of those baseball things, you know? Bouncing around the bushes, never home, playing winter ball in Puerto Rico. She just wasn't a baseball wife.'

'Who is?' I said. 'Like with Eddie.'

'Yeah. Like with Eddie. It happens. How is Eddie, anyway? How's he doing?'

'I haven't seen him in a while,' I said. 'He wasn't doing that great last time I saw him.'

'Understandable.' Vaughn shook his head. 'Too bad. And he was one of the best prospects I ever saw, too.'

'How about Gus Geralchik?' I said. 'What do you know about him?'

'Poor Gus. He died a couple of years ago, you know. Stomach cancer. He deserved better. One tough son of a bitch, Gus. Hung around the big leagues quite a while. Back— oh, in the mid-fifties, it was. Always a second-stringer, but the kind of guy you just wanted to have around.'

'He was with the Cubs.'

'Right. We signed him originally, though. Right out of high school. Chicopee, it was, out there by Springfield. We let him go after a couple of years in the low minors, and Chicago picked him up. I was glad to see him make it. Work his ass off, Gus would. I bet in all the years he hung on with them he didn't get to bat five hundred times. Doubt if he minded. He liked being around the game.'

'I didn't realize he was originally Red Sox property.'

'Yup. You stay close to your own guys, even when they move on. I was real sorry when he died.'

'What did he do after baseball?'

Vaughn stroked his chin. 'Seems to me he bought into a filling station. Something like that. Maybe it was a car dealership. Outside of Chicago. And, no, I can't think of anything unusual about him. Absolutely straight shooter. Married his high school sweetheart, stayed married to her. Just your average guy.'

'That's not so average,' I said.

A waitress approached us, pencil and pad poised. 'Are you gentlemen ready to order?'

Neither Vaughn nor I had glanced at the menus that had been laid before us earlier. I picked mine up. Vaughn didn't refer to his. 'Spinach salad,' he said. 'No dressing. Just bring a wedge of lemon.' He looked up at me. 'Have the lobster, if you want, Brady. The Red Sox are paying for this.'

I was tempted to tell him that I could well afford the lobster myself, but I checked myself. He wasn't trying to patronize me. 'The open-faced steak sandwich. Medium rare. French fries. Bottle of Molson's. I don't want any salad.'

She bobbed her head, retrieved our menus, and whirled away.

Vaughn propped his chin atop his fist. 'Anybody else you want to talk about?'

'Bobo Halley.'

He squinted at me. 'What do you know about him?'

I shrugged. 'That he pitched for the Tigers for a couple of years. That he was killed in an automobile accident a few years ago.'

'That's it?'

I nodded. 'It's in the *Baseball Encyclopedia*.'

He cleared his throat. 'Well, this wasn't in the *Baseball Encyclopedia*, Brady, or the newspapers, either. I'm going to tell you about it because I know you won't abuse the information, and because you're trying to help out Eddie. At least, that's what I assume you're doing.'

He looked expectantly at me. I shrugged.

'Anyway,' he continued, 'what happened to Bobo isn't a big secret. Just that there's no sense of messing up the reputation of a dead guy.'

He hesitated again, and I nodded.

'When Bobo retired from baseball he was a young man. Thirty-one or -two. He'd had a few decent years with the Detroit club. They said it was arm trouble. They gave it a name—fancy medical jargon. Got a doctor to verify it. But—'

'But it wasn't arm trouble.'

'No,' he said. 'There was nothing wrong with Bobo Halley's arm when he retired from baseball.' He stared out the window, then turned to peer at me. 'Brady, what the hell has this got to do with Eddie Donagan's kid?'

I shook my head. 'I don't know. Maybe

nothing. Look. I have no intention of besmirching the memory of Bobo Halley or anybody else, believe me. Hell, I don't know if any of this means anything. I've got no hypothesis. I'm just poking around. Don't worry. You can trust me.'

He sipped his cranberry juice and gazed off at a point beyond my right shoulder. 'I know,' he said. 'Sorry. Anyway, Bobo Halley retired under duress, you might say. He was asked to retire. He was forced to retire, to be perfectly accurate. They made a deal with him. It was one of those deals where everybody is better off, you know? Bobo, the Tigers, organized baseball, the fans. It was like a plea bargain.'

'What did he do?'

'He bet on games.'

I lifted my eyebrows. 'I imagine lots of ballplayers gamble.'

'Bobo bet a lot of money. He used bookies. Illegal bookies. He bet on baseball games.' Vaughn stared at me with those icy eyes. 'He bet on games he played in. Sometimes he bet on his team to lose.'

'Yeah, I see,' I said. I leaned back and drained my old-fashioned. 'Say it ain't so, Bobo.'

Our lunches arrived. Vaughn squeezed the lemon over his spinach leaves. I poured A-1 Sauce on to my steak and a big glob of catsup all over my French fries. Vaughn watched me. He puffed out his cheeks as if he had a mouthful of vomit. I grinned at him and ceremoniously picked up a French fry in my fingers and lowered it into my mouth.

Vaughn wielded a knife and fork to chop his spinach into delicate little bite-sized pieces. He speared a couple and jammed them into his mouth. He was a firm believer in thorough mastication.

'So the league office thought it would be better if Bobo just retired,' he said.

'Bad PR for the grand old game, eh?'

'Yes,' he said solemnly. 'It could've been disastrous. Like the Black Sox scandal. The lesser of evils was to hush it up. At least that was the thinking.'

'Amazing they were able to get away with it.'

'It was in everybody's interest.'

'Except the media's. And maybe the public's.'

He shrugged.

'They thought he was throwing games,' I said. 'Was that it?'

He shrugged. 'There was no actual evidence of that. But, yes, of course, that was the real issue. There was plenty of motivation for it.'

'There's a lot of betting on baseball,' I said.

'Sure. Big money out of Vegas. Not to

mention Chicago and New York and Atlantic City.'

'And Boston.'

'Yes. Boston, too. They bet on margins, of course. Hell, you can read gambling odds in the papers. Little service the sports departments provide for their readers, right alongside the columns that crucify any athlete who wagers a couple of bucks on a game. Who will win and by how many runs. But there isn't much they don't bet on. Total runs, runs per innings, how many innings a pitcher will last, number of hits, almost anything that can be quantified, people will bet on. And where there's people to bet on something, there's bookies to pick up their bets.'

'Tempting for a player. Inside information, thinks he knows more than the oddsmakers.'

'Which, of course, he really doesn't,' said Vaughn. 'What there are, of course, are plenty of crooks around to try to arrange things to work out the way they bet on them.'

'Yes. And players weak or greedy enough to go along.'

'The thing is,' he said, 'they don't see the harm in it, as long as they can still play to win. They think they haven't done anybody any harm if they boot a grounder, or strike out with a couple of runners in scoring position, or groove a fastball to a good hitter, as long as they end up winning the game. And if they happen to win a little money because of it, so much the better. It happens in all sports, of course. A heavily favoured boxer will carry a weak opponent for seven rounds, when the odds said he'd put him down in six, for example. Split ends drop passes when their team's ahead. Basketball players—well, you remember B.C. a few years back. Athletes aren't always the brightest or most ethically well-grounded citizens. Their ethic is simple. Win. Win at all costs. You rarely find athletes in any sport betting against themselves, or against their team.'

'Bobo Halley did.'

He nodded. 'Yes. Bobo did. Most of them don't. The point is, they figure, as long as they bet on themselves they're living by the ethic. Win. Nothing else matters. They hear that in Little League. They hear it in the big leagues. It's easy to rationalize gambling. Hard to blame them, really.'

'Professional athletes should know the law,' I said.

'Yes. They should.'

'But there was no evidence that Bobo actually shaved points or threw games?' I made it a question.

'Well, no. No evidence. He bet a lot of money. Evidently he lost a lot. And that's another problem, of course.'

'Being in debt to bookies can be a problem.'

'Can make one vulnerable,' said Vaughn.

'What about Bobo's death? How was that connected?'

'It wasn't, as far as we know. He just died in a car crash. Thousands of people die in car crashes. Hell, thousands of people die in car crashes on the Southeast Expressway, seems like. He was on his way home to Lynn when it happened. Drove into the guardrail, car flipped, and Bobo's skull was fractured, along with all the rest of him.'

'Nothing suspicious about it?'

He shrugged. 'Guess Bobo'd had a couple of pops on his way home. Is that suspicious?'

'I suppose not. He lived in Lynn? I didn't remember that.'

'Sure. His home town. We signed him out of Lynn English. He was a helluva athlete over there.'

'So he was Red Sox property originally, too?'

'Oh, sure. I thought you were asking me about guys who started out with the Sox.'

'I guess I was. The other two I was going to ask you about, Arnie Bloom and Johnny Warrick. They were originally with Boston, too, I know.'

'Yup. We signed Bloom out of UConn.

166

Warrick went to a parochial school in Manchester, New Hampshire. But those two weren't involved in anything like you're looking for, as far as I know.'

'I don't know what I'm looking for,' I said quickly.

He grinned at me. 'Right. Anyhow, Warrick had a nice little career with the Sox, as I'm sure you remember, and Bloom was a good player for the Twins.'

'And Warrick owns a hog farm and Bloom sells life insurance.'

'Right. They're both good kids.'

'As far as you know.'

He nodded. 'As far as I know.'

I thought for a minute. 'Who signed them?'

'I did.'

'I mean, who scouted them? Who recommended them?'

'Oh, that was Stump Kelly. He had the region for about twenty years. You remember Stump.'

'Sure. He signed Eddie. I met him a few times.' I hesitated. 'Was there ever any talk of Eddie being involved—you know, like Bobo Halley?'

Vaughn shook his head slowly. 'No,' he said. 'None. Eddie wasn't that kind of a kid.'

'Was Bobo?'

Vaughn cocked his head and stared at me.

'Well, now, I guess he was, wasn't he?'

We finished eating. I watched Farley Vaughn chew methodically on his spinach leaves and sip his cranberry juice, while I finished my steak and swigged my Molson's.

'I don't know how you can eat that damn rabbit food,' I said to him.

'Makes for a healthy colon,' he answered. 'Roughage, you know. Keeps your stools nice and soft.'

'Oh, sure.'

'You ever think about cholesterol?' he said.

'Never. I don't think about smallpox or runaway Budliners or guys who go to McDonald's with machine-guns, either.'

'I see your point,' said Vaughn.

He paid the bill with a credit card and we plummeted down through the middle of the Prudential Building on the express elevator. I left my stomach, crammed with steak and French fries and Molson's Ale, on the fifty-second floor.

CHAPTER TWELVE

Julie's typewriter was clattering when I got back to the office. When she saw me come in, she stopped, raised her arms into the air,

168

arched her back, and stretched grandly, pushing her breasts taut against her blouse.

'I wish you wouldn't do that,' I said.

'Huh?'

'Never mind. Any calls?'

'Nothing I couldn't handle. I left your messages on your desk. Only one seemed urgent.'

'What was that?'

'Doctor Adams called. He said the bluefish off the mouth of the Merrimack in Newburyport were biting like snakes. He said it was very important you get back to him.'

'Like snakes? Did Doc say, "Like snakes"?'

'Those were his exact words,' said Julie. 'You don't think I'd say that, do you?'

'My mother was right,' I said. 'I should have been a dentist like Doc Adams. Then I could go fishing whenever I wanted to. Nothing else?'

'Like I said. All the rest of the calls were just from your clients, all boring stuff concerning your law practice. Which I took care of for you. I figured you had to talk with Doctor Adams yourself. I wouldn't want to fool around with important things like bluefishing expeditions.'

I patted the top of her head in the condescending way I knew irritated the hell out of her. 'You're a good kid,' I said.

She stuck out her tongue at me and returned to her typing. I went into my office. I glanced at the pile of little slips she had left there. She had made several appointments for me. There were a couple of calls I had to return. They could wait. I buzzed Julie.

'I know,' she said into the phone. 'Cancel all appointments for tomorrow. You're going fishing with Doctor Adams.'

'Aha!' I said. 'You're wrong, for once. No. See if you can get Farley Vaughn on the phone for me.'

'You just had lunch with him.'

'Right.'

'Well, okay.'

A moment later she buzzed me. 'I have Mr Vaughn for you.'

'Farley. Sorry to bother you,' I said to him.

'No problem. You having trouble with your digestion? You really should get more roughage, you know.'

'Yes, you're probably right. Listen, Farley. How can I reach Stump Kelly?'

'Well, he's living in Chatham now. He's been retired for three or four years.'

'Do you have an address and phone number for him?'

'I can look it up. Hang on.'

I lit a Winston and waited, drumming my

fingertips on the top of my desk. A few moments later Vaughn came back on the phone and read me an address in Chatham. 'It's a condominium, I think,' he said. 'No phone number. Unlisted.'

I jotted down the address, thanked Farley Vaughn, and tried the information operator, who confirmed that she could not divulge the number of Arnold C. Kelly—with one 'e'—of Chatham, Massachusetts.

I went back out to where Julie was working and stood beside her until she stopped typing, sighed, and looked up at me with a 'now what is it?' expression on her face.

'I'm, ah, headed for the Cape now.'

She cocked her head. 'How nice. And what shall I tell Mrs Bartlett, with whom you have a three-thirty?'

'Tell her I had to go fishing.'

'Oh, sure.'

*   *   *

Fishing, of course, is exactly what I was doing. I didn't know what I expected to learn from Stump Kelly that I didn't already know, and I was tempted to agree with Marty Stern that the list of names was nothing more than a smokescreen, and that Annie was trying to put me off the track rather than on to it. But if

Kelly knew those five men as well as he had known Eddie Donagan, there was a good chance he might be able to help me see what I was supposed to see in that list of names—if, indeed, I was supposed to see anything at all.

Chatham is located on the point of the elbow of Cape Cod, a lovely old village still relatively free of the Burger Kings and Pizza Huts and roadside tee-shirt and sneaker outlets that keep popping up along Route 28 all the way from Hyannis to Harwich as regularly and as uncontrollably as teenage zits.

I had some Vivaldi and Dvořák for the tape deck in my BMW, and I felt deliciously irresponsible in abandoning the office so impetuously in the middle of my working hours. But what the hell. I had stubbornly stuck to my lone-wolf law practice precisely so that I could do madcap, devil-may-care things like driving to the Cape for an afternoon with virtually no hope of accomplishing a damn thing, and leaving Mrs Bartlett in the lurch.

On the other hand, if my timing was right I might be able to swing by Mildred's on my way back and have a big bowl of the best clam chowder in the world. That, certainly, would be justification no one could quarrel with.

I left the city a little after two o'clock, crossed the Sagamore Bridge an hour later, and, to appease that vague tug at my Puritan conscience for doing something so impulsive, chose Route 6 as the most direct route to Chatham, depriving myself of the infinitely more pleasant drive along 6A. Exit eleven took me straight into Chatham. I stopped at a Gulf station where an obese young man with greasy hands and 'Frank' stitched above the pocket of his dark blue shirt gave me directions to the Fox Hill Estates.

The entrance to the Fox Hill Estates was marked by a discreet wooden sign with carved gold lettering set into the ground in an island that divided the long driveway. Along either side of the pea-stone drive swept a broad expanse of Cape Cod meadow—bull briers and low-bush blueberries and knee-high grass already turning yellow. It looked like terrific country for quail. The driveway dipped down, and over the rise I glimpsed the grey line of ocean touching the hazy Cape Cod sky.

The condos were laid out on a low bluff in a shallow horseshoe that followed the waterline below. They were finished with natural cedar shake shingles weathered to silver, with dark green shutters and red brick chimneys poking up at regular intervals. The Fox Hill Estates nestled into the landscape comfortably, as native to Cape Cod as sand dunes and scrub pines. I estimated there were twenty-four townhouses, all connected to each other, distinguished one from the other only by the colours of the doors.

Number fourteen belonged to Stump Kelly. It had a moss green door. I parked in front of it and rapped on the brass knocker. The door opened abruptly, and I faced a woman with hair the same colour as the door knocker and eyes remarkably close to the colour of the door. She was, I guessed, in her mid-forties—about my age. Once she had been a beauty, and now, perhaps, some might think she still was. She wore scarlet shorts and a white tee-shirt. Her upper arms and thighs were just beginning to pouch and pucker, but the skin on her face was marshmallow smooth and her green eyes were clear and sharp.

'Yes?' she said, her smile more than a formality but short of a flirtation.

'Mrs Kelly?'

'Yes.'

'Is your husband home?'

'Arnold is at the club. Arnold is always at the club in the afternoon.' She looked me up and down, conducting, it seemed to me, an assessment. 'Can I help you? Do I know you?'

'My name is Brady Coyne. I knew your husband when he was in baseball.' I gave her my disarming, lopsided, good-old-boy grin. 'I was in the neighbourhood and thought I'd look him up.'

Mrs Kelly lifted into view a square-cut old-fashioned glass, which she had been holding discreetly at her side. She rattled it in front of my face, indicating it had been drained except for a few ice cubes. 'It's martini time,' she said. 'Why don't you come in and join me? He'll be home in an hour or so.' She stepped back from the door expectantly.

'Oh, thanks, but I haven't got much time. If you could just tell me how to find the club...?'

She shrugged, sucked a shrunken ice cube into her mouth, and crunched it loudly. 'Back to the road, go right, take your third left and you'll see the sign. The Wedgewood Country Club. You can't miss it, with all those old ladies in pink shorts buzzing about in those silly little buggies hacking away at those garish orange balls. I'd look for him in the locker room. He likes to sit around in his underwear with all those sweaty men telling dirty stories and drinking beer and pretending he's still in the big leagues.' She cocked her head at me. 'Were you a ballplayer?'

I nodded vigorously. 'Oh, sure. I played.'

She smiled. 'I thought so. I can always tell.'

I thanked her for the directions and backed away from the door. When I had climbed into my car I looked back. She stood there, holding her glass aloft, wiggling her fingers at me and smiling with what I assumed was supposed to be seductive intent.

The Wedgewood Country Club, like the Fox Hill Estates, was clearly not designed to service the leisure pursuits of the vulgar mob. I wedged my BMW between a current model Fleetwood and a classic old Corvette, got directions to the men's locker room from a veiny old guy in Bermuda shorts, and found Stump Kelly sitting with three other men at a table near the bar in the dark panelled room adjacent to the showers. The room was empty except for those four and the young man perched behind the bar watching television.

They were playing bridge. I pulled a chair close and sat near Kelly's left elbow. He glanced at me, muttered, 'Hiya, fella,' frowned, and returned his attention to the cards he held in front of him. He clenched a straight-stemmed unlit pipe in his teeth. A can of Budweiser sat beside him. He looked exactly as I remembered him—leathery seamed face, sharp little blue eyes, and a smooth hairless dome.

'*Three* spades, then, if you insist,' he said to the man across from him. 'I ain't gonna argue with you.'

The guy on Kelly's left mumbled, 'Pass,' and Kelly's partner said, 'Okay, then, four goddam spades. Your lead,' he added to the man at his left.

'I haven't passed yet,' protested the fourth in a deep Harvard-cultured tone. 'The rules stipulate—'

'You *gonna* pass?' interrupted Kelly.

'Of course.'

'Me, too,' said Kelly.

'Me three,' said his left-hand opponent.

'The rules *stipulate*,' mocked Kelly, 'that you gotta make the goddam opening lead, then, Norman, and you better make a goddam good one 'cause this is for a seven-hundred rubber.'

'Don't bully me, Arnold,' muttered Norman. He slid a card on to the table and Kelly laid his hand down in front of him.

'Nice,' said his partner.

'Betcher goddam ass,' said Kelly. He pushed himself back from the table and turned to peer at me. 'Help ya, there, friend?'

'I'm Brady Coyne. We—'

'Hold it. Wait a minute.' Kelly held up his hand and squeezed his eyes shut. 'Yeah. I got it. Donagan, right? You were Donagan's agent. Friend of Sam Farina's. Am I right?'

I grinned. 'Right on the button.' I held out my hand and Kelly grasped it firmly.

'So. You playing golf, or what? Never saw you here before. Not a member, are you?'

'Actually I came to see you. Your wife told

177

me I might find you here.'

'Was she sober?'

I shrugged. 'Seemed to be.'

'Well, then, I'll wait awhile before I go home. Hey, how 'bout a beer?'

'Sounds good,' I said. 'I don't want to take you away from your game.'

'The game's over. Provided my partner doesn't screw up this hand completely. We all gotta get back to our old ladies, soon's they've had a few martinis and get human. So we'll pound a coupla brews, huh?'

Kelly went to the bar and persuaded the kid behind it to abandon the rerun of 'Get Smart' long enough to fetch us two cans of Bud. We took them to a table and Kelly fussed with his pipe, finally got it lit, and thrust his face at me through a cloud of perfumed smoke.

'You wanted to see me, huh? Something to do with Donagan? I heard about his kid. Damn tragedy. That what you wanna talk about?'

I took my time lighting a Winston before I answered him. 'Not exactly,' I said carefully. 'I wanted to ask you about some other men you scouted.' I spoke the names of the five ballplayers from Annie's list, then looked at Stump Kelly. 'What can you tell me about them?'

'Christ, what a question! I can tell you

everything about them. I practically wiped their asses for them when I was birddogging them. You wanna know what brand of tobacco they chewed?'

'I want to know what they might have had in common with each other. And with Eddie Donagan.'

He puffed his pipe and stared at the ceiling. 'Bello. Warrick. Halley. Bloom. Geralchik.' He sounded as if he were reading off a lineup. 'Sure. I scouted them. Sox signed them. And they made it.' He turned his gaze to me. 'And that's it. Except for Donagan, they were the only ones who did. Not a goddam superstar in the bunch of 'em, though God knows when they were kids there wasn't a one of 'em who didn't have the tools. Not Stump Kelly's fault they didn't turn out better. Lookit Donagan, for Christ's sake. How the hell was I supposed to know he was gonna be a head case?'

'They didn't blame you, did they?'

He waved his hand. 'Naw. But after a while, you know how it is, the fat guys behind the desks begin to wonder about old Stump. You know, maybe Kelly ain't all that sharp, maybe Kelly ain't got the instinct for a prospect's mental makeup. Can't judge their sense of the game, their attitude, how they react to pressure. Only one with the attitude was Geralchik, poor old Gus, he died, you know, and he maybe didn't have the talent. But the rest of 'em?' Kelly took a long draught from his Budweiser.

'What about Bobo Halley?'

On the other side of the room the three bridge players burst into loud conversation. Kelly's partner called over to him, 'We made it. With an overtrick.'

Kelly raised his beercan towards him. 'Good. They didn't lead trumps, huh?'

The one they called Norman said, 'It wouldn't have mattered. If he'd played it properly you'd have had a slam. Which proficient bridge players would have bid.'

'There was no God damn slam in there,' said Kelly's partner. 'We did damn good to make five.'

The three men came over to our table. Kelly said, 'This here is Brady Coyne. This is Norman, and Pete and Francis. Brady's an attorney. Old friend of mine.'

I shook hands with each of them.

'D'you finesse that diamond, or what?' said Kelly to his partner, the one he'd introduced as Pete.

'Didn't need to. Francis led one for us. That was the overtrick.'

'Good, good,' chuckled Kelly. He swivelled around and called to the bartender. 'Give these boys a drink. Put it on my tab.'

The three men went to the bar. Kelly turned back to me. 'Where were we?'

'I was asking about Bobo Halley.'

He cocked his head and narrowed his eyes. Then he said, 'Bobo was a pretty good ballplayer.'

'I meant, anything about him, you know, different?'

He shrugged. 'A decent ballplayer, that's all. I guess that makes him different from the others.'

Whether Stump Kelly knew about the pitcher's gambling problems and felt he ought not to divulge it to me, or whether he had been kept in the dark about it, I couldn't tell. I tried a different track. 'He was killed in an automobile accident, I heard.'

'Yup. Damn shame, too. Listen. Why're you asking me about these guys, anyway? What are they to you? This have something to do with Donagan's kid, or what? Or are you still agenting for ballplayers?'

'No, I'm not agenting any more,' I said. I leaned across the table and lowered my voice. 'But it is legal business, if you know what I mean. I can't, you know, really talk about it. But any help you can give me . . .'

He nodded solemnly. 'Oh, sure, I see. Of course. Anything I can do to help.'

I sat back. 'Why don't you just talk about

these ballplayers, those five guys. Whatever comes into your head. How's that?'

He placed his pipe on the table. 'Sure. I can do that.'

He could do that, all right. He turned out to be quite a talker, and two hours and several Buds later he was only beginning to wind down. By that time my mind had begun wandering to the bowl of clam chowder that waited for me at Mildred's in Hyannis, nearly an hour's drive from where I sat at the Wedgewood Country Club in Chatham, and I had given up murmuring, 'Hmm,' and, 'Oh, yes,' into the occasional spaces Kelly left for me in his monologue. He told me nothing I hadn't already learned from my reading or from Farley Vaughn. The only way I was going to rescue this silly trip to the Cape from the ranks of an utter wild goose chase was with that bowl of chowder.

By the time Stump Kelly lapsed into an abstracted and prolonged silence, his bridge partners had left the locker room, the bartender had switched the TV to the evening news and turned up the volume, and we had lined up ten empty red and white Budweiser cans on the table between us. I seized the opportunity to thank him and followed him to a row of urinals, where we stood side by side for a long time, staring at the tile wall directly before us.

I took my leave of Stump Kelly in the parking lot, where he climbed into a white Chevy sedan that seemed scaled much too large for him. I pointed my BMW towards Hyannis, not the least depressed by the realization that I had thoroughly wasted my afternoon. Nothing that Mildred's chowder wouldn't take care of.

CHAPTER THIRTEEN

I beat Julie to the office the next morning—my way of assuaging the guilt I couldn't shake, despite some elegant rationalizations, at leaving Mrs Bartlett and the rest of my clients in the lurch the previous afternoon. I gave Mr Coffee a drink and switched him on, took the telephone off the answering machine, and strode purposefully to my desk, determined to put in a full, boring day of lawyering.

Julie had left one of her neat little stacks of new memos in the middle of my desk. 'Mrs Bartlett heartbroken. Rescheduled Thursday 2:00,' read the one on top. 'Mr Franklin insists on conference re Webb case. Call ASAP.' Doc Adams had called twice in the afternoon. 'Questioning your priorities,' Julie had noted editorially. 'Don't forget Billy's tuition payments,' read another.

And so it went. I shoved them aside and went back to the coffee maker, thanked it for its reliability (as opposed to my own, as Julie's messages had succeeded in pointing out), and poured myself a black mugful.

When the telephone rang I automatically answered, 'Hello,' before I remembered to add, 'Brady L. Coyne, Attorney at Law.'

'Mr Coyne, can we meet again?' I remembered her dark, tilted eyes, and her voice, even on the phone, accelerated the throb of pulse in my temples.

'Yes, of course,' I said quickly. 'There are several things—'

'Please. Not now. Listen. Three o'clock today in the Sanctuary of the Old South Church. You know where that is. The last pew in the back on the left. Don't be early. Don't be late.'

'Okay, sure. Three o'clock. I hope you plan to—'

But she had hung up, and I was left with the brief memory of her voice, a sudden gust of cool scented air in an otherwise humid summer morning.

This time, I vowed, I wouldn't let her off the hook. This time I would get some answers. I'd had plenty of cryptic clues, thank you. The names of five ballplayers meant nothing to me. It was time she told me what it was she wanted me to know about E.J. Donagan. It was time to get tough with her.

At a quarter of three that afternoon I told Julie I was going out for cigarettes and sauntered across Copley Square to the big hulking old stone church. I stopped at the corner to thumb through a *Field & Stream* at Maxie's outdoor stall until my digital watch read 2:58, mindful that my instructions had been to be neither early nor late. Then I entered the dark coolness of the old church. The Sanctuary was on the first floor on the right. I entered it through the narrow doorway and paused just inside to allow my senses to adjust to the dim light and the moist musky odour of dead old souls. The dark oaken pews, the scrolled wood carved into the high vaulted ceiling, and the muted tinted light that filtered through stained-glass Bible scenes, all suggested a severe God presiding with harsh justice, and I felt, as I always do in places of worship, alien, unable to speak the language.

Gloria, when we were married, had been a Catholic. I went to church with her sometimes, having no convictions in conflict. I liked the Latin obscurity of the old-fashioned Mass. I liked the Gregorian music. I liked Gloria's God, too, and the mystical predictability of the rituals, the bells, the incense, the colourful garb of the priests, the ordered sequences of standing, sitting, and genuflecting. All, strangely, soothed my soul even as my mind rejected the mystery of transubstantiation that lay at the root of it.

Somewhere along the line the priests turned around to face the worhippers, and they translated the ritual into vulgar English. They put long-haired guitar players up on the altar. Gloria proclaimed it all a vast improvement, and couldn't understand it when I stopped going with her. It was just one more of the issues between us.

But this place housed a stern Protestant God, a grouchy, judgmental, inflexible old curmudgeon who would tolerate no guitar music or other frivolous nonsense. I hoped, if He were home on that particular afternoon, He wouldn't think too unkindly about the mission that brought me there.

I slid into the last pew on the left, as Annie had instructed. She wasn't there. I was left alone with that awful God to tot up my considerable accumulation of sins while I waited. Someone had left a tattered paperback book on the seat. I picked it up and glanced at it. It was an anthology of Sherlock Holmes tales. Most appropriate for a lawyer playing at detective, I thought. I resolutely refrained from opening it, and instead held it on my lap where I should have been grasping the Book of Common Prayer.

It was five after three. I wondered how late she'd be, and if, when she arrived, we'd converse in hushed, reverent tones. I thought some more about Gloria, and the sense of sinfulness her eyes had conveyed but her mouth had never articulated when we had first discussed our divorce.

I wondered why Annie had chosen this place to meet.

I waited an hour. She never came, and when I slid out of the pew to leave I had to resist the impulse to genuflect—or at least nod—towards the altar. And it wasn't until I got back to the office that I realized I had carried the little Conan Doyle volume with me. I shrugged and tucked it into the pocket of my sports jacket to bring home. It might be fun to reread those tales sometime. It wasn't, I told myself, as if I had actually stolen the book.

I hoped the God who lived in the Old South Church agreed with me.

★   ★   ★

Sylvie and I grilled steaks on the hibachi on my balcony, and after we finished eating we sat out there, sipping the last of our bottle of Bolla Valpolicella and watching lightning dance across the harbour. We could see the storm roll towards us, and we remained outside to watch. I loved the power and fury of it. Sylvie clutched my hand and winced when the thunder rolled and crackled. When the rain came driving in at us, we carried our glasses inside and sat at the table by the big sliding doors to watch it some more.

Sylvie, who found thunderstorms less entrancing than I, picked up the copy of Sherlock Holmes stories I had left on the table and began thumbing through it.

I put on a tape. E. Power Biggs playing Bach's F Major Toccata on the big Flentrop organ in the Busch-Reisinger Museum. The big chords were supposed to accompany the storm outside. I thought it would amuse Sylvie. All she did was frown and settle into the Holmes book.

When the phone rang, I thought it would be Annie. We needed to reschedule.

But it was Gloria. 'The storm,' she said. 'I thought of you, how you loved thunderstorms.'

'I know. You were scared. Are the boys all right?'

'I was *not* scared. That's just your damn stereotyping. The boys are fine. Except Billy's a little worried that his tuition payment is late. But that's not why I called.'

'I bet.'

'It's not.'

'Have I ever failed to come through?'

'No. I told him.'

'He called me at the office today to remind me. Tell him not to worry.'

'That was me who called.'

'Oh. You called to remind me of Billy's tuition at the office, then.'

'No. That's just what I told Julie.'

'Aha. Perfectly clear.'

'Look, I—are you alone?'

'Of course I'm alone.' I wondered why I lied to her. 'What's the matter, Gloria?'

'Nothing,' she said. 'We can't all, and some of us don't. That's all there is to it.'

'Huh?'

'Gaiety. Song-and-dance. Here we go round the mulberry bush.'

'Oh, Jesus. Winnie-the-Pooh.'

'Remember how you used to read to the boys, Brady? When Joey was little, and Billy tried to pretend he was too old for Winnie the Pooh, but he'd sneak up close and sit by your feet when you were sprawled on Joey's bed? And you had that funny melancholy voice for

189

Eeyore that always made them laugh.'

'Bon-hommy,' I quoted. 'French word, meaning bon-hommy. I'm not complaining, but There It Is.'

Gloria laughed once, then was silent. I glanced over at Sylvie. She was slouched in the kitchen chair, her feet up on the seat so that her skirt had slid off her legs and was bunched around her waist. She had the Sherlock Holmes book propped on her bare knees. She was studiously ignoring my telephone conversation.

'What's the matter, Gloria?' I said again.

'I was wondering how Jan and Eddie are doing.'

'E.J. is still missing. It doesn't look good.'

'Oh, God.'

'And Eddie took off again. Jan is—bearing up, I guess.'

'But what are they doing?'

'The FBI is working on it. I'm—there's not much else to be done, I guess. Wait, hope.'

'Isn't there something you can do?'

'Me?'

'Well, somebody.'

'No,' I said. 'I don't think so.' And when I said it I realized it was probably the truth.

Gloria was silent for a moment. Then she said, 'Well, I was just thinking of you, and them, and I thought I'd call. The thunder and lightning and all.'

'Nice that you called.'

'We could have a drink sometime.'

'Sure. Sounds good. I'll call you.'

'Okay. Call me.'

I hung up the phone and went back to the table to sit with Sylvie. She looked up at me, her finger marking her place in the book.

'Are you all right?'

'I'm all right.'

'Look at this.' She pushed the book across the table to me, holding it open to the table of contents. Twelve of Conan Doyle's short stories were listed. One of the titles, 'Silver Blaze', had been underlined with a red pen. 'You said you found this book?' she said.

'In a church. Yes.'

'There are markings in the story, too. Look.'

I opened the book to the page indicated in the contents, then began to thumb through it. Towards the end of it I found what Sylvie had referred to. I read the lines that had been underlined with the same red pen, glanced up at Sylvie, then reread them.

Inspector Gregory says to Holmes:

'"Is there any other point to which you would wish to draw my attention?"

"To the curious incident of the dog in the night-time."

"The dog did nothing in the night-time."

"That was the curious incident," remarked Sherlock Holmes.'

'It is funny, no?' said Sylvie.

'It is funny, yes,' I said, realizing for the first time that Annie had not stood me up at the church after all.

*   *   *

The sky beyond the windows was still dark when I awoke with a start. I sat up and flicked on the light beside my bed. Sylvie, lying on her side facing away from me, sighed in her sleep and wiggled her bottom against me. I picked up the Sherlock Holmes book from the bedside table and read again the underlined part.

The significant thing that Holmes had perceived was this: The dog didn't bark. The thing that should have been present was absent, and that was Annie's message to me. She had given me a list of names. An incomplete list. One name was missing from it. The name that should have been present, that would have completed the list, was absent from it.

Sylvie stirred, rolled over and kissed my shoulder. 'Is something wrong?' she murmured.

'Yes,' I said. 'Something is wrong.'

'I can make it better,' she said, nestling her body against me.

'There's nothing you can do.'

She sat up and frowned at me through sleep-swollen eyes. 'What is it?'

'It's Eddie Donagan,' I said, hugging her against me. 'I'm afraid something has happened to him.'

CHAPTER FOURTEEN

Sam Farina was practising his stroke on the lambchop-shaped putting green beside his house. He glanced up when he heard me coming, mumbled something about stiff wrists, and bent over like a question mark to address the ball. In his baggy plaid Bermuda shorts he looked like an overweight flamingo. I sat on a lawn chair beside the green to watch him.

He had six balls lined up, and he stroked them methodically towards one of the holes about ten feet away. Two of them went in. He grunted. 'I think I need to move it back towards my rear foot more,' he said. 'Maybe close up my stance a little. I keep jerking them to the left. It's driving me nuts.'

'Try keeping your elbows closer to your body,' I said. 'Your arms should act more like a pendulum.'

'I know about the pendulum, for Christ's sake. You can do better, huh?'

'Better than two out of six from ten feet. Damn right.'

He smiled. 'You probably can. I got the yips these days.' He put down his putter and came over to sit beisde me. 'And it's not just my putting.' He held his hands out in front of him and made them tremble.

I nodded. 'E.J., huh?'

'Yes. And Jan. And Josie.'

'That's why I came over. To bring you up to date.'

Sam reached down into the cooler beside his chair and handed me a can of Tuborg. He cracked one for himself and took a sip. 'Good. Shoot.'

I told Sam about Annie and the list of names she had given to me. I told him about my visit with Stump Kelly. I told him about finding the paperback volume of Sherlock Holmes stories in the church. 'It all points to Eddie,' I concluded.

Sam shook his head. 'I don't know. One of those guys used to come over once in a while. That Halley, the pitcher. He and Eddie were asshole buddies for a while, right after Eddie

194

quit baseball. Seemed like a nice enough fella.' He took a long swig from his beer can, then set it down gently on the table. 'I don't know, Brady,' he repeated. 'It all sounds pretty far-fetched to me. What makes you think she was the one who left the book in the church, anyway?'

I shrugged. 'Look. Even if she didn't, even if the book has nothing to do with this, it still makes sense that Eddie is the answer. What else could that list of names mean?'

'It probably doesn't mean anything.'

'Yeah, that's what Stern says.' I lit a cigarette. 'Sam, do you have any idea where Eddie might be?'

His smile was sad, and I noticed for the first time that he had grown puffy blue bags under his eyes since the last time I had seen him. 'Eddie's gone,' he said. 'We haven't seen him. The last time was the night you delivered the ransom money. Since then, not a word. He just can't face up to grown-up responsibilities. You know that. Okay. Good riddance. Fuck Eddie Donagan.'

'Every other time he took off he at least called. This time nothing. I think he's in trouble, Sam. I think that's Annie's message.'

Sam gazed down along the side of his big nose. 'Maybe she's saying that Eddie did it. Maybe Eddie took E.J. That makes about as much sense.'

'I thought of that,' I said, nodding. 'Either way, we've got to find him.'

Sam reached into the cooler and pulled out two more cans of beer. 'Eddie Donagan,' he said slowly, 'is a baby. He didn't have the balls to make it in the major leagues, and he didn't have the balls to stick around and take care of his wife and son. That doesn't make him a criminal, though. You know that.'

'I agree. It doesn't make sense. Which leaves us with the conclusion that he's in danger.'

'Well, I don't know how I can help. He's got no family—except us. Nobody in the world he cares about. Far as I know, nobody who cares about him, either, except maybe E.J. and Jan, I guess. Josie's bitter as hell at him. Figures he should of stuck around for Jan's sake instead of running away again.'

'You're sure Jan hasn't heard anything?'

'Absolutely.'

'How is she doing?'

Sam lifted his bulky shoulders and let them sag. 'How does a mother do whose little boy has been kidnapped and been gone for three weeks after the ransom has been paid off? She went on TV, like you told her, and now she's got involved in some goddam group of broads who don't shave their armpits, want to get laws passed so the government will help find runaway children. Which is okay, I guess, but it ain't the point. E.J. didn't run away. That FBI guy, what's his name, Stern, has called her a couple of times, and each time Jan ends up crying. And there's some crackpot who keeps calling, asking for Eddie. Keeps pushing. Where's Eddie? You heard from Eddie? How can he get ahold of Eddie? He's got something for Eddie, he says, something important, he can only give it to Eddie. Like that. I told Jan going on TV was a bad idea, Brady.'

I shrugged. 'Maybe you're right.'

'She goes into E.J.'s room every morning, as if she expected him to be there. Which, of course, he isn't. Once a week, if you can believe it, she changes the sheets on his bed. How's my little girl doing, you want to know? She's driving herself nuts is how she's doing.'

Sam took a long swig of beer and stared off into the distance. 'And Josie and me, we aren't doing a hell of a lot better, to tell you the truth. Brady, you can't imagine what it's like. It's as if there was this cancer eating away at your belly, this constant burning ache down there to keep reminding you that there's something terribly wrong, some horrible thing is going on. You forget about it sometimes, like when I was putting. But it's always there.

You wake up in the nighttime, and your mind doesn't register it for a minute, and then you become aware of that pain in your gut and it reminds you that the boy is gone.'

He leaned over the table towards me. 'Listen, Brady. I wanna tell you something, God forbid Jan or Josie should hear me say this, but this is what I believe. We'd be better off knowing that little E.J. was dead. I mean, you could deal with that. You could bury him, put flowers on his grave. You could cry and pray for his poor little soul and get on with things. Understand? This way, you feel he's probably dead. You imagine the worst things. And gnawing at you is the thought—the possibility—that he's alive. And that keeps the knife down there going, slicing and poking holes in your stomach.'

'Sam, I—'

'No. Wait. I'm not saying it'd be better if E.J. was dead than alive. But you know and I know in our hearts that he's dead. But we don't *know*, understand? You gotta see a body, go to a funeral, have the priest say his thing, to really *know* it. That's what I mean. *You* don't think he's alive, do you?'

I shook my head. 'I guess I don't, Sam. But there is hope, still.'

'Ahh!' he exploded, bringing the palm of his hand down on the table. 'That's just

bullshit, Coyne. And you know it.' But Sam's
tone lacked conviction, and I realized that he
still hoped, and that the pain in his belly fed
on his hope, and that the day Sam woke up
without that ache in his gut would be a sad day
for him.

I put my hand on Sam Farina's thick wrist,
and he covered it with his own hand and
turned his face away from me. I gave his wrist
a quick squeeze and pulled my hand back. I
stood up. 'I'm going to try to find Eddie,' I
told him. 'I want you and Josie and Jan to
know that I'm doing what I can, and maybe it
doesn't make much sense, but it's something,
at least. And I know that Stern hasn't given
up, either. I think Annie is telling me that
finding Eddie will help us to find E.J. I don't
know how or why, but that's what I'm going
to do.'

Sam looked at me. 'Do me a favour, will
you?'

'Sure. What is it?'

'If you find that cocksucker Donagan, slug
him in the stomach for me. Make him feel the
pain that we're feeling. Will you do that for
me?'

'Sam,' I said, 'I have the feeling that
Eddie's got the same pain you do already.'

He nodded slowly. 'I don't know whether
he does or not, but I hope the hell you're

right. I'd think better of him if he did.'

★   ★   ★

The telephone beside my bed jarred me from my sleep. I fumbled for it, cleared my throat, and said, 'Yes?'

'This is Nathan downstairs,' came the voice of the night man.

'Christ, Nathan. What time is it?'

'It's nearly three o'clock, sir.'

'What do you want?'

'There are two men who want to see you.'

'At three o'clock in the morning?'

'They're policemen.'

'Oh. What do they want?'

'They didn't say.'

'Well, send them up, then.'

'I already did, sir. They're on their way.'

I switched on the light, found a Winston and lit it, and pulled on my jeans. Then I rescued my sneakers, one from the bathroom next to the toilet and one from under the kitchen table, and slipped them on without socks. The knock on the door was soft and polite.

The two men at the door wore State Police uniforms. 'I'm Garrity and this is Laski,' said the younger of the two. 'We'd like you to come with us, Mr Coyne.'

200

'Is it one of my boys? Jesus! Did something happen to Billy or Joey?' I felt a flush of panic rise in my cheeks.

Laski glanced at Garrity. 'No, sir. It's nothing like that. Lieutenant Travers asked us to come for you. He'll explain.'

I exhaled hard, as if I were blowing out a match. Travers was the State Police inspector who had been at Sam Farina's house with Stern when we were discussing the delivery of E.J.'s ransom money.

'Does this have something to do with E.J. Donagan, then?' I asked the two cops.

'We're not at liberty to say, sir,' said Garrity. 'The Lieutenant will explain. Are you ready to go?'

I pulled on a shirt and tucked a pack of Winstons into the pocket. 'Okay.'

In the elevator Laski and Garrity stood at attention, staring at the numbers as they blinked backwards from six to one. We got out and marched through the lobby. Nathan, sitting at his table by the front door, raised his hand to me, and I smiled and nodded to reassure him that I didn't think I was under arrest.

The cruiser was parked directly in front of the door. The two policemen got in front and I climbed into the back seat. Laski took the wheel. He pulled sedately out of the short

201

driveway and on to Atlantic Avenue. Then he turned on the siren, tromped on the accelerator, and the car shot forward through the dark, abandoned city street. We cut up State Street, through the banking district, then over past Government Center on to Cambridge Street. We circled the rotary near Mass. General and suddenly took a sharp right where there was no road and sped across the narrow grassy strip that separated the Charles River Basin from the highway. As we careened through the dark I could see ahead of us the pulsing flash of blue and red lights, and reflected in their strobelike glare was the Hatch Shell, where the Boston Pops puts on its annual Fourth of July extravaganza.

We skidded to a stop, and Garrity and Laski got out. 'Come on, Mr Coyne,' said Garrity. 'This way.'

I followed the two policemen towards the group of erratically parked vehicles. A tough-looking, white-haired guy wearing a short sleeved white shirt with a striped tie pulled loose at the throat detached himself from the crowd of mostly uniformed men and approached me. Garrity and Laski melted away.

He held out his hand. 'Travers,' he said.

I gripped his hand. 'I remember,' I said. 'We've met. What's this all about?'

'Stern said you should come. He's over here.'

Travers turned and walked back towards the cluster of people. I followed him. He tapped a short man on the shoulder. When he turned I saw that it was Marty Stern. Stern looked at me through his thick horn-rimmed glasses. He didn't bother to offer his hand.

'Come over here, Coyne,' he said.

We pushed through the crowd. They had gathered around a woman slumped on a bench. She wore dark blue slacks and a red shirt. She had long, straight dark hair. Stern gestured towards her, then bent over and lifted her head gently with both of his hands so I could see her face. What I saw, though, wasn't her face, but the bright red semicircle under her chin, and the big splash of blood down the front of her. Her dark tilted dead eyes stared past me.

I looked away and gulped back the bile that rose in my throat.

'Look at her,' said Stern. 'Is this the one?'

I nodded without turning my head.

'Are you sure?'

'For Christ's sake, I'm sure.' I forced myself to look at her again. The slash across her throat cut deep, through the tendons and tubes that connected her head to her body. They stood out white against the red of the rest of the wound. Annie's shirt, I noticed, had once been white, but the entire front of it was soaked in crimson blood, still gleaming moist in the lights from the flashlights and automobiles.

Stern lowered her head back on to her chest, wiped his hand on his pants, and took my arm. He steered me to another bench nearby, and we sat beside each other. I turned my body sideways so I wouldn't see all the professionals working at Annie's body.

I tried to light a cigarette. My hands shook. I steadied one with the other so that I could direct the flame of my Zippo on to the tip of my Winston. I dragged deeply on it. 'That's her,' I said. 'That's Annie. She was right.'

'What do you mean?'

'Talking to me. Helping. She said it was dangerous. She shouldn't have done it.'

Stern shrugged. 'I wouldn't blame yourself. She knew what she was doing. You didn't force her.'

I looked sharply at him. 'Don't bullshit me. It's my fault she's dead.'

Stern smiled at though he'd heard it all before. 'That's ridiculous,' he said mildly.

My mind whirled with half-formed thoughts. 'It means she *was* helping us, though, doesn't it? What she was trying to give us, it was important, then. Otherwise, they . . .'

'Maybe,' said Stern. 'Maybe not. It could mean they knew she was in touch with you, anyway.' Stern touched my arm so that I would look up at him. 'The interesting thing is that they did it here, where they knew she'd be found, and they did it this way, so that we'd know exactly why they did it. To shut her up. They could have dumped her body into the bay, or in a dumpster, or into a concrete form on Route 95 if they'd wanted to. But they wanted us to see this. Yes. I agree. There is a message here, Coyne. Do you get the message?'

I nodded. 'I get the message.'

'Time to leave it to the pros.'

'That's the message. Yes.'

What Stern didn't need to say, because he figured I understood it perfectly already, was this: If somebody was willing to cut Annie's throat and leave her to bleed to death on a bench by the Hatch Shell because she had given information to a nosy lawyer, what was to prevent them from seeing that the nosy lawyer met the same fate?

That was the message.

'The other thing,' began Stern.

'I know the other thing,' I said quickly. 'The other thing is that it doesn't look very good for E.J. Donagan. Right?'

Stern shrugged, then nodded. 'That's what I was thinking. Yes.'

'Or Eddie Donagan, either.'

'What do you mean?'

I told Stern what I had inferred from the list of names Annie had given me, that it pointed straight to Eddie, and about the Sherlock Holmes book I assumed she had left for me.

'Could be,' mused Stern. 'I don't see how he's connected, though. Donagan didn't kidnap the kid, we know that. Maybe he knew something, or figured something out. He hasn't been heard from, huh?'

'No. I talked to Sam Farina just today. Yesterday, that is. No one there has heard from him.' I flicked my cigarette away. 'Maybe Eddie's floating in the bay or taking up space in a bridge abutment somewhere.'

'One good thing, anyway,' said Stern.

'Yeah?'

'We'll be able to figure out who the hell she is. That could lead us somewhere.'

'Do you think they'd leave her body like this for us if we could trace them through her?'

'It's possible. We'll see. In the meantime, I think you better go back to drawing up wills and separation agreements.'

'That's probably good advice.'

I glanced over to where Annie's body

slumped on the bench. A police photographer was snapping pictures. The blinks of light from his flash were being soaked up by the brightening sky overhead. Bursts of static came from the radios in the official vehicles, which crouched there with their motors running and their doors open like animals of prey. Now and then came the unruffled voice of a female dispatcher, droning numbers and code words. The policemen and medics stood around, talking in low muffled tones, waiting for their turn to perform their given function.

I knew Stern's advice was sound. I had to admit that he was right. There was a message there for me, and it would be stupid to ignore it.

PART FOUR

E.J.

CHAPTER FIFTEEN

The sky along the horizon was turning from black to purple when officers Garrity and Laski dropped me off at my apartment. I prised my sneakers off with my toes and kicked them against the wall, loaded up my electric coffee pot, and shucked off my clothes. The shower felt good, and I let it run as cold as I could bear it. It failed, however, to wash away the image of that gaping half-moon wound on Annie's ivory throat. The tighter I squeezed my eyes shut, the redder I remembered her blood. She couldn't have been dead long. The blood that had splashed over her breasts and puddled in her lap had only just begun to cake and turn brown.

I dried myself, shaved, and slipped on some clean clothes. The coffee was ready, so I poured myself a big mug. Suddenly I was hungry. In the face of that awful death, I was starving, and I felt ashamed to be so aware of my own life processes.

In the back of the refrigerator I found four white cardboard cartons with little wire handles—salvage from a jaunt Sylvie and I had taken a week earlier to the Yangtze River Restaurant in Lexington. I took them out, lined them up on the counter beside the stove, and opened them one at a time. Beef and pea pods in thick brown gravy. Sub Gum pork fried rice. Sweet and sour shrimp with chunks of pineapple and blood-red cherries. Moo Goo Gai Pan—little bits of chicken with mushrooms, bamboo shoots, water chestnuts, and other good stuff.

I dumped the contents of the four cartons into a big skillet, stirred them all together, sloshed on some soy sauce, put it on low heat, and covered it. A real country breakfast. Then I took my coffee out on to the balcony to see if the sun would come up.

It did, right on schedule, spilling crimson over the rippled surface of the ocean and staining the high clouds with a colour not unlike what I had seen a few hours earlier on Annie's white blouse.

New England mariners knew what it meant: 'Red sky in the morning, sailors take warning.'

I fiddled with a couplet of my own as I sipped my coffee. Bloody blouse at night/ Should give dumb attorney fright.

It didn't scan, but the message was there, and I knew it. Marty Stern had been telling me all along I was in over my head, but some mix of guilt and adolescent adventurousness had prevented me from leaving the cops and robbers stuff to the cops and robbers.

The lower rim of the sun cleared the horizon. Its motion was visible proof that our planet continued to rotate, as did all the other planets in the solar system, and all the other clusters of celestial bodies in the ever-expanding universe. What had begun as a big bang a few billion years ago wouldn't be affected much by the behaviour of a few clusters of protoplasm on one of those whirling chunks of matter.

What egoism, to think that anything we did in the eyewink of our lives meant a damn thing in the grand cosmic scheme of things— or to postulate a God who watched over it and gave a damn.

I went back into my kitchen and lifted the lid on the skillet to sniff the steam that burst out. It looked awful—a brownish, glutinous mush—and smelled terrific, which reminded me of a really raunchy joke Charlie McDevitt had told me once. I dumped it on to a plate, poured myself a second mug of coffee, and sat at the table to eat my breakfast. The most important meal of the day.

I was chasing the last bits of fried rice around the edges of my plate when the phone rang. I glanced at my watch. It wasn't even six yet.

'Yeah?' I answered.

'Stern. Thought you might want to know. We've ID'd the girl.'

'You guys work fast.'

'This is the sort of thing we're good at. One of the marvels of the computer age. Send a set of fingerprints down to Washington electronically, the big machine clanks and whirrs, and up on the screen pops the information.'

'Your machine didn't say who killed her, did it?'

'Nope. Not yet. It might. We've just got to ask it the right questions.'

'So who was she?'

'Name of Mary Ann Mikuni. Japanese name.'

'I might have guessed.'

'Yes, I suppose you might have,' he said, implying that it was equally likely I might not have. 'Anyway, she was arrested once in Providence back in seventy-eight.'

'Don't tell me,' I said. 'Let me guess. Prostitution. Soliciting. What do they call it?'

Stern laughed. 'Nothing like that. God, you do have a conventional mind, Coyne. Or is that just a chauvinistic mind? You think any time a beautiful young woman is involved in a crime it has to be for selling her body?'

'I take enough of that shit from my secretary,' I said. 'What did she do?'

'Legally, she did nothing. She was never brought to trial. But she was involved in an extortion scam. A Providence contractor gave kickbacks to some guy in the Mayor's office for a big school building contract, then turned around and blackmailed the guy. They made some arrests—including Mikuni—but the guy in the Mayor's office shot himself, depriving the state of its best witness. So they never prosecuted.'

'What else do you know about her?'

'That she grew up in San Diego, graduated from Brown in seventy-two *cum laude* with a major in chemistry. Went to work for a concrete manufacturer—how do you like that, you want bridge abutments?—a concrete manufacturer in Providence. Started out in the lab, but got promoted to an executive position after a little more than a year. Some kind of sales manager. That's what she was doing when she was arrested. After that, we don't have anything.'

'How does that help us?'

Stern chuckled. 'Oh, we should be able to extrapolate where she went, who she knew, what she did. Like that.'

'And how she got involved in E.J. Donagan's kidnapping?'

'Eventually. Maybe. It'll take awhile.'

'I have the feeling we don't have a hell of a long time.'

'Not "we", Coyne. Not you. Me, the Bureau, the cops. Not you.'

'Sure. I hear you.'

'I hope so.'

'So she would've been in Providence in 1971, then, right?'

'Brown University is in Providence,' he said. 'Right.'

'Eddie Donagan was at Pawtucket then.'

'So?'

'How far is Pawtucket from Providence?'

'In Rhode Island how far is any place from any place else?' said Stern. 'You know what the best thing was that ever came out of Rhode Island?'

'What?'

'Route 95.' I didn't say anything. Stern said, 'That was a joke.'

'I thought it was supposed to be,' I said. 'Guess I'm not in a real receptive mood for jokes this morning.'

'Listen, damn it. Forget it, will you? Case closed, okay? Go to your office. Read the Constitution. Write a will. You want real excitement, chase an ambulance. You're not in our league now.' I imagined Marty Stern jabbing at the telephone with his glasses.

'Are you guys going to look for Eddie Donagan?'

'We guys are going to try to find out who kidnapped the boy, if that's what you mean. And the State Police and the Boston cops are going to try to figure out who carved up Mary Ann Mikuni. And if the two things appear to be related—'

'*Appear* to be! Jesus, Stern. It's obvious—'

'It's *not* obvious. It's possible. It's supposition. Maybe even likely. Look. We'll see where the evidence leads us.'

'Are you saying that you won't be working with the police on this?'

I heard his sigh hiss over the phone. 'You should understand about jurisdictions, Coyne. It's not clear that there's overlap here. Not yet.'

'Wait a minute,' I said, struggling to keep my voice calm. 'I identified the girl as the one who contacted me to make arrangements to deliver the ransom money. And she's the one I met who gave me information about the kidnapping. And she's the one who got killed. What question can there be about overlap, as you call it?'

'You *think* it was her voice. You *think* those

names have something to do with the kidnapping.'

'Yeah. I do think so. I *know* so.'

'Listen,' he said, exasperation dripping from his voice. 'I'm calling you out of courtesy. I got you out of bed this morning and put you through an unpleasant experience because I thought the girl might be the one you had met. The description was right. That proves that I haven't discounted her connection with the kidnapping case. The fact is, Travers called me when they found her body because he and I have been communicating about this thing. Okay? So now I'm keeping you informed. I don't have to do this. But you're an attorney. You're supposed to be able to handle it intelligently. In return, I don't expect you to criticize our methods, or interfere, or do stupid things.'

'E.J. Donagan has been gone a long time.'

'I know, I know. We're doing our best.'

'Well...?'

'Be patient, will you? And stay the hell out of it.'

'I hear you,' I said, and hung up.

★   ★   ★

I found the street where Eddie lived in back of Tufts University in Medford. It was narrow,

215

made more so by the cars parked on both sides. I drove slowly. Kids riding noisy three-wheeled plastic vehicles zipped in and out from behind the cars and played ball in the street. The stark grey stumps of dead elms poked up next to the sidewalk at regular intervals. They had been cut off at about twenty feet so they wouldn't topple over and smash into any houses. They were marked with big orange spray-painted 'Xs'. Some day maybe the city would come by to finish the job.

The three-decker houses were all the same—square, close to the street, needing paint, and lined up close together. I squeezed my BMW into an empty place. A cluster of children came over to stare at my car. It looked out of place among the old Fords and Volkswagens. Then the kids stared at me, as if a man wearing a necktie was *ipso facto* cause for suspicion.

Not all the houses bore street numbers. On those that were numbered, the numerals had been painted over, so that I had to mount the front steps to read them. Eddie's apartment was at forty-six. I found fifty. Then I found forty-two. There was a house between them. I muttered, 'Eureka!' to myself. Sherlock Holmes would have been proud of me.

Beside the door were three bells. Over each

was taped a faded scrap of paper with a name on it. The top bell was labelled 'Donagan' in blue ball-point pen. I rang it, expecting no answer and getting none. The bottom bell was named 'Sandella'. When I pushed it I heard the shrill buzz echo from inside. On the third ring a short man with a hooked nose and blue suspenders over his tee shirt opened the door.

'Whadda you want?' he said.

'I'm looking for Mr Donagan.'

He shrugged his narrow shoulders. 'He lives upstairs.' He started to shut the door.

'Wait, Mr Sandella. Please.'

'Yeah?'

'Mr Sandella, I'm Eddie Donagan's lawyer. I need to see him. He might be in trouble.'

The old man's face broke into a broad, gap-toothed grin. 'It's no surprise. He no pay his rent, he in trouble, you bet.'

'When did you see him last?'

'Never see Eddie. He come and go, you know? Just when he pay his rent. He come downstairs, bring me wine and money. He a good kid, Eddie. But he no pay rent, two weeks. Two more weeks, Eddie out ona street.' Sandella looked me up and down. 'No lawyer stop me. I kick him out, he no pay.'

'You saw him two weeks ago?'

Sandella hesitated, then opened the screen door that separated us and stepped out on to

217

the stoop. He thrust his face close to mine. He smelled of tobacco and garlic. 'I see Eddie *six* weeks ago, mister. Last time I see Eddie, when he pay his rent. I have a month advance from when he take his lease. When it gone, Eddie out ona street.' He cocked his head at me. 'What all you people want Eddie for? He a good kid. He do something bad?'

'Somebody else was here?'

Sandella nodded solemnly. 'Sure. Cops was here. Coupla weeks ago. I tell them same thing. Eddie no here. They make me go upstairs, let them in. They look around, they leave, no Eddie.' The old man chuckled. 'Eddie disappear, huh?'

'Would you take me upstairs?'

Sandella hooded his eyes and gazed beyond me. I took my wallet from my hip pocket and extracted a twenty. I folded it twice and pressed it into his hand. He didn't look at it, but shoved it quickly into the pocket of his baggy pants. He turned and went back inside. A moment later he came back to the door.

'Come on. This way.'

I stepped into the narrow foyer. Sandella unlocked a door and led me up a dark stairway. At the top he unlocked another door and we entered Eddie Donagan's apartment. There were two rooms—a large kitchen, and a smaller room where a narrow bed, a bedside

218

table, and a bureau were the only furnishings. Two ajar doors revealed a small bathroom and a closet as well.

The place smelled like a dirt-floored cellar—damp, musty, unused. A film of dust covered every surface. Some dishes were stacked in the sink. There were two empty beer bottles on the table in the kitchen. I opened the door of the small yellowed refrigerator. It was practically empty—catsup, salad dressing, mustard, beer. There was a bowl half full of blue mould. I couldn't tell what it had originally been. I closed the door quickly against the odour of rot and decay it emitted.

Sandella was standing by the doorway watching me. I turned to him. 'Do you mind if I look around for a little while?'

He shrugged. 'Help yourself. He's not here. Close the doors when you go.'

Sandella left. I went back into the bedroom and sat on the bed. On the bedside table stood a lamp and an old clock radio. The alarm was set for nine-thirty. In the drawer I found a framed picture of Jan and E.J. when E.J. was about two. They were both smiling. E.J. had a bushy head of curly red hair and freckles sprinkled across the bridge of his nose. Jan's hair was longer then. She wore it loose, a set of dark parentheses around her heart-shaped

219

face. There was a bottle of Excedrin and a handful of coins in the drawer. That was all.

I rummaged through his bureau. All the drawers were packed with clothes, none too carefully folded. In one corner of the room was a big plastic trash bag. It, too, contained some clothes. In the closet I found a couple of suits and sports jackets, half a dozen dress shirts on hangers, and several pairs of shoes on the floor. In a cardboard box on the shelf were some sweaters. In the back was a scarred leather suitcase.

I wandered back into the kitchen and sat in one of the two chairs at the table. The room smelled of fried onions, rotten fruit, and burned cooking oil. The ceiling was grey and cracked. The wallpaper was stained and greasy. Some place for the guy who had once been the best pitching prospect in the American League to end up.

On the wall beside the refrigerator hung the telephone. I went to it and lifted the receiver. I got a dial tone. When I replaced the receiver I noticed that several phone numbers had been scribbled on the wallpaper beside it. Most of them had been written in pen. A couple were in pencil. It looked as if Eddie might have jotted them down while talking on the phone. Some had faded and smudged on the greasy wallpaper. A couple looked recent.

I recognized Sam Farina's. Two of the numbers were mine—one my office and one my home phone. There were half a dozen others. I jotted them down into my appointment book.

Off the kitchen was the bathroom—a cracked porcelain sink, a toilet, and an old-fashioned tub with feet like lion paws. On the sink a squeezed-out tube of Crest lay curled like an empty snakeskin. Beside it a ratty toothbrush was propped up in a plastic glass. The medicine chest held a razor, a dispenser of Gillette Platinum blades, a can of Rise, another bottle of Excedrin, a stick of Old Spice underarm deodorant, a bottle of English Leather, and a box of Band-Aids. I dumped the pills out into my hand. They were all Excedrin tablets. I put them back into the bottle, returned it to its place, and closed the door.

I took a can of Eddie's Schlitz from the refrigerator and sat again at the table. Eddie's apartment told me two things: no one had lived there for a long time, and Eddie hadn't packed before he left. He had neither paid Sandella in advance nor cancelled his lease. He had not disconnected his telephone.

He had just left.

I closed the doors behind me. Downstairs I rang Sandella's bell, and when he came to the door I thanked him. He shrugged and said, 'No lawyer gonna stop me, mister. Two more weeks, he's out. I got a cousin wants the place. I like Eddie, he no make trouble, but he's out ona street.'

'That's certainly your right, Mr Sandella,' I said. 'I agree with you. If Eddie doesn't come back and pay you, you give it to your cousin.' I took one of my business cards from my pocket and handed it to him. He glanced at it and hooded his eyes again. I found another twenty and held it up in front of his face. 'If you hear anything from Eddie, call me, will you? Just so there won't be any trouble for anybody.'

Sandella took the money and shoved it into his pocket. 'I'm supposed to call the cops, too.'

'That's okay. Call them, too. Just don't forget me.'

Sandella looked more closely at my card. Then he smiled at me. 'I call you, Mr Coyne. The cops, they don't give me nothing. I call you first.'

CHAPTER SIXTEEN

Julie was on the phone when I got to the office. It was nearly noon. She made a big exaggerated 'Oh, it's *you!*' face at me, which I ignored. I continued on into my office, slamming the door behind me. A moment later I heard her knock.

'Come in,' I growled.

She opened the door and stood there, frowning at me.

'Just don't say anything,' I said. 'I know exactly what time it is, I know I have a busy law practice, I know old Mrs Bartlett is thinking of finding a nice staid old firm that will pat her arm and say, "There, there," and at this point I don't give a fat shit. I've been up since three.'

'Have you had a pleasant morning, otherwise?' she said sweetly.

'No. I haven't. And no, I don't want to talk about it.'

'Fine with me. Call Mr Stern.' Julie shut the door behind her. I sighed and walked back out into the reception area, where she was hunched over her typewriter. I touched the back of her neck. She shook off my hand.

'Hey,' I said. 'I'm sorry.'

She turned to look up at me. 'You don't need to apologize to the hired help, Brady. It would just help if I knew you weren't going to be in, and if you wanted me to consult with your clients, or what. You're the boss. I'm not complaining.'

'Things came up. Bad things.'

'You don't have to tell me.'

'Why don't you take the afternoon.'

'I'd rather have tomorrow. Okay?'

'Sure. Fine. Tomorrow's Friday. We'll just close up the shop for the day. I could use a day off myself.'

She smirked at me, but refrained from commenting on the time I had been taking off lately. 'I'll have to change a couple of appointments,' was all she said.

'That's okay. Do it.'

'Brady, really. Your clients—'

'I know, I know. I'll take care of them. What did Stern want?'

'You think he'd tell me?'

I squeezed her shoulder. 'No. Not Stern. I'll go call him.'

Back at my desk I lit a Winston and took my appointment book from my jacket pocket. I stared at the six telephone numbers I had copied from the wall in Eddie Donagan's apartment. Then I picked up the phone and punched out a number.

'Mr McDevitt's line,' answered Charlie's secretary, a little dumpling of a lady who looks like her picture should be on the label of a can of apple pie filling.

'Shirley, you gorgeous creature,' I said. 'How can Charlie get any work at all done with you sitting there to distract him?'

She giggled. 'Talk like that will get you a sexual harassment suit, Mr Coyne. Hold on a minute, I'll get him for you.'

A minute later Charlie came on the line. 'Hey,' he said. 'You wanna go golfing?'

'Sure. Sometime. Right now I need a favour.'

'What's it worth?'

I paused, pretending to calculate. 'How about scallops at the Union Oyster House?'

'With good wine?'

'The house white.'

'Sold,' said Charlie. 'Listen. We really gotta get out.'

'Last time we played, I seem to recall, I lost my shirt,' I said.

He chuckled. 'Speaking of that, did I tell you about this guy I know, Carl, who lost his boat?'

'I'm really not in the mood, Charlie.'

'Carl's got this nice little eighteen-foot sloop,' he said, ignoring my protest. 'Moors it on the Annisquam River right in front of his house. Carl loves his boat. He's always down there polishing the brass, scraping and varnishing and swabbing it out. Anyhow, he goes down to the dock after supper a couple of nights ago and his boat's gone. Carl is very upset, as you can imagine.'

'Um,' I said.

'So he goes wandering around the neighbourhood, knocking on doors, asking everybody if they've seen his boat, and, of course, they haven't, but they're neighbourly types, so they invite Carl in for a quick snort. Which Carl doesn't turn down. A few hours later he has paid a visit to just about everyone on the river, and he's feeling no pain. Finally his wife looks out the front window, and there's Carl, with his arms around the flagpole on the front lawn. She goes out and says, "Carl, what in the hell are you doing?" And Carl looks at her and he says, "My boat, my boat. I found my boat."'

I lit another cigarette and waited.

'You there, Brady?'

'I'm here,' I sighed.

'Carl's wife told me about it,' Charlie continued. 'Know what she said to me?'

'What'd she say, Charlie?'

'She says to me, she said, "Poor Carl. He still doesn't know his mast from a pole in the ground."'

'Is that a true story?'

'As God is my judge,' he said solemnly. 'So. What can I do for you that's worth scallops at the Union Oyster House?'

'I've got some phone numbers. I need names.'

'Local?'

'All but one. That's a 413.'

'That'd be Western Mass. Shouldn't be too much of a problem. Give 'em to me.'

I read the six telephone numbers to him. He repeated them to me. 'It'll take me a couple of hours. Okay?'

'Fine. Listen. One more thing. Can you check with your fellow federal employees over at the Medford Post Office and see what they're doing with the mail of a guy named Eddie Donagan? Can you do that?'

'Donagan the ballplayer.'

'Right. The ex-ballplayer.'

'Give me the address.'

I gave it to him, and we hung up. I swivelled my chair around, stared out the window for a minute, then turned back to my desk. I found the number for the Shawmut County Bank branch in Medford, tapped it out, and was finally connected to somebody named Mr Marley.

'My name is Edward Donagan,' I said, crossing my fingers. 'I have a question about my chequing account.'

'Certainly, sir. May I have your account number, please?'

'Ah, jeez. I left my chequebook home. You can look it up, can't you?'

'Well, normally . . .'

'Listen,' I said. 'I think you guys have screwed up my account, okay? I think someone's been writing cheques on my account, or else you guys are taking money out of my account, because it don't seem to add up, see, and if they are, or you are, then you've got trouble. So just look it up for me, will you? I want to know all the cheques you think I've written in the past three weeks, and what my balance is. Okay? I don't want to have to bother my lawyer.'

'How did you spell your name again, sir?'

I spelled 'Donagan' for him, and he put me on hold. I lit another cigarette and waited. I was just stubbing it out when Mr Marley came back on the phone. He sounded quite jovial.

'According to our computer, Mr Donagan, you have written no cheques on your account since the seventh of July.'

'Let's see,' I said. 'That was a little more than three weeks ago, right?'

'Yes, sir.'

'Which cheque was that? The last one.'

'New England Telephone. Twenty-two

dollars and forty cents.'

'Okay. And what's my balance?'

'Seven hundred and thirty-six dollars and nineteen cents.'

'No other cheques?'

'No, sir.'

'What about deposits?'

'Your last deposit was on the second of July. Five hundred and eighteen dollars and seventy-one cents.'

'Right. My paycheque. That's it, huh?'

'Yes, sir. That's it.'

'Hm. Guess I was wrong. My mistake, I guess. Well, thanks, anyway.'

'Any time, sir. Glad to be of assistance.'

I pondered the information Mr Marley had given me for a moment, then called Stern.

'Coyne,' I said when he answered. 'You called?'

'Keeping our bargain,' he said. 'You keeping your part?'

'Sure. I'm here at my office being an attorney. What do you have?'

'Couple of things that might interest you. First, you remember one of the names on that list the Mikuni girl gave you, the ballplayer, Halley?'

'Sure. Bobo Halley.'

'Just thought you might want to know that he was drummed out of baseball. Gambling.'

'Gambling,' I repeated. 'No kidding.'

'Yeah. They decided to cover it up. I guess he was tight with some bad boys in Detroit. Owed them some money. Suspicion that he might've thrown some games.'

'What do you make of that?'

'Well, I don't know,' he said. 'We checked the other guys on the list and there was nothing like that with them. I talked to the cops who investigated Halley's death. All they could say was he'd had a few drinks when he cracked up.'

'Hmm,' I said, pretending that was all news to me. 'What was the other thing? You said you had a couple of things.'

'The other thing is, I decided to send one of my guys through Donagan's apartment.'

'Good idea.'

'Yeah, I thought so.'

'Of course,' I said, 'you know the cops have already been there.'

'Like hell they have. This is my case. No cops do anything without my say so.'

'Well, according to the landlord, two cops were there two weeks ago.'

'And just how in the hell do you know that, Coyne?'

I didn't answer.

'You keep playing Dick Tracy, Coyne, you're gonna wind up with some big holes in

230

you, know that? Understand, I'm not worried about you particularly. I just don't want this case fucked up. You're interfering with an FBI investigation, and I'm about ready to have you locked up. I mean it. You are pissing me off, Coyne. So you went to Donagan's apartment. I suppose you handled everything and moved stuff around and left your fingerprints everywhere.'

'Look, I don't see how—'

'Butt out, Coyne.'

'Okay. You're right. I'll be a good boy.'

'Sure. And I'm gonna swear off Cutty Sark, too.' I heard him sigh. 'Look. Do you want to cooperate with me on this, or what?'

'Sure I do.'

He sighed again. 'Yeah, well anyhow. I'm gonna have Travers get Donagan's description out, see if we can find him. They're good at that kind of stuff. Better than you. So you can relax, okay? We'll take it from here. Nice work, and all that shit.'

'Okay. I hear you.'

'Of course,' he said, 'you're probably right.'

'How's that?'

'Donagan's probably dead.'

*   *   *

It was close to three hours later when Charlie

231

McDevitt called me back. 'You got paper and pencil?' he said. 'You want to write these down?'

'I'm all set. Go ahead.'

'Okay. The 5081 number's in Billerica. Name of Suzanne Anders.' He spelled it for me, and gave me the street address. 'Next, 2170's the number for the office at the Herman's store in Burlington. That's at the mall. Okay? And 2663 is someone named Anthony Sandella in Medford, forty-six East Street. Now this one here, Brady, this makes me wonder what you're up to. This 9957 is in Dorchester. It's for Bond's Variety Store. You know about Darryl Bond?'

'Never heard of him.'

'Well, Darryl Bond's a bookie, among other things. Not a nice man. Likes to break people's thumbs.' He hesitated. 'You're not planning to talk to Darryl Bond, are you?'

'You seem to be implying, in your usual circumspect manner, that perhaps it might not be a wonderful idea.'

'Right. Not wonderful at all. You don't want to go near that neighbourhood, and you don't want to go near Darryl Bond.'

'He's a bookie, huh?'

'Oh, yes. He's been picked up a few times. Hard to nail him down. Does a little dope, runs a few hookers, too, just for recreation.

Stay away from him.'

'Okay. What about those other phone numbers?'

'That's what took me so long,' said Charlie.

'Even with all the resources of the United States Justice Department at your fingertips?'

'Even then. Now this 3327 number is a pay phone in Central Square on a corner by a Gulf station on Mass Ave. And this 413 number's in Lanesborough. It was disconnected a year and a half ago. It's a bitch to run down disconnected numbers, you know. It's for somebody named Jacob Grabowski.'

'I know who that is,' I said. 'Did you have a chance to check the post office?'

'Did you ask me to? Sure I did. They're holding Donagan's mail for him.'

'Did he request it?'

'No. Evidently it started building up in his mailbox, so the mailman checked with the landlord, who said Donagan was away. So they put in a notice that they were holding it for him. I guess that's what they do.'

'For how long?'

'Nearly a month.'

'Okay. Listen, thanks a lot, Charlie.'

'Brady, old buddy, I've got this feeling maybe you should tell me what's going on. You do tend to, you know, get involved.'

'Nothing to worry about. I've learned my

lesson.'

'Sure.' He didn't sound convinced.

'Don't worry. If I need you I'll holler.'

'Well, I hope you will. I really do. I'm looking forward to those scallops. Don't want something to happen, you can't pay up.'

★   ★   ★

I spent the rest of the afternoon making Julie happy by talking with clients, filling in the blanks on wills, and even keeping an appointment with Mrs Bartlett. I assured her that things at probate could be straightened out, that I'd get to it at the beginning of the week. She was smiling and calling me 'dear boy' by the time she left. Plucking the heartstrings of rich old ladies was what I did best.

Off and on throughout the afternoon I rang the number of Suzanne Anders in Billerica. It was five-thirty when someone answered the phone.

'Is this Suzanne Anders?' I said.

'Yes, this is Suzanne.' She had a husky, Lauren Bacall voice.

'My name is Brady Coyne. I'm Eddie Donagan's attorney.'

'Yes?' The voice was cool.

'You know Eddie, don't you?'

'I did, yes.'

'I'd like to talk to you about Eddie.'

'I've got nothing to say about Eddie Donagan.'

I sensed she was about to hang up on me. 'Wait, please,' I said. 'It's important.'

She hesitated. 'Why? Why is it important that we talk about my former friend, that son of a bitch Eddie Donagan?'

'I have reason to believe that he's in trouble.'

'That's not news. I could have told you that. He is in big trouble.'

'What do you mean?' I said.

'He stood me up on a date about a month ago. No call, no apology, nothing. The hell with him.'

'I mean *real* trouble, Miss Anders.'

'Miz,' she corrected—automatically, it seemed. But her tone softened. 'What do you mean, real trouble?'

I paused dramatically and dropped my voice, a ploy that always works. 'I'm not at liberty to say right now,' I said.

'Oh, my goodness,' she said. 'Really heavy lawyer stuff, huh?'

'You're mocking me,' I observed.

'Why, yes, I suppose I am,' she said. She paused. 'Okay, Mr Coyne. You've done it. I'm curious. If it's really that important, why don't you meet me at work when I get my break, and then we can talk. I'm on nights at Lauriat's. At the mall.'

I told her how she could recognize me, and we agreed to meet at the Häagen-Dazs stand at the Burlington Mall at nine o'clock where she said we could get the best ice-cream in the world and where we could sit and talk. It sounded good to me.

CHAPTER SEVENTEEN

The shopping centre is here to stay, as closely attuned to the American psyche as the department store was a couple of generations ago. Where else can Americans do everything they want to do all at once? They can drive in their cars, mill around with hordes of strangers, and buy things they didn't know they wanted until they got there.

America. It's not the Grand Canyon or the Empire State Building. It's not the Harvard Yard or the Old North Bridge. It's not the Boulder Dam or the Statue of Liberty. America's not an Iowa cornfield or the Chicago stockyards or the Rocky Mountains or Silicon Valley.

America is the Burlington Mall shopping

centre.

The sporting goods store where Eddie Donagan had sold running shoes was located there near Lauriat's, and I found it easily, thanks to one of the several big maps that had been erected by the entry for my shopping convenience. As soon as I walked into the store, the credit cards in my hip pocket began to squirm and twitch, reminding me that I was not entirely immune to the lure of Things. I strode resolutely past shelves of golf equipment, past racks of warm-up suits, past a display of two-man tents, and found the fishing department. Here, I knew, I'd be safe. I already had more fishing gear than I could ever use, the result of numerous other trips to other sporting goods stores.

I was slobbering over some expensive English fly reels in a glass-topped case when a young man with a wispy blond moustache sidled up to me and said, 'May I help you?'

'Is that a Hardy reel?'

'Yes, sir. Would you like to look at it?' He went behind the glass case, took out the reel, and laid it reverently on top of the glass counter.

'I'm, ah, just looking,' I said. The salesman looked a lot like Larry Bird, except for being about five-seven and chubby. 'Actually, I was wondering if Eddie Donagan was working tonight. Is he here?'

'Eddie? Oh, he used to be over in shoes. He doesn't work here any more.'

I picked up the reel. It was a beauty. 'He's not here any more?'

'You a friend of Eddie's?'

'I used to know him,' I said.

The boy—he couldn't have been more than twenty, and I estimated his moustache was eight years in the making—looked me up and down for a moment, then said, 'He hasn't worked here for a few weeks. He quit.'

'Quit?'

'More or less. He stopped coming to work. The boss was bullshit, needless to say. But that's Eddie for you.'

'You knew him, then.'

'Does anybody know him? Funny guy, Eddie. One day, friendly as hell, next day he won't talk to you. We had beers after work a few times. Listen, you like that reel?'

I put it back on to the counter. 'No. Well, yes, I like it, of course. But I'm not going to buy it. Look, did he happen to mention anything about quitting to you before he left?'

'Nope. Just one Monday he didn't show up. The boss called a few times, I guess, and got no answer, and that was it. But you know Eddie, I guess. Hell, I think they still got a paycheque waiting for him. Betcha he never

238

comes for it.'

'You're probably right. You haven't heard from him since he quit, have you?'

'Nope. Wouldn't expect to. We weren't close, exactly. Somebody told me he used to be a ballplayer. Is that true?'

'Yes. He was. Once. Pretty good one, too.'

'Funny guy, Eddie. Never talked about it. Hey, let me show you something about this reel.'

★　　★　　★

At nine o'clock I made my way down to the other end of the mall where the Häagen-Dazs booth was located, clutching a shopping bag with the Hardy reel nestled in the bottom. It was in a big open horseshoe-shaped area, in the middle of which were scattered seventy-five or eighty white tables with white aluminium chairs. Big skylights were set into the arched ceiling. Trees grew among the tables, giving the illusion of privacy to the shoppers who paused there for a snack and a smoke.

The booths were lined up along the outside of the horseshoe. Besides ice-cream, you could get hot dogs with chili or sauerkraut, barbecued chicken, seafood, shish kebabs, soup, salad, pastries. Chinese or Mexican platters, and coffees and teas from all nations. All fancy, all quick, all expensive.

I claimed a table and lit another Winston, and Suzanne Anders appeared a couple of minutes later.

My ex-wife would have said Suzanne Anders had a 'cute figure', which would be a little like calling New York City a 'good-sized town', Shakespeare a 'fair poet', or Rembrandt a 'decent draftsman'. Her hair was cut short and straight in the style popularized a few years ago by the figure skater, Dorothy Hamill. The dimple in her right cheek could have buried a marble. Behind her rimless Gloria Steinem glasses her dark eyes were smiling at me.

'Mr Coyne, I presume,' she said.

'And you must be Suzanne Anders,' I said.

She sat across from me and sighed deeply.

'Oh, what a boring job,' she said.

'It's not what you do regularly?'

'I'm not knocking it,' she said carefully, 'but cashiering at a bookstore isn't my idea of a career. No. I'm at law school. Suffolk. I'm working my way through.'

'Good. Good for you.'

'Can I have my ice-cream now?' she said, her voice mimicking a small child.

'Okay.' We went to the Häagen-Dazs booth. 'What do you recommend?' I said.

'They're all good. I've had 'em all. Elberta Peach, Rum Raisin, Carob, Macadamia Nut. The sorbets are delicious. I especially like the Boysenberry and Cassis.' She arched her eyebrows at me from behind her glasses. 'I think I'll have the Carob this time.'

I studied the list of flavours. To my relief, they had what I wanted. 'Chocolate,' I said.

She smiled at me. I shrugged. 'It's what I like.'

'I could have guessed,' she said. 'Chocolate. I could've figured you for chocolate.'

The small cones—and they *were* small—cost $1.10 each. It had been a long time since I'd had an ice-cream cone. The last time, I seemed to recall, they cost fifteen cents for a double dip.

We took our cones back to our table. Suzanne licked hers delicately, her pink tongue flicking in and out, her cheeks working to savour the flavour. She saw me watching her. 'Want a lick?' she said. I smiled. 'Oh, God,' she said. 'A genuine, old-fashioned, dyed-in-the-wool dirty old man.'

'Gimme a lick,' I said.

She handed me her cone. I tasted the Carob. Something like chocolate, only not as good. I gave it back to her. 'Not bad,' I said. 'Not chocolate, of course. But not bad.'

'That's silly.'

241

'I just figured out the colour of your eyes,' I said.

'Oh?'

'Yes. Hot fudge sauce.'

'Well, gee whiz,' she said, 'enough about me. You wanted to talk about Eddie.'

'Yes. He's disappeared. I want to find him.'

'What do you mean, disappeared?'

'Just that. He hasn't shown up for work. He hasn't been at his apartment. No one has heard from him.'

Suzanne nodded. 'He disappeared from my life, that's for sure. It's just like him though, isn't it? Eddie's a funny guy. I pretend to be mad at him, but I'm not. Maybe a little hurt. More bewildered than anything. We weren't lovers, or anything like that, you know. It hadn't gotten anywhere near that. It probably never would have.' She shrugged and twirled her cone against her tongue. 'I used to see him around. Herman's is practically next door to Lauriat's, you know. One night I was here, having an ice-cream after work, and he came in. We nodded to each other. He got a cone and sat at another table. I went over and sat with him. He didn't seem surprised, or pleased, or anything. Very casual guy, he seemed. We started talking. More accurately, I started talking. He listened. When our cones were gone we said goodbye. I realized he

242

hadn't said a damn thing about himself. He was a good listener, though. Anyway, a few nights later we met here again, and we sort of got in the habit of it. He took me for drinks a couple of times. That was our relationship. I did like him a lot. But I had the feeling that he could take me or leave me, you know?'

'That's hard to believe,' I said. 'Listen, you don't have to tell me this. Your relationship with Eddie is your own business.'

'I'm just trying to explain why I probably can't help you. He gave very little of himself. I can tell you one thing. He really loved his wife and his little boy. When he talked about them he lit up. Otherwise he was a sad, lonely man. You know,' she said, leaning towards me, 'he never touched me, never even tried to kiss me. I'm not used to that. At first I figured it was his way of coming on to me. It's one of the tricks. I'm familiar with it. They make you think they don't want you, and you begin to wonder what's wrong with yourself, and pretty soon you find yourself trying to seduce them.'

'But that's not what Eddie was doing.'

She shrugged. 'No. I don't think so.' She smiled. 'I guess we'll never know, huh?'

'Well, I hope he comes back,' I said. 'Did he ever mention anyone—a friend, a relative, anybody besides Jan or E.J.? Can you think of anything he ever said that might give us a clue about where he went?'

She thought for a minute. 'Well, of course, he did talk about baseball. He seemed to know a lot about it, although he was always making fun of it. "Stupid game," he always called it. "Stupid people play baseball," he said. It was a long time before I realized he'd played baseball himself. He told me he hadn't seen a baseball game since the last one he played in. He said he'd never go to a baseball game, never watch one on television. I think he really hated the game. It did something bad to him, though he never came out and told me that.' She looked at me. 'Do you like baseball?'

'Yes. Yes, I do,' I said. 'I love baseball.'

She nodded. 'Me, too. I wanted him to talk more about it. He did, but it was still all negative. He said it was phony, just a show. He said it wasn't important enough for anyone to pay attention to, or for people to get paid for. He was very bitter about baseball.'

'He had a right to be,' I observed.

'But, you know, there was a funny thing.' Suzanne frowned at me.

'What was that?'

'He always wanted to know the scores. We were at this place one night. There was a television over the bar. We were at a table

244

having a drink and talking. Suddenly Eddie jumped up and went over to the bar to stare at the TV. A minute later he came back shaking his head. I asked him what was so important that he had to leave so quickly without saying excuse me. He said he wanted to catch the weather report. But I could see the set. It wasn't that. They were giving the baseball scores.'

'I think he bet on the games,' I said.

She looked puzzled. 'But he hated baseball.'

'I know. I don't think that made any difference. Did he ever talk about the players? Do you remember any names he might have mentioned?'

'No. I don't think he ever talked about anybody except his family.'

'Jan and E.J.?'

'Yes. That's what I meant. Just them.' She bit into her cone. 'You know where he might have gone?'

'Where?'

'Alaska. He talked about going to Alaska. As if it were a place where he could start over again. I never took it seriously. It seemed to be just a kind of figure of speech for him. I mean, that's like going to the moon.'

'It seems as if that's where he went.'

'Alaska?'

'No. The moon,' I said.

We walked out of the shopping mall together. When we were outside, Suzanne said, 'Where's your car?'

'Over there somewhere,' I said, gesturing. 'You?'

'Other direction.'

'I'll walk over with you.'

'Don't bother. I can manage, thanks.'

I shrugged. 'Well, thanks for talking with me.'

'I guess I didn't help much.'

'Hard to say. It was nice to meet you, anyway.'

She smiled. 'Sure,' she said. The lamps that illuminated the parking lot glittered on her glasses so that I couldn't see her eyes. She held out her hand. I took it.

'Maybe we could have a drink together some time,' I said.

'I don't think so,' she said.

She released my hand and turned away. Then she stopped and came back to me. 'Eddie said a funny thing to me. It was that time when he went to check on the baseball scores. When he came back to the table, he said, "I just bought the farm." What do you think that meant?'

'It meant he died,' I said. 'Figuratively, of course. To buy the farm is to die.'

'He must have lost a lot of money on his bets.'

'I imagine that's what he meant.'

Suzanne Anders nodded and walked away from me. She did have a cute figure, no matter how you looked at it.

CHAPTER EIGHTEEN

Friday dawned cloudy and cool. Wispy fog floated around my apartment building and gauzed the skeletons of the boats that drifted like dried leaves on the harbour below. Julie had the day off. I had left my 'Gone Fishin'' message on the answering machine.

I had two mugs of coffee out on the balcony, savouring the rich sea smells that wafted up on the moist air. Then I went inside and ate a cold slab of leftover deep-dish pizza. I decided not to shave, slapped together a couple of peanut butter sandwiches, and gathered my fly-fishing gear together. I stowed my fly boxes, spare leader tippets, insect repellant, fly and line dressings, and spare reels into my fishing vest, chose an old Orvis eight-foot split bamboo rod, and slung my chest-high waders over my shoulder. Thus burdened, and feeling wickedly independent and carefree, I rode the elevator down into the basement of the building to where my car was parked. Minutes later I was heading west, the city behind me and the Deerfield River three hours ahead.

I slid a Julian Bream tape into the deck and allowed my mind to ride on the lyrical voice of his classical guitar. The trout, I figured, would be taking terrestrials off the surface—black ants and grasshoppers. I imagined an old acquaintance, a monster brown trout, rising at the head of Diamond Drill Hole, and upstream, in Lookout Run, the rainbows would be working.

Inevitably, my mind turned to Eddie and E. J. Donagan, and I realized, with sudden, surprising clarity, that they were both probably dead. The concurrence of their disappearance had to be more than coincidental, and I felt stupid for ever believing that Eddie would choose the occasion of his son's kidnapping to take off for Alaska. He loved E.J. too much, I knew. No, whoever took E.J. had somehow taken Eddie, too. That, I figured, was what Mary Ann Mikuni had been trying to tell me before she, too, was killed.

The fish all follow the sharks, she had said. It could be a metaphor, although I didn't suppose she had intended it that way. Eddie gambled. Bobo Halley, whose name appeared on the list Mary Ann Mikuni had given me, had gambled, too. Bobo Halley had died. E.J. had been kidnapped. A big ransom had been delivered. The dog did nothing in the night-time, Sherlock Holmes had pointed out. Eddie told Suzanne Anders that he had bought the farm.

I was on Route 2. I passed the exit to Fitchburg, where, some fifteen years earlier, Sam Farina had taken me to a baseball game at the State College to introduce me to Eddie Donagan. I had drawn up his first contract, I had negotiated deals for him, I had befriended him and his family. And now, I knew, I should mourn his loss.

Now he had really bought the farm.

The phrase repeated itself in my brain and as I thought back over those times I remembered Jake and Mary Grabowski. They lived on a farm. Eddie had written Jake Grabowski's phone number on his wall. Eddie had loved them, back then at the beginning. They were old folks, even fifteen years ago. When I first met Eddie they were the only family he knew. He had endowed a scholarship in the name of their son at Fitchburg State, and then, as far as I knew, he had forgotten them.

I had been to their place once, that first

winter I knew Eddie. He was just beginning his marriage to Jan then, and I hadn't yet terminated mine with Gloria. The four of us had driven through the snow-covered Massachusetts Hills to the Grabowski farm in Lanesborough over this same Route 2. In his pocket Eddie carried round-trip plane tickets to Florida, along with a four-week reservation at a Hilton hotel, a package that included meals, sight-seeing tours, a deep-sea fishing trip, and passes to Disney World and several shows. Eddie had been very pleased with himself, and when Jake quietly refused the gift, anger glittered from Eddie's eyes.

'We can't leave the cows,' the old man explained. His face, tough as cowhide and eroded into deep gullies from a lifetime outdoors, attempted to smile, to dispel the disappointment he read into Eddie's silence. 'We ain't had a vacation in sixty years. We're happy here. This is where we belong. I don't reckon Mary and me'd know what to do with ourselves in Florida.'

We were sitting in the kitchen of the big old farmhouse. Mary stood at the stove basting the roasting chickens, whose rich aroma filled the room. Jake reached over to touch Eddie's arm. 'You're a good boy, son. You just keep on being a good boy. That's the only present we want.'

Eddie pulled back from the old man and stood up. He walked over to the window, and I could see the tears in his eyes. I realized they were tears of frustration, and even fury. It was the first time Eddie had shown me that side of himself.

On the way home in the car Eddie had railed at Jake and Mary. 'Goddam old fools,' he said. 'It's not fair that they won't let me pay them back. Brady, you gotta make them go.'

'They don't want to go,' I said. 'You're being selfish.'

'Oh, fuck you,' he muttered. 'Fuck them, too.'

After that, Eddie never mentioned Jake and Mary Grabowski to me.

The road climbed up through the foothills of the Berkshires. I flipped the Julian Bream tape over. Lanesborough was only an hour or so beyond the Deerfield. I could visit Jake and Mary and still be on the river for the best fishing in the afternoon. It was a futile hope, and I refused to invest any optimism in it, but it was possible that Jake and Mary Grabowski could help. Even with a disconnected phone, perhaps somehow they had heard from Eddie. At least I knew that Eddie had patched things up with them. I was glad. Anyway, it would be nice to see the old folks.

The section of Route 2 that runs due west

251

across the Connecticut Valley and into the mountains is called the Mohawk Trail. It's a winding, two-lane highway that climbs the hills and cuts through the valleys, past old paper mills and working farms, through worn-out little villages like Erving and Turner's Falls. After it crosses the Connecticut River it rises into the Berkshires and picks up the Deerfield River, which it parallels for several miles. The Deerfield is a classic trout river, big by Massachusetts standards, deep and swift, its waters kept frigid year-round by the hydroelectric dams that feed it. It boils around the great boulders that are scattered in its bed, and the trout like to lie in the eddies and suck in the insects that are funnelled to them.

I stopped in Charlemont and carried my two peanut butter sandwiches to the bank of the river. I sat with my back against the trunk of an old oak. The water was high, surging over the tops of the boulders that normally lay exposed. That meant the Fife Brook Dam, a few miles upstream from where I sat, was releasing water into the river. Those of us who fished the Deerfield for trout did so cautiously, because we knew that when they let water go from the bottom of the dam, the level could rise two or three feet in a matter of minutes. We learned to listen for change in the pitch of the water's melody. It comes rumbling, like a distant train, and it warns us to get off the river fast.

As I munched my sandwiches and watched the river rush by, I remembered the one time I had failed to heed the warning. It was near sunset of a June evening several years earlier. I was wading the Yankee Flats, only a few hundred yards downstream from the dam. Charlie McDevitt was working a pool a little downstream from me and around the bend. Down in that deep gorge where the river flowed, the sun had not touched the water for hours. It had already become too dark to tie on a new fly, so I heard the rising trout before I was able to see him. Glug, it went. A big fish swirling at the surface, sucking in insects, a solid, heavy, no-nonsense noise. I'd heard such sounds before, and this one made my pulse race as I remembered the size of the other fish. It was no ordinary trout. I imagined one of the eight- or ten-pound brown trout I knew fishermen occasionally took from the river—fish as long as a man's arm.

I flicked the fly dry with a couple of false casts, then with a strong thrust of wrist and forearm I cast towards the place where the fish had risen. The fly fell short. I stripped more line from the reel and cast again, striving to combine just the right proportions of delicate

253

timing and sheer strength necessary to cast long distances with a fly rod. But I was still short. I needed to get a little closer to the fish.

I reached with my left foot, probing with my toe for the river bottom. I already stood waist deep, and I knew somewhere ahead of me the river bottom dropped off abruptly, but I was still surprised when my foot came down nearly a foot deeper than where I had been standing. I remained there, poised, left foot ahead of right, with most of my weight still on my rear foot. Slowly I shifted my weight and edged my right foot forward beside my left. Later I remembered hearing the grumble of heavy water moving towards me, but at the time my brain was focused on the big trout, and the warning didn't register.

The rising water arrived at the moment my right toe struck against a submerged rock. I felt my upper body begin to fall forward. My left foot slid sideways on the slippery gravel on the riverbed. My right foot bumped the boulder again, and in that instant of imbalance the full force of the rising river struck me at the waist, hip and knee. I waved my arms awkwardly, seeing equilibrium, my fly rod a useless balancing staff. My body twisted so that I found myself facing directly upstream. The top half of my body began to topple backwards so that it seemed I would end up lying on the water, my face to the dark sky overhead, and shoot downstream head first.

I struggled to remain upright. My feet bounced on the bottom as the growing force of the water began to carry me downstream. Water roared around my shoulders and splashed against my face. Then I went under. My mouth and nose filled, and I felt a surge of panic. I found myself twisted around facing downstream, out of control, the river surging against my shoulders. I strained to find the bottom with my toes. The dark riverbank seemed to race past. It appeared to be so close that I thought I could touch it, grab a root, hang on, and I tried to manoeuvre towards it. But I could reach nothing. My toes kept scraping river bottom, but I couldn't stop. My waders filled with water, pulling me down. My legs grew heavy. I thrust my head back in an effort to keep my face above water. I went under again, and the roar of water filled my ears. Avoid tipping over, I thought. Remain upright. Above all, don't tip. Then I would be totally at the whim of the river. Then I'd tumble against the bottom. I'd lose track of where the top was. I'd be crushed against underwater rocks.

I bobbed downstream, moving faster and faster, still instinctively gripping my fly rod. Sometimes I'd touch bottom with one of my feet, but then the river would pick me up and sweep me along. I willed the panic from my brain. I dropped my rod and tried to use both arms to maintain my balance by laying them flat on the surface and finning. I found I could steer a little and keep my head up that way. I tried to move away from the middle of the river, hoping to find shallower, less swift water. I kept circling and probing with my feet, reaching for the bottom. But my waders had filled, and the weight of the water in them seemed to pull me lower and lower into the river. My arms were underwater. I treaded desperately. My heavy legs moved reluctantly. The water felt as thick as mud around them. I tipped my head back to breathe. I was spinning, now facing upstream, now twisted around by the relentless force of the water. Two, three times my head went under. My toes reached nothing. I had lost the river bottom.

Suddenly, with the force of a speeding automobile colliding with a tree, I felt myself smash against a boulder. A white flash of pain surged across my hip and shoulder. I clawed frantically at the rock, but the river yanked me away. Then I was tumbling. I could no longer distinguish the surface of the river from its bottom. I bounced, shoulder and knee and head scraping and banging against the gravel and rock. I was a wet rag in the mouth of a bull mastiff, at the complete mercy of the driving power of the river.

I groped wildly with my hands for the river bottom that raced under me. With a desperate heave I pushed myself upward. My head broke the surface, and I gulped a breath of sweet air before I was wrenched under again. Then something hammered the side of my head. A great sinking blackness sucked away the last of my strength.

Charlie's voice came to me from miles away. 'How're they bitin'?' he was saying.

I opened one eye. Charlie's face was a shadow above mine.

'Hey, Brady, drink this,' he said.

I opened both eyes. I pushed myself up on to one elbow and accepted the flask that Charlie held towards me. The undiluted liquor burned my tongue and throat.

'Excuse me,' I mumbled, and, propping myself on my hands and knees, I belched, gagged, then vomited gloriously, seemingly endless stomachfuls of water, mixed with undigested bits of the ham and cheese sandwich I had gobbled before wading into the river. 'I gotta learn to chew my food better,' I observed.

'Are you okay?'

'Oh, yeah. Fine.' I touched my right cheek.

257

A jolt of pain stabbed through my head. My hand came away bloody. I sat up and flexed each limb, one at a time, and twisted my torso gingerly. 'Nothing broken. Except my spirit. Damn big trout rising back there.'

Charlie stared solemnly at me. My teeth began to chatter. I hugged myself.

'Try some more of this.' Charlie gave me his flask. This time the bourbon stayed down, searing its way into my stomach where it created a glowing centre of warmth that quickly diffused through my limbs. Charlie left, and a moment later returned with a brown Army blanket, which he wrapped around my shoulders.

'I thought you were a goner,' he said. 'Lucky you washed up at my feet. When I saw your rod floating at me I knew you couldn't be far behind.'

'Did you get my rod?'

'Aye-yuh,' he drawled. 'Figured you'd want me to save it first. Then you.'

I nodded. 'It's my favourite rod.'

'I told you to listen for the dam,' said Charlie, his face, for once, serious. 'You can't fool around with this river.'

'Jeez, Charlie. There was a huge trout rising up there. I wasn't paying attention.'

He touched my arm. 'You gotta pay attention to the Deerfield,' he said.

* * *

I finished my peanut butter sandwiches and heaved myself to my feet, the memory of that unplanned float trip down the Deerfield vivid in my mind. In the years since that evening when Charlie McDevitt dragged me from the river, I had fished it many times. I did so respectfully, ever alert for the rumble of heavy water surging from the bottom of the dam.

There was a big trout there I still had a grudge against.

'I'll be back later,' I said aloud to the river.

I climbed the steep bank and slid into my car. I could visit Jake and Mary Grabowski and be back in time for the best fishing. The water would have returned to its normal level by then.

Beyond the Deerfield, the Mohawk Trail climbed through steep mountains. In several places the roadside fell away into deep, rock-strewn gorges, at the bottom of which thin ribbons of water flowed, small tributaries to the greater Deerfield. I executed the hairpin turn high on the sheer western face of the mountains, from which I could see the broad valley beyond the Berkshires stretch towards the next range of mountains. North Adams lay below, and beyond it Williamstown, where I would turn south to Lanesborough and the Grabowski farm.

It was a little after two in the afternoon when I pulled into the farmyard. Grey sheets flapped on the clothesline beside the peeling and flaking white farmhouse. The carcass of a rusted tractor huddled in the high weeds beside the barn, and out back lay a rocky pasture where a dozen or so black and white cows grazed lazily. In the distance I could hear the chug of farm machinery.

I mounted the steps to the front of the house and rapped on the door, waited, and knocked again. When I received no answer I walked over to the barn. Through the open door I could see only darkness inside. I stood outside and called, 'Hello! Anybody home?'

Again, I got no answer. I stepped to the open door. I could smell the ripe mixture of aromas—newly cut hay and fresh manure. A trapezoid of sunlight fell from the doorway where I stood on the rough wood floor. Inside, the barn lay in shadows.

Again I called into the darkness, 'Hello?'

I moved into the barn. I stood just inside the doorway, squinting to adjust my eyes to the dimness. I sensed a faint movement behind my right shoulder, a whisper of air in motion, no more, and I started to spin my head around to confront it. My mind registered in an instant a man's figure, teeth clenched white in the shadow, and the long object he held like a baseball bat slashing towards my right cheek. I had time only to tuck my chin into my hunched shoulder before the blow struck. It glanced off the point of my shoulder and ricocheted high off my skull. Strobes of white light flickered into my ear, and then I felt myself melt on to the floor.

CHAPTER NINETEEN

I did not lose consciousness but I felt dazed and paralysed by the pain. I was aware of lying on the hard floor for a moment before rough hands grabbed me by my armpits and dragged me into the darkness. My shoulders were propped against something that scratched the back of my neck. I squeezed my eyes shut in an attempt to cool the searing burn in the centre of my brain. When I opened them the filmy outline of a man appeared. Gradually he came into focus.

'Hi, Eddie,' I mumbled.

'What the fuck are you doing here?'

'Can I ask you the same question?'

I wiggled into a sitting position, blinked,

and groaned. 'Oh, man,' I said. I touched the point of the most intense pain. My hand came away wet. 'What the hell did you have to do that for?'

Eddie Donagan looked like a hillbilly out squirrel hunting. He wore faded blue overalls with a bib in front and no shirt underneath. His beard had grown long and scraggly, and his arms and shoulders looked hard and ropy. He was sitting on a hay bale in front of me. Across his knees rested a pump-action shotgun. The bore looked as big as the open end of a coffee can. It was pointed at my sternum, and it didn't waver.

He stood up and tucked the gun under his arm. 'Don't move,' he said.

'Not likely,' I said.

He moved beside the doorway and stood with his back against the inside wall. He held the shotgun in his right hand like a pistol, his finger curled around the trigger, the barrel pointed straight up. Slowly he peered around the corner. He stood that way for a long minute, and then, evidently satisfied, came back and resumed his seat opposite me.

'Were you followed?' he said.

'I don't know. I don't think so. Why should I be followed?'

He ignored my question. 'How did you find me? How did you know I was here?'

'I didn't know you were here. I just came to see Jake and Mary. I was in the vicinity.'

'In the vicinity,' he repeated, sarcastically, as if he didn't believe me. 'Who else knows you're here?'

'Nobody, for Christ's sake. Why?'

He shook his head slowly and shifted his position. The bore of the gun remained fixed on me. 'If they followed you . . .'

'Who? Who's "they"?'

'Never mind. Let me think for a minute.'

I touched my scalp again. The blood had started to congeal. 'If that gunbarrel hadn't hit my shoulder first you would've killed me, know that?'

'I was trying to.'

'You never were much good with the bat.'

'Yeah, I was a lousy hitter. I didn't know it was you. I'm sorry if I hurt you.'

'*If* you hurt me? Jesus, Eddie!' I fumbled for a cigarette and lit it. 'Eddie, what the hell is that gun for, anyway? Do you have to point it at me?'

He adjusted the gun so that it aimed over my shoulder. 'It's a long story, lawmaster. I don't think I want to tell it to you.'

'What are you afraid of? Not me, surely.'

'I told you. A long story.'

'Where's E.J.?'

He hesitated. 'E.J. was kidnapped.'

263

'I know that. And?'

He stared at me. Then his eyes shifted away. 'I helped them,' he whispered.

His words jolted me. 'Eddie, for Christ's sake!' I jerked to my feet. Eddie stood, too, and levelled the shotgun at my nose.

'Sit down, Brady.'

I sat.

Eddie resumed his seat on the hay bale but held the stock of the gun snug under his armpit so that it remained pointing directly at me. 'They called me that Saturday night,' he said. 'The day E.J. didn't come home. You had already talked to me, so I knew what they meant. They let me talk to him. He was okay. Scared, but okay. I told him everything was fine. Then they told me I had to help them. Or they'd kill him, see? I believed them. What could I do? I said I'd do what they wanted. They said if I fucked it up E.J. was dead. I had to go along with them, right?' Eddie's eyes appealed to me.

'Sure. I see that. Then what happened?'

'They said I should call you back, pretend I didn't know nothing. So I called you. Then I was supposed to play dumb, go along, they'd let me know what to do. I waited. All day Sunday, nothing. Sunday night they called again. I was going batshit, believe me, wondering if E.J. was okay. They asked me if

264

Sam was good for one and a half big ones. I said I thought so. They asked me who I could trust. I said you. Then they said if I wanted to see E.J. alive, I should keep playin' dumb and the night after they got the money I was supposed to meet them, and they'd let me have E.J. What could I do? They'd of killed him. I drove to a place. There were three of them there, in a car. Two of them got in with me. One drove, the other got in back with me and shoved me down on to the floor. He was holding a knife against my neck. We drove somewhere else, and when we got there I saw E.J. They said they'd let us both go after they were sure I hadn't given them away.'

'And you believed them?'

He snorted. ''Course not. What else could I do, though, huh?'

'I don't know,' I said. 'Eddie, for God's sake, what happened to E.J.?'

He gazed at me for a moment, then nodded slowly and stood up. 'Come here,' he said. He swung the barrel of the shotgun, gesturing for me to move ahead of him. We walked down the centre of the barn, past empty stalls and stacks of hay bales. At the back of the barn was a wide double door, pulled shut. Eddie slid it open a crack. 'Take a look,' he said.

I moved to the door and looked out beyond a fenced in area to a hay field adjacent to the

265

pasture where the cows grazed. A tractor was chugging along, mowing hay. It was moving directly away from the barn, so that all I could see was the back of the man who was driving it. He wore a broad-brimmed straw hat against the summer sun.

'Is that Jake?'

'Yes. Wait.'

The tractor reached the end of the row, pivoted neatly, and started back towards the barn. Then I could see E. J. Donagan perched up on old Jake Grabowski's lap, steering.

I stepped back from the door and Eddie quickly slid it shut. We returned to the hay bales and sat down again.

'Jake and E.J. are great pals,' said Eddie softly. 'Jake's happy to have us here.'

'What does he think?'

He shrugged. 'I'm not sure what he thinks. I asked if we could stay for a while, that's all. Little summer holiday. Hell, we didn't bring any luggage, didn't announce ourselves. Old Jake knows more'n he lets on, probably. But he likes the company, and he's an old Yankee. Minds his business. Anyway, since Mary died he's been alone. We help him keep the farm going. It makes him happy.'

'Mary died,' I said. 'I'm sorry to hear it.'

Eddie nodded. 'Yeah. Tough on Jake.'

'That when he had the phone

266

disconnected?'

Eddie arched his eyebrows. 'How'd you know that?'

I smiled. 'A lot of people are pretty worried about you two, as you might have guessed. You could've called.'

He frowned and shook his head. 'I haven't left this place since we got here. I don't dare. I'm sorry about Jan being worried and all. But there wasn't a damn thing I could do about it.'

'You're hiding.'

'Oh, yeah, we're hiding, all right. So far we've been lucky.'

'Why haven't you gone to the police?'

'You don't know them. Like I said, I don't dare move. We never leave the farm. I keep the gun with me, stick close to E.J. All I can think is some day they'll come. When they do, I'm gonna be ready.'

He moved to the open barn door again and cautiously looked around. Then he came back and sat down. 'I didn't see your face,' he said. 'When I heard you yelling, all I could figure was . . .'

'I understand. How did you get away?'

Eddie chuckled. 'They had us at this house in the woods, one of those ranch houses all on one floor. At night they kept me and E.J. locked up in separate rooms. They'd sit around the living-room watching TV and drinking. My room had one of those skinny casement windows, you know, the kind you crank to open. Anyway, one night I crawled out. I guess they didn't figure I'd try because they'd still have E.J. I don't know. Anyhow, I went to E.J.'s room and tapped on his window, and he crawled out, too. It was simple. I was planning just to run, but my car was there. I always keep a spare key taped on to the back of the bumper, and it was still there. I stuck a wad of E.J.'s gum into the ignition of their car, and then he and I got into mine, and we just drove away.'

'You took quite a chance.'

'Not really, when you think they were going to kill us anyway. We drove like hell. At first I was gonna head for Maine, but then I realized I didn't have any money, so I thought of Jake. I was gonna borrow some iron from him and keep going, Canada, maybe, but he was so damn glad to see us, and I thought maybe it'd be a good place to stay for a couple of days, and the more I thought about it the more I figured we'd be better off here than trying to move.' He shrugged. 'So we're here.'

'Well, now you can come back. We'll go back home tonight.'

He shook his head. 'No we won't.'

'Why the hell not?'

He sighed deeply. 'It's not that simple, old

lawmaster.'

'Of course it is. You'll be safe.'

'That's not the point.'

I stared at him. 'Do you think you're in trouble?'

'I know I'm in trouble.'

'No one can blame you for helping them get money from Sam, if that's what you're worried about. Christ, Eddie, you're a hero for getting E.J. away from them. We'll go back, bring E.J. home, and you can talk to Marty Stern. It's simple.'

'It ain't simple. We'd never get there.'

'I think you're being paranoid.'

'Think whatever you want. I ain't going back.'

'And what about E.J.? What about your son?'

'Yeah? What about him?'

'You can't hide him forever.'

Eddie narrowed his eyes, but otherwise made no reply.

'Look,' I said. 'At least let me take E.J. back with me. You can do whatever you want. Just give me names and places. Tell me who these people are and where we can find them. Then we can make it safe for you to come back. What do you say?'

For a moment he didn't answer me. When he finally spoke, his voice was a hoarse whisper. 'Brady, I am in deep shit, believe me. I have really fucked up my life. I can only think of two good things I've ever done. One was helping to make E.J. The other was helping him to get away. I ain't worth a pig turd. I been trying to run away from all this bad shit for sixteen years. All I can do is keep running.' His eyes appealed to me. 'I don't want to go back. And if I let you go, you'll tell them where I am. The police, Stern, all of them. You have to. You're a lawyer. And they'll come for me. So I can't let you go.'

I nodded. 'You're right. I won't bullshit you. I'll have to tell them. But listen. I'll give you three days. You give me E.J. and I promise you three days. Three days to keep running. Or three days to decide to come back and get your life together.'

'Can you do that?'

'Sure. I can do that.'

He shook his head slowly. 'You goddam lawyers. Nothing's right and wrong with you guys, is it?'

'What do you mean?'

'I mean, it's either right that you tell them about me, or it's wrong. But you, you find something in the middle.'

'We learn to do the best we can. Everything's a compromise. Three days is a compromise.'

'What if I say okay?'

'If you say okay, you tell me who these people are, you tell me who's done what. And you tell me the rest. You tell me what you're really afraid of, so I can give you some good legal advice. And if you still won't come with me, I'll leave here tonight with E.J. I'll take him back to Jan, and I'll talk to the FBI. Sure, they'll ask me where you are. I'll tell them I don't know. I'll make up something. They won't believe me, but I don't think they'll beat me with rubber hoses. In three days I'll tell them you're here. You can run away, or you can come back, or you can stay here and wait if you'll feel safer. Okay?'

'You know,' said Eddie slowly, 'me and E.J.'ve gotten along real good here. We work together, play catch, do a little fishin' in Jake's pond. I've gotten used to having him around. I *like* him. I never really had that feeling before. He's a nice kid. Jan's done a good job with him.'

'What about E.J., anyway?' I said. 'Does he understand what's going on here, the kind of trouble you and he are in?'

Eddie shrugged. 'He doesn't say much. But, yeah, he knows. He's a tough little monkey. And smart. He doesn't know about me, but he knows he was kidnapped, all right, and he knows we're hiding out. He can handle it.'

'What about his mother? He must miss Jan?'

Eddie smiled thinly. 'Sure. Sure he does. I've been telling him he'll see her soon. Whenever that will be.'

'She deserves to have him back.'

'I know. Okay. It's a deal. Three days.'

I sighed. 'Good. Now. You've got to tell me everything.'

'Like a confession, huh?'

'Sure. Tell Father Coyne all about it.'

He chuckled. 'A priest you ain't, Brady.'

'Tell me about it, my son.'

'This ain't easy. Sixteen years I've lived with this. When they took E.J. my feeling was, well, I deserve this. This is what I get. This is my penance. See, it started that year I was at Pawtucket. I didn't know what the hell was going on. I was just a kid. You gotta believe that.' He stared earnestly at me, and I nodded. 'First, it was the girl. Oh, Jesus, was she a beautiful girl . . .'

Eddie talked for a long time, his soft voice brimming with self-reproach. His story spilled out in bursts of disconnected thoughts linked by long moments of silence when I thought he had finished, or decided not to continue. His knee jiggled constantly as he talked, and the shotgun he held across it bounced with it. I

272

smoked several cigarettes while I listened. When he mentioned names, I wrote them into my address book. Once he stopped, his eyebrows lifted to request assurance. I told him it was okay, it wasn't so bad, and he said, 'Don't give me your lawyer bullshit.' But he kept going, driving himself through the pain of the words. I couldn't see how his soul was benefiting from his confession, but he made a full one to me, and when he was done I told him I wanted to help him.

'Oh, I know you can help me with the legal stuff,' he said. 'I've always known that. There were times when I had my mind all made up to tell it all to you. When I left Jan and E.J. I wanted to spill my guts to you, I really did. But I didn't want to see that look in your eyes, Brady, like I see now. I wanted you to respect me, and I didn't want you to pity me. All I ever wanted was a little genuine respect from people. The only way I was going to get that was by working it out for myself.'

'So you kept running. That didn't work, Eddie.'

He shrugged. 'I never thought the bastards would do something like kidnap my son. The worst I figured was they'd kill me.'

From outside the barn came the roar of an engine. It belched three or four times, then died. 'Well, that's them,' said Eddie. 'E.J.

and Jake.'

I nodded. 'Come back with us tonight, Eddie. Let's set things right.'

He shook his head. 'No. I need to think.'

'You're making a mistake,' I said. 'But, okay. We're agreed?'

'We're agreed.'

Eddie sighed and we stood up. He pumped the shotgun, ejecting three shells on to the floor of the barn. Then he hung the gun on pegs on the barn wall. He stooped to pick up the shells, thrust them into the pocket of his overalls, then went outside. I followed him.

The tractor was parked in the dusty farmyard under the shadow of a big solitary beech tree. E.J. and Jake stood side by side next to it. Their backs were to us. Jake had one hand thrust into the engine, and with the other he was making little circular movements. E.J.'s head was cocked up to watch the old man speak. It could have been a Norman Rockwell painting, Jake's seamed old face furrowed like freshly ploughed earth, and E.J.'s as pink as a new-born heifer, Jake's full of love and E.J.'s full of trust.

When we approached, they turned.

'Hi, Dad,' said E.J. 'Jake was just telling me about carburettors. They mix the gas with air so it'll burn good.'

'Gol-danged thing's all gunked up,' said

274

Jake. He peered at me and frowned.

'This is Brady Coyne,' said Eddie. 'Remember him?'

I held out my hand and Jake gripped it strongly. 'Nope,' he said, squinting at my face.

'It was many years ago,' I said.

'Must've been,' said Jake. To Eddie he said, 'E.J.'s gonna be a race car driver, he tells me. So he's gotta know engines. He did a helluva job cuttin' hay.'

'I can do it by myself as soon as my legs get longer,' said the boy. He looked at me and grinned. 'Hi, Uncle Brady.'

I ruffled his hair, 'Hi, pal.'

Eddie glanced at me, then put his hand on E.J.'s shoulder.

'Uncle Brady came to take you home,' he said. 'Vacation's over.'

E.J. looked from Eddie's face to mine. 'Aw...'

'Now, never mind,' said Eddie. 'You didn't think you were going to stay here forever, did you? Your mother misses you.'

'You mean today?'

'Tonight,' said Eddie. 'Right after supper.'

CHAPTER TWENTY

E.J. and I had been on the road for half an hour before I became suspicious of the grey station wagon. It had appeared in my mirror shortly after E.J. and I left Jake and Eddie at the farm, and by the time we turned on to the highway in Williamstown I had to acknowledge that it could be following us.

I pulled into a Getty station and asked the attendant to check my oil and fill the gas tank. 'Want a Coke, partner?' I said to E.J., who had thus far succeeded in fending off my conversational sallies.

'Okay. Sure.'

I dumped a pocketful of change into his cupped hands. 'Get me one, too,' I told him.

The grey wagon, a late model Buick, slid past us. It contained two men, neither of whom turned his head in my direction. Nor did the car slow down or in any other way suggest that we were of any interest to its occupants. I jotted down the licence number anyway.

E.J. climbed back into the car and handed me my Coke, along with the leftover change. We cracked the cans open and I held mine out to him. 'Here's to coming home,' I toasted.

'My mother doesn't let me drink Coke,' he said, touching cans with me.

'Well, you're with me, now.'

'Not for long.'

'She's missed you. So have your grandparents. They've been terribly worried. They'll be happy to see you.'

E.J. didn't answer. He slouched against the car door and sipped his Coke.

I realized that I didn't know much about talking to ten-year-old boys, especially one who had been kidnapped, whose father had rescued him, who had hid for several weeks, and who, now, was being taken back to the place where it had started.

The Buick picked us up again as we entered the North Adams business district. It maintained a discreet distance, leaving half a dozen cars between us. I knew there were many ways to explain it. But I remembered that fear that had glittered in Eddie's eyes when we said goodbye in the Grabowski farmyard. He hugged E.J., who responded with a self-conscious grin, and then he leaned down to speak to me through the car window. 'Be careful, will you?' he had said.

I smiled. 'Sure. Don't worry.'

'Look. I'm worried.'

I reached up to squeeze his arm. 'I'll be careful. Promise.'

Eddie had nodded without conviction. 'You don't know them.'

Outside of North Adams Route 2 climbs quickly into the mountains. There was a hairpin turn in the road where a parking area had been cleared for motorists to stop and admire the view westward towards New York and north to Vermont. I pulled in and turned off the ignition.

'Let's get out and look at the sunset,' I said to E.J.

He shrugged his thin shoulders without looking at me. 'I'm not really big on sunsets,' he said. But he opened the car door and got out.

We walked to the edge of the parking area, which was lined with boulders nearly the size of Volkswagens. Beyond the crude barricade the sheer face of the mountain fell straight down for what looked like half a mile. I hoisted E.J. up on to one of the rocks so he could see, keeping a firm grip on his belt. He wiggled and twisted, hinting that I should let go of him, that he was old enough to keep his own balance. I released my grip on his belt, but stayed close to him.

'It *is* pretty,' he said after a moment. 'Do you think we can see Jake's farm from here?'

'Nope. Too far away.'

As I was talking to E.J. I kept part of my

attention focused on the road. The Buick moved past us. Again the two men failed to look in our direction as the car continued along the route that I was taking, heading east towards Boston.

I smoked a cigarette and watched the pink fade on the western horizon. E.J. clambered down from the rock, and we climbed back into my car.

I switched on the headlights. The road wound through the mountains. Signs warned us to beware of any number of dangers— falling rocks and crossing deer and slippery pavements and soft shoulders and fog.

At the crest of the hills the road levelled off and sliced through desolate pine and oak forest. I noticed headlights behind us, distant twin pricks of light. They seemed to be gaining on us rapidly. It could have been any vehicle, but my hands tightened on the steering wheel and I tromped on the accelerator. The little BMW jumped forward. I kept the speedometer on sixty-five, about as fast as I dared move along the twisting two-lane highway. When I glanced again into my rearview mirror I was startled to see headlights no more than fifty yards back, and gaining visibly. I pushed it up to seventy, then seventy-five, and had to brake hard as the road bent sharply to the left on to a long curving descent.

The car behind us matched our speed. I touched the brakes, then hit the accelerator, and was gratified to see the headlights behind us recede momentarily. But then the car reappeared, now only a few car lengths back. I pushed it up to eighty. The BMW purred sweetly and gripped the pavement through the curves.

But I could put no distance between us. I thought of simply pulling to the side of the road to allow our pursuers to pass, but I didn't dare take the chance that they would stop, too. So as we approached the sharp left turn that I knew so well, that led to my favourite fly-fishing stretch of the Deerfield River, I said to E.J., 'Hang on!'

I touched the brakes hard, released them, then hit them again, creating a long, controlled skidding spin. The rear of the BMW swerved around as I wrenched the wheel, and then we shot up the bumpy roadway that paralleled the river along some railroad tracks.

I turned off the headlights and downshifted to reduce speed without showing the brake lights. For a moment all was black outside, but my eyes quickly adjusted to the dim moonlight and I was able to follow the narrow pot-holed road that cut through the dense pine forest. I kept moving as fast as I dared, and was gratified to see nothing but darkness in the mirror. The Deerfield flowed along the left of the road, and I imagined big brown trout chasing minnows there.

We kept heading deeper into the woods on the rutted roadway. I crossed the river at an old railroad trestle and continued north, the river now on our right and far below us in the bottom of a rocky gorge. We were approaching the place I had taken that unplanned float trip, just below the dam.

I had nearly forgotten about E.J. I said to him, 'You all right, old buddy?'

'Fine, sure. They were following us, huh?'

'I'm not sure. I think so. They're gone now.'

'No, they're not,' said E.J.

I glanced into the mirror but saw nothing. I eased to the side of the road and coasted to a stop. Then I turned in my seat. Far behind us I saw a glitter of lights flashing through the trees. They seemed to be moving slowly along the road towards us. They were still a quarter of a mile or so back. I put the car in gear and pulled ahead until I came to a parking area where I had left the car many times before to fish.

I tucked the BMW up under the boughs of a pine tree, well away from the road and, I hoped, out of sight.

'C'mon. Let's get out,' I said to E.J.

We slid out of the car. 'This way,' I said. 'Give me your hand.' The bank sloped down sharply to the river. I knew there were pathways leading to the pools and riffles popular with fishermen, but it was too dark under the trees to find them, so we skidded and scrambled over and around boulders and fallen tree trunks. Saplings whipped my face and briers picked at my clothes. By the time we reached the bottom of the gorge I had acquired a hard knock on my shin and my chest was heaving from the effort. I still held tight to E.J.'s hand.

The river gurgled cheerily over the gravel bottom. The dam upstream had not begun its evening release. When it did, the place where we stood beside the river would lie under three feet of powerful current.

'Let's just sit and be quiet,' I whispered to E.J., giving his hand a quick squeeze before I released it.

We sat side by side on a flat boulder. The burble of the river and the occasional shriek of a night bird seemed to intensify rather than disturb the vast wilderness silence. I wanted a cigarette, but decided not to chance it. After a few minutes I heard the murmur of a car moving in low gear. High above us, where the road passed, I could see lights playing through the trees. So they had a flashlight, or a spotlight on the car. Judging by the movement of the light, they were driving very slowly. As they drew close I heard the engine stop. Two doors slammed. Then I heard voices.

'Yeah, this is it. It's his.'

Again, the sound of car doors opening and closing. They had found my BMW. I touched E.J.'s shoulder and squeezed gently. 'Shh,' I hissed to him. 'We've got to be very quiet.' I felt his muscles tense under my hand.

I could hear them moving around up on the road, and I could distinguish snatches of their conversation.

'. . . can't be far . . . Yeah, well, which side? Let's stick together.'

E.J. pressed himself against me. I suspected he recognized those voices.

'Let's go down and look,' said one.

'There's a river down there, for Christ's sake. They wouldn't go down there.'

'We've got to check it out anyway. C'mon.'

I leaned close to E.J. 'We'll have to cross the river,' I whispered. 'It's not too deep here. Just hold tight to my hand and follow along. Okay?'

His hand found mine and grasped it firmly. 'Don't be afraid,' I said. 'We'll be all right.

283

Let's go.'

From above us came the crackle of underbrush. The flashlight flickered through the trees, slowly coming closer. E.J. and I stepped into the water. The river was fed from the coldest water at the bottom of the dam. It immediately numbed my feet and ankles, and even though it was at its normal level, it sucked and pulled with surprising force.

The riverbed was strewn with big boulders. As we approached one, my foot abruptly sank into a hole which the water had gouged into the bottom as it swirled around the big rock. I stood in the eddy behind the boulder in water nearly up to my hips and drew E.J. close to me. The water came to his armpits.

'It gets shallower again,' I whispered. 'Don't worry.'

We moved forward, and the water was again at my knees. I glanced over my shoulder. The light had advanced halfway down the embankment. We had to get across the river before they arrived at the bank, or we'd be sitting mallards in the middle of the river. The rock-paved bottom was slick with algae and moss over smooth gravel, and once I slipped and had to scramble to regain my balance. E.J. struggled against the swift current that came to his waist. It was frustratingly slow going. We came to another

284

boulder. I sank to the middle of my chest in the hole beside it. Before I could warn him E.J.'s head slipped under. I grabbed him under his armpits and hoisted him up. 'Ahh!' he sputtered.

'What was that?'

The light played through the trees on to the water, flickering on and off like a strobe as it found openings through the foliage. I could see that we still had thirty feet to go before we reached the sanctuary of the far shore, and the two men with the light had already nearly reached the water's edge. I knew we wouldn't make it.

'I heard something,' said one of the voices.

'Goddam owl or something.'

'Like hell. That was them. They're down here somewhere.'

'Listen,' I hissed to E.J. 'We've got to hide right here. Okay? We'll move around this rock and get down so just our heads are sticking up. They won't see us. You with me?'

'Okay,' he said. There was no hint of fear in his voice.

I kept one arm around his back as we eased to the side of the boulder. The current tugged hard at us, and I felt E.J. grab on to the back of my pants. With my free hand I tried to cling to the big rock. By bending my knees I managed to duck into the shadow of the boulder.

The light played across the water and over our heads.

'Nah. I told you. Nothing down here. They're back up there in the woods across the street.'

Then I heard it, a low rumble. I could feel a new vibration in the riverbed. I recognized it instantly and felt a quiver of panic. They were releasing water from the dam. In a couple of minutes a two-foot wall of water would hit us like an out-of-control truck. It would lift us and tumble us down-stream, smash us against the rocks, suck us under. The furious power of the river was still a palpable memory for me.

'E.J. Listen carefully,' I whispered. 'We've got to try to get across now. Climb on to my back and hold tight. I'll stay as low as I can. Okay?'

'Sure,' he said.

I helped him crawl up so that he had a firm grip with both arms around my neck. I held his legs in the crooks of my arms and, crouching as low in the water as I could, I slid quietly away from the shelter of the rock.

Already I could feel the growing power of the river. We had, at most, one minute before the full force of the released dam water hit us.

'Look! Over there! There they are!'

We were centred in the beam of the flashlight. I tried to move out of the light. I slipped into darkness, then the light found us again. I heard an explosion, then another, and it took me an instant to realize that they were shooting at us.

'For Christ's sake,' yelled one of them angrily. 'I can't hold the goddam light and shoot, too.'

'Give me the gun.'

Momentarily we were in darkness. The light swept across the rising river. E.J.'s grip around my throat made me gasp for breath. We were only ten feet from the brushy, rock-strewn shore. Ten feet from safety.

Then the light found us.

'There! For Christ's sake, shoot!'

It felt as if someone had touched the back of my leg with a red-hot brand, the pain sudden and surprising. 'Ow!' I yelled. My leg buckled under me, and at that instant the surging wave hit me. I felt E.J.'s grip on my throat loosen as I stumbled, knocked off balance by the force of the water and staggered by the abrupt numbness in my right leg. I clutched E.J.'s ankle, had it for an instant as it slipped through my arm, and then it was wrenched away from me. I tried to pivot around to grab him, and as I did the water lifted me by my shoulders and rammed me under. I came up gasping, my mouth and nose full. My feet searched for the bottom. It was all so familiar. I tried to keep my head up and my hands out to fend off the rocks. My feet touched, bounced, and were swept along.

I crashed against something solid, and instinctively I clawed at it. It felt rough, and I found a grip on it. It was the trunk of an ancient tree that had toppled into the river. I found handholds and hoisted myself along it until I was able to crawl into the thick brush that grew alongside the river.

I lay there gasping for breath. My stomach was full of water and my head swirled dizzily. My right leg had no feeling. I touched it. It felt dead, foreign to my body, but my hand came away warm and sticky. I realized I was bleeding heavily. I felt no pain. My mind seemed to float, and I clenched my jaw in an effort to think clearly.

'You got him. They're gone,' shouted a voice above the crashing roar of the river.

'Let's get the hell out of here,' said the other. 'We got more business.'

'Hang tight for a minute. Play the light along there. I want to be sure.'

The light swept across the river. I lay flat, my cheek grinding into the soft earth, and didn't move. The light touched me, moved on, then came back and paused. Then it moved away. I heard the voices, but couldn't make out what they were saying. The rhythm of the pounding river lifted my brain so that I seemed to be drifting high over the water. I forced myself to regain control. There was something important. I couldn't remember. My eyelids were heavy. I wanted to sleep. I was very tired. No. I had to stay awake. There was something . . .

I willed my eyes to open and, clawing at the bushes around me, heaved myself over on to my back. The arching branches of the trees overhead spun crazily. I narrowed my eyes, trying to make them focus, to halt the whirling in my brain.

I turned my head so that I could look back across the river. The light bobbed and flickered up the embankment. They were moving back to the road. I concentrated on the light. It gave me something to do, a reason to fight the sleep that my brain cried for.

The light disappeared. Then I saw it again, moving at a steady pace down parallel to the river. They were in their car. They were leaving. We were safe.

We. Then I remembered. E.J. Where was E.J.?

I tried to yell for him. The roar of the river filled my ears. My voice was a hoarse gurgle, a pitiful, weak whisper. I tried to prop myself up on to my elbows, and I collapsed with the effort, my head falling back on to the muddy earth. 'E.J.!' I croaked.

Then a black hood fell over my head.

CHAPTER TWENTY-ONE

Sharp, rhythmic lashes of pain against the side of my face dragged me up into reluctant consciousness. I heard the roar of the river, and higher up the whine of wind through the pines. Another sound mingled with the wind and the water, a voice, chanting what sounded like a prayer. 'Come on, come on, come on,' it crooned, in synchrony with the sharp stings on my cheek.

I forced my eyelids to lift. The pain against my face was sharp but superficial. The pulses of hurt in my leg went deeper, into the marrow of the bone and up into my armpits with each contraction of my heart. I moaned and shivered. I was wet—drenched, I realized, and my body began to quiver and shake uncontrollably.

I raised my hand to brush away the stinging on my face.

'Come on. Uncle Brady, wake up. Come on.'

I shifted my eyes. E.J. knelt beside me, slapping methodically at my face. 'Hey! Cut that out,' I said.

I turned my head. He sat back on his haunches to peer down at me.

'Are you all right?' he said.

'Are you?'

'I'm okay. I took a swim. I thought you were dead.'

'Not quite.' I tried to sit up and the woods began to whirl around me. I sank back to the ground and let my eyes close. 'Can't make it,' I said. 'Got to rest for a while. Tired. Real tired.'

E.J. grabbed my shoulders. 'You've got to get up.' He shook me. 'Come on. We can't stay here.'

I opened my eyes. 'How long have we been here?'

'A long time,' E.J. said. 'It took me a long time to find you. I got out of the water way down there and I waited until they were gone. Then I came to find you. You've been sleeping. I think the water is going down. It isn't as loud as it was. You've got to stand up. I'll help you.'

He tugged at my shoulders and the pain in my leg sharpened my mind. I struggled up on to my elbows. E.J. moved behind me and pushed me into a sitting position. He held me that way until the dizziness faded and I could sit unaided.

'Are you okay now?' he said.

'I think I can make it. Find me a stick or something to lean on. I don't think my leg's going to work too well.'

'Did they shoot you?'

'Yes. On the back of my leg.'

He was back in a minute with a piece of a dead limb. I tested it between my hands and it seemed sturdy enough. I propped it on to the ground with my right hand and E.J. moved under my left arm and together we heaved me to my feet. I fought off a wave of nausea and dizziness and then I was okay. I was gratified that my right leg was no longer numb. It was far from numb. But the pain seemed centred in the big muscle in back, and I knew no bone had been broken. And I felt strong enough. I couldn't have lost too much blood. It had been the shock that knocked me out when I was hit. I thought I'd be all right. I tried an experimental step. With E.J. at my left side and the stick supporting my right, I managed to shuffle forward a couple of paces.

'See what happens when you get old?' I said to E.J. with a feeble grin.

'Very funny,' he said. 'Let's go. We've got to get across the river.'

E.J. helped me across the river and up the

slope to where my BMW waited. The two gunmen must have been pretty confident that they'd killed us, because they hadn't bothered to yank out the wires or shoot holes in the tyres.

We drove back to the main road and found the Riverview Inn, a stately old Federal period place where I'd eaten a few meals after a day of fishing on the river. A grandmotherly old lady herded me and E.J. into a big, sunlit dining-room, studiously ignoring the dampness and disarray of our clothing. We ordered breakfast and then I excused myself to use the pay phone I had seen in the lobby.

I dropped in a quarter, dialled 'O' and then Marty Stern's number, told the operator to make it collect and person-to-person, and muttered, 'Be there, Stern. God damn it, be there.'

He answered on the second ring, agreed to accept the charges, and said, 'What now?'

'Hi,' I said. 'Listen. I'm at the Riverview Inn in Charlemont. It's right on Route 2. Here's what you've got to do.'

'Now just a damn minute, Coyne—'

'No, you listen to me. I've got E.J. Donagan with me. I've seen Eddie. I've been shot in the leg. I've got the story. Will you listen?'

'I'm listening.'

'There's a guy named Stump Kelly. Arnold, his name is. Lives in Chatham at the Fox Hill Estates. Two other guys, I don't know where they live but Kelly can tell you. One named Peter Lucci and the other is Vincent Quarto. They drive a grey Buick station wagon, licence P29–257. Might be Kelly's. They kidnapped E.J. and Eddie Donagan. They killed Mary Ann Mikuni and Bobo Halley. They tried to kill me last night. Got that?'

'Yeah. Slow down. Yeah, okay, I got it. Explain to me—'

'I'll explain it all. But you've got to get out here. We've got to go get Eddie. Come pick me up. It's right on the way. I'll explain it all to you then. And listen. Call Sam Farina and have him come here to get E.J. Tell him E.J.'s fine and wants to see his mother. Okay?'

I heard Stern sigh. 'Okay. I hope the hell you know what you're talking about, Coyne. We can pick up these guys, but you know we can't hold them. Not without evidence.'

'Eddie'll give you that,' I said. 'Guaranteed.'

'Right. Hey, listen, Coyne. You all right?'

'You're a darling to ask. I am just fine, thank you so much.'

I bandaged my leg, then had three eggs, over easy, four slices of toast, a big slab of ham, and a glass of orange juice. After I finished eating, E.J. and I sat on rockers on the front porch of the inn and watched the traffic on Route 2 while I worked on my third cup of coffee. Aside from the stiffness and dull ache in the back of my leg, I was feeling stronger by the minute. E.J. chattered continuously. He had been a man, he probably had saved my life, but now he was a boy again waiting to see his mother after a month's separation. As I listened to him talk, I rehearsed what I would tell Eddie when I saw him. I had promised him three days. Now I had decided to give him less than one. I hoped he was still at Jake's farm.

Stern pulled into the circular drive two hours almost to the minute from when I had phoned him. He had two other men with him. One was a young guy with black hair and piercing black eyes, whose face seemed permanently fixed in a scowl. Stern introduced him simply as Catlett. The other one, Swan, was pushing fifty. They both referred to Stern as 'Chief'.

I told E.J. that his grandfather would be right along for him, shook his hand and told him I'd see him soon, and left him with Swan. Stern and Catlett and I climbed into Stern's car. Catlett got behind the wheel, and Stern and I sat in back. I gave Catlett directions then settled back in the seat.

'Okay, so talk,' said Stern.

I told him how I had found Eddie and E.J. at Jake Grabowski's farm. I explained how Kelly and his two henchmen had kidnapped E.J. and then lured Eddie into it, and how Eddie and E.J. had escaped and fled to Lanesborough. I told him how E.J. and I had been followed and shot at and left for dead.

'I don't get it,' said Stern. 'What's the connection? Kelly's the baseball scout. He knew Donagan. It's not just a coincidence that it was his kid they kidnapped.'

'No,' I said. 'It's not a coincidence. It goes way back. I'm not sure it's relevant.'

'Everything's relevant, Coyne.'

'Yeah, I guess you're right. Okay,' I said. 'It goes like this. After Eddie was signed by the Red Sox they sent him to the minor league team in Pawtucket. There he got involved with a girl.'

'Mikuni,' said Stern.

'Yes. Annie. Eddie was a kid. She was beautiful. It happens. Anyway, she liked to gamble on ball games. Pretty soon she had Eddie betting, too. Just on his own team, on himself, but still gambling. It was easy money, because Eddie was so good he could win, and beat the odds, almost every time. There didn't seem to be anything wrong with it, even though he knew the rules. The girl laid off his bets for him and gave him his money when he won. Then one night he met her in a bar after a game. Stump Kelly was sitting at the table with her. Eddie thought it was all over right then. If a baseball official knew he had been betting it could've cost him his career right there.'

'Kelly was in on it,' said Stern. 'It was a scam. Right?'

'Yeah, something like that. The girl and Kelly worked together. I guess they had worked the same thing on other young players. Bobo Halley, for sure. Eddie will explain all that. Anyway, Kelly had Eddie over the proverbial barrel. Made it seem like he had found out about Eddie's gambling, but out of the goodness of his heart wouldn't tell. So Eddie was in his debt. It soon became clear that Kelly had something else in mind for Eddie.'

'He wanted him to throw games.'

'Not right away. He wanted Eddie to get to the big leagues, first, where the real gambling money was. But he did manoeuvre Eddie into the position where he'd give up a run or two so that Kelly could beat the spread, all the time reminding Eddie that one word from him would mean disgrace and the end of the only profession Eddie knew. And Kelly was clever enough so that there never would've been any case against him. Everything went through the girl. And they made Eddie continue betting, too. He usually won, in the beginning, which made it easier for him to go along.'

I lit a cigarette, and Stern waved the smoke away.

'The first year Eddie was called up to the Red Sox,' I continued, 'Kelly left him alone. Eddie figured it was all past him. It wasn't until his second year up that Mary Ann Mikuni got in touch with him. Eddie had established himself by then. He was a great pitcher. The team was favoured to win every time he took the mound. She managed to remind him where he stood with her and Kelly. There was a game with Cleveland which Eddie was scheduled to pitch. The Sox were favoured by two and a half runs. Eddie was instructed to keep it close. Win, okay. But by no more than two runs. Eddie resisted. He was a big leaguer, he had his pride. But Kelly had him. So he kept it close. He won the game, and he won the bet they made him lay down, and that was the beginning of the end for him.'

By now we were cruising into Williamstown. I told Catlett where to turn to get on to the road that would take us to

Lanesborough and Jake Grabowski's farm.

I touched Stern's leg. 'I hope all this can be kept quiet,' I said. 'The thing that's eaten away at Eddie's soul all these years has been the fear that his son would find out that he ended up throwing baseball games.'

'I can't promise that,' said Stern.

I shrugged. 'I suppose if it has to, it'll come out anyway.'

'So then what happened?'

'Then they had him. He tried to do whatever they wanted. At first he was allowed to win, but they were betting against him, just trying to beat the odds. And, of course, they made Eddie bet against himself. He was a good pitcher, but in the big leagues no one's that good. Eddie sometimes lost games. And gradually it wore him down. He lost his confidence, and with it went his gift. He wasn't always favoured to win any more. So if the Sox were a one-run underdog when he pitched, he had to lose by more than one run so Kelly could cover the spread. It did something to Eddie's head. A psychologist could probably explain it. He'd always had great control. It's what enabled him to groove a pitch in a certain situation so someone could get a hit that would allow a run to score, and then get the out he needed. But he lost it all. In a way, I think his mind rebelled against what he was doing. Subconsciously he decided to be so bad that he'd no longer be allowed to pitch. That seemed the only way out of it.'

'So he lost his job.'

'He quit. He had been sent down. He still had a healthy arm. It happens to pitchers. They lose their control. The Red Sox hoped he'd work it out. But Eddie knew better. So he retired. He hoped that would be the end of it, and for a while it was. But then Kelly got ahold of him, reminded him of what he knew, and demanded money.'

'Sure. Blackmail. Extortion,' said Stern.

'Yes. Eddie had a good job with his father-in-law, he had access to company funds, and Sam trusted him. Kelly figured he could bleed Eddie. Eddie refused. Kelly threatened him, said he'd leak it all to the papers. Eddie told him to go ahead. He was ready to face it. Instead, Eddie's friend, Bobo Halley, who was in the same boat, was killed. Kelly made it clear that something like that could happen to him, too. Or to his wife and child. That's when Eddie quit his job with Sam and left Jan and E.J. He hoped to put as much distance between himself and his family as he could. He didn't care what Kelly did to him. But he didn't want Kelly to think that his family mattered to him.'

'Jesus,' said Stern. 'That poor bastard.'

'Yeah, I know. And none of us had any inkling of what was going on. Yesterday, when I saw him, Eddie told me he hoped Kelly would just kill him and be done with it. He wanted to run away, but he didn't dare leave E.J. and Jan. He *wanted* Kelly to know where he was. But Kelly made it clear that he wasn't done with Eddie. He wanted money. Eddie didn't have any. He tried to get some easy money, betting on games. But you know how that works.'

'Yeah,' said Stern. 'No one wins in the long run.'

'Nope. So Eddie just got deeper in the hole. And he couldn't run away because he feared for E.J.'

'And he was right.'

'He was right,' I said. 'They snatched E.J. Then they called Eddie. They knew he'd cooperate. They knew Sam had money. After they got it, they would've killed the two of them. But they got away. And Mary Ann Mikuni realized she was into something a whole lot deeper than she had intended. That's when she got ahold of me. I guess Kelly found out.'

'Sayonara, Mary Ann Mikuni.'

'It's just a mile or so down this road,' I said to Catlett. 'On the right. A white farmhouse and a big old barn.' To Stern I said, 'They

301

were following me, I guess. They figured I'd lead them to Eddie. Which I did.'

'It's not your fault,' said Stern.

I nodded. 'I know that. And we do have E.J. Now I just hope the hell Eddie hasn't run away again.'

Catlett braked the car to a stop.

'We're not there, yet,' I said. It's around this bend.'

Then I saw the uniformed police officer approach. Catlett turned his head to the open window, and when the cop bent down, Catlett said, 'What's the trouble?'

'I'm sorry, sir. You'll have to turn around. There's fire apparatus in the road.'

I felt a hand twist my guts. I leaned forward. 'Is it the Grabowski place?'

The cop's face was expressionless. 'Please, you can't go any farther.'

Catlett produced his wallet and held it open to the cop. 'FBI,' he said. 'What's the story?'

'I'm sorry, sir. I didn't realize—'

'It's all right,' said Catlett impatiently. 'What's going on?'

'The Grabowski place. Yes. Burned to the ground early this morning. The arson man from the State Police is here, and—'

'Let's go,' said Stern.

He and Catlett leaped from the car and began to jog along the roadway. I eased myself

302

out and followed them, hopping as well as I could on my stiff and aching right leg.

Around the corner and past the row of big oaks that lined the road lay what was left of Jake Grabowski's farmyard. Where his barn had once stood lay a black heap of charred timbers. Wisps of smoke still drifted up from them, and a fire truck stood nearby with several fireman clad in black rubber coats and black boots watching. The farmhouse was a dark corpse. The once peeling white exterior was stained a sooty black. The empty windows looked into a blackened interior. The front door was missing. A hole gaped in the roof. From the pasture came the low mournful cries of Jake's cows, asking to be milked.

I hobbled through the muddy farmyard to where Stern and Catlett stood talking with a grey-haired man in shirt-sleeves. Stern glanced at me and said to the man, 'This is Mr Coyne. He's a lawyer. He's with us. Coyne, this is Captain Melcher. Arson. Why don't you start over?'

'Okay,' said Melcher. 'I guess somebody passing by on the main drag saw the sky all lit up and called the fire department. By the time they got here there was no chance to save the barn. They did the best they could with the house, but ...'

303

'What about—?' I began.

'Two bodies. Adult males. They found them in the barn, along with some cows.' Melcher smiled sympathetically.

'Not much left of them, I'm afraid. The ME's got them. Try to make an identification.'

'I can tell you who they were,' I said.

Melcher darted a glance at me. 'Not by looking at them, you can't.'

'So what do you figure?' said Stern.

'No doubt,' said Melcher. 'Both places were torched. Gasoline. The barn was full of hay. It must've gone up in a matter of minutes. The house was slower.'

'And the bodies?' said Catlett.

Melcher shrugged. 'They were lying together in the middle of the barn. Of course, it's hard to say exactly what happened. They were fully clothed, it would appear. Now that right there is suspicious, if you know what I mean. We figure the fire broke out around four in the morning. That's kind of early even for farmers to be up and around.'

I had heard enough. I wandered away from the skeletal remains of Jake's farm and sat down heavily on the ground beside the road, my back to the horror I had just seen. It was clear to me what had happened. After the two guys in the Buick left me and E.J. on the banks of the Deerfield River, they'd returned here to take care of Eddie. Kelly's henchmen, Peter Lucci and Vincent Quarto, I had no doubt. I hoped, at least, they had had the decency to kill Jake and Eddie before they left them to burn.

And I knew it was my fault. I had led them here. Stern had been right about me all along. I should have left the sleuthing to him. I butted in where I didn't belong, I didn't know what I was doing, and I'd made things worse.

This time I had got Jake and Eddie killed.

I pounded my bad leg with my fist. The jolt of pain felt good. It was what I deserved. I wanted to make it hurt worse. I hit my leg again and again.

CHAPTER TWENTY-TWO

I felt an arm around my shoulder. I looked up to see Marty Stern squatting beside me. 'Hey, easy, there,' he said softly. 'Just take it easy.'

'Don't you see?' I said. 'I brought them right here.'

'Now, we don't know that, do we? We don't know anything, yet. Let's just wait a bit, okay? Catlett's on the horn right now.'

I nodded and fumbled a cigarette from the

305

pack in my shirt pocket. My hands trembled, but I managed to get it lit. Stern sat on the ground beside me. We both stared across the road, away from Jake's farm, at the broad meadow that was blanketed with yellow and purple wildflowers. Beyond the meadow rose some low hills, and beyond them darker mountains climbed to the clear blue sky. It was a beautiful August morning in the country.

A few minutes later Catlett came over and scootched down in front of us. 'Some good news, Chief,' he said to Stern. 'They picked up Kelly and Quarto and Lucci. They were all there at Kelly's house. Kelly was very cool, said nothing, called his lawyer. The other two're nervous. Maybe something'll happen.'

Catlett glanced at me and frowned. 'There's something else . . .'

'Yeah, okay,' said Stern, starting to stand up.

'No, go ahead,' I said. 'I've got a right to know.'

'Now, look—' said Stern.

'I want to hear it.'

He stared at me for a moment, then nodded and sat beside me again. 'Okay,' he said to Catlett. 'What is it?'

'I talked to the Medical Examiner. One of the bodies is definitely Jake Grabowski's. A local dentist made his false teeth. And the other one fits the description of Donagan. And . . .'

'Go ahead,' said Stern.

Catlett lifted his eyebrows. Stern glanced at me. 'I'm all right,' I said.

Catlett nodded. 'Okay. Both men had been shot. Once in the forehead. The bodies were burned pretty bad, but the ME was able to determine that they were dead before the fire.'

'What about E.J.?' I said.

Catlett nodded. 'I checked on that, too. He's fine. He's on his way home with his grandfather and his mother.'

'No, I mean—'

'He doesn't know. None of them know. We'll have to call the local police. That'll be their job.'

'Don't,' I said. 'It should be my job. I want to do it.'

Stern stared at me. 'Are you sure?'

'I'm sure. I've been thinking about it. I want to do it.'

'Well,' said Stern, 'you better wait until they positively identify the body.'

'The ME's checking,' said Catlett. 'He's getting Donagan's dental records. They'll know pretty soon.'

'I'd like to go home now,' I said to Stern. 'Can we do that?'

Stern shrugged. 'I guess so. Catlett can drive us to your car, and you and I can go back in it. He'll have to come back here for a while to keep an eye on things.'

We went over to the FBI car. Stern and I got in, and Catlett paused to talk with Melcher for a minute. Then he climbed behind the wheel. 'I told him I'd be back. I explained the case to him a little. We'll cooperate with each other. No problem.'

We drove back to the Riverview Inn where Stern and I transferred to my car. Stern drove while I rode beside him. I tried to rehearse in my mind the speech I would have to make to E.J. Donagan. It never came out right, so after a while I gave up and smoked cigarettes and watched the countryside roll by.

Stern stopped by an MBTA station near my apartment and got out of the car. I climbed out, moved around to the driver's side, and slid behind the wheel.

'You sure you're okay?' he said, leaning in to me.

'Sure. Pisser.'

'I mean, can you drive?'

'Sure.'

'Get that leg looked at.'

I nodded.

'And for Christ's sake stop acting like a baby. What happened, happened. The bad guys killed them, not you. Okay? Self-pity doesn't suit you.'

'Appreciate the advice,' I said.

Stern slapped the roof of my car. 'I'll call you when I hear anything.'

'Thanks.'

He started to leave. 'Wait a minute,' I said.

He turned back. 'Yeah?'

'What are the chances of keeping the stuff about Eddie's gambling out of the papers? It'll be awfully important to E.J. Especially now.'

'I told you,' said Stern. 'I can't promise anything. It all depends. It's complicated with Donagan and Grabowski dead. Now the media'll latch on to it. You've got to be ready for that.'

'You'll do what you can?'

He nodded. 'I will.'

When I got back to my apartment I shucked off my clothes and unwrapped the bandage from my leg. By standing with my back to the full-length mirror on my closet door and craning my neck I was able to see my wound. It looked too small and clean to hurt as much as it did. It was simply a scabby gouge maybe four inches long across the back of my thigh. What they called in the movies a superficial flesh wound. Probably needed stitches. Otherwise there'd be an unsightly scar to mar the classic beauty of my leg. I'd see somebody about it tomorrow.

I limped, naked, into the bathroom and turned on the faucets to fill the tub. I found a bottle of bubble bath that Sylvie had left in the linen closet and poured some of that in, then went to the kitchen and poured about six fingers of Jack Daniels into a tumbler. I looked through my tapes and found Beethoven's Ninth, Sir Georg Solti conducting the Chicago Symphony. I smiled. Lots of years earlier Eddie Donagan had called the second movement 'Huntley-Brinkley music' and had proclaimed the awesome Choral Symphony a 'great show'. I slid the cassette into the slot, turned it up loud, and as the magnificent first strains of the deaf man's music filled my little cell high above the harbour, I carried my glass of corn mash into the bathroom and sank into the tub.

I drank and soaked and hummed the bars of the Beethoven and dozed, and I felt the poisons start to seep out of my body. I tried to keep the troublesome question on the fuzzy edges of my consciousness: How do you tell a ten-year-old boy that his father has been murdered? How do you tell him it's your fault?

When my glass was empty and the tub water cool and all the bubbles gone, I heaved myself out and tried to dry my body with a big bath towel. I kept dropping it, and every time I stooped over to pick it up I lost my balance. Somehow it struck me funny. I finally finished the job while sitting on the floor. I was wrestling with my jeans when the phone rang. I brought my empty glass to the kitchen phone and poured some more Jack Daniels into it before I lifted the receiver.

'Howdy,' I said.

'It's me. Stern.'

'Hi there, old pal.'

'You all right, Coyne?'

'Tip top.'

'How's the leg?'

'Better than ever. I'll be *en pointe* again in no time. *Pas de deux*, know what I mean?'

'No, I don't. Listen, maybe you should get somebody over there to stay with you tonight.'

'Oh, yeah, heh heh. The lubricious Sylvie Szabo, maybe.'

'Look,' said Stern. 'I've got some news. You think you're sober enough to understand me?'

'I'm as sober as a churchmouse. That's right, isn't it? A churchmouse?'

'I guess so. Will you listen to me?'

'Okay, okay. Don't yell at me.'

I heard him sigh. 'Bad news and good news. Bad news first. They made a positive ID on the other body. It was Donagan.'

311

'They're sure?' I said.

'They're sure. That's the bad news.'

'Okay,' I said, feeling, suddenly, at least as sober as a churchmouse. 'What's the good news?'

'A couple of things, actually. Vincent Quarto has spilled his guts. Everything. We got a signed confession from him. So I would say the case against them all is open and shut.'

'That's real good.' I sipped from my glass. 'What else?'

'Quarto and Lucci didn't follow you to Lanesborough yesterday. They had tracked down Donagan before that. They were already there. If you hadn't showed up they would've killed the boy along with Donagan and Grabowski. If you'd stayed overnight, they would've killed you too. But when you left with the boy they figure they had to stop you. They thought they had succeeded. Then they went back to the farm. You understand what I'm saying, Coyne?'

There was a sudden constriction in my throat. I felt my eyes mist over. Booze sometimes does that to me. I nodded.

'Coyne, are you there?'

'Yes.'

'The only thing you did yesterday was to save that little boy's life. If Donagan had listened to you, if he had followed your

312

advice, he and Grabowski would still be alive. You did everything right, see? Nothing to blame yourself for. Nothing at all.'

'Yes. I see,' I managed to say.

'Listen, Coyne. I mean it. Get somebody over there to stay with you. I think you could use company tonight.'

'Good idea. Thanks.'

Stern paused. 'Look, I'll be in touch. You want anything, call me. Any time. I'm home. You've got my number. I'll be here all night. Okay?'

'Yes, okay.' I cleared my throat. 'And thanks. Thanks, Marty.'

'Coyne, for Christ's sake, sober up.'

'You shouldn't try to deceive me, Marty.'

'What the hell do you mean?'

'It's not a churchmouse. It's a judge.'

Stern hung up on me.

I replaced the receiver gently. Then I took my glass of Jack Daniels over to the sliding doors. I stood inside for a few moments, sipped, and watched the ocean. A motorboat inscribed white scrolls over the smooth surface of the water. Gulls cruised and darted. Overhead puffy fragments of fair-weather cumulus drifted across the darkening evening sky.

I went back to the telephone and dialled a familiar number. It rang half a dozen times before I heard Gloria's voice, breathless, as if she had just dashed in from the garden.

'Hullo?'

'It's me.'

'Oh, Brady. Well, how are you?'

'I'm okay,' I said. 'I was just wondering. How are the boys?'

Photoset, printed and bound in Great Britain by REDWOOD BURN LIMITED, Trowbridge, Wiltshire